MAD FE

Matt Burgin

Disclaimer

This is a work of fiction. None of the events in this book happened. Although some of the names used correspond with people the author may know, all the characters are made up and, except for figures clearly in the public domain, any resemblance to persons living or dead is purely coincidental. All events take place in a non-existent time parallel which have been arranged to suit the convenience of the book, with all events clearly subject to satire and parody. Any events or dialogue involving those in the public domain is pure satire and has no factual base. The opinions expressed are those of the characters and should not be confused with the authors.

FIRST EDITION   October 2021
COVER DESIGN   Carl Kennedy
COVER PHOTO   Christian Hopewell
                  (Courtesy of the Leadmill Team)

Chapter 1

The Meet Cute

WEDNESDAY, OCTOBER 21ST, 2015

Her nose twitched and she stirred, as he lay on his side watching her sleep. Expelling a slight groan, she rolled onto her side, facing him. Her face was round, pale and flawless, apart from a small pockmark above her left eyebrow, which was noticeable courtesy of the morning sun pouring through a gap in the curtains.

Her arm balanced on her side, tucking the duvet just above the elbow, but low enough for him to see the top of her breasts. Gravity sunk the surrounding duvet, the contours highlighting a lithe yet curvaceous outline around the hips.

The shoulder-length blonde hair cascaded from behind her ears, slowly covering her face. Gently, he scooped the hair with his forefinger, avoiding her skin, returning the strands to their origin. Its softness to the touch and shimmering in the daylight suggested she invested part of her student loan on a decent conditioner.

Despite his caution, he had disturbed her. Having previously occupied the no-man's-land between sleep and consciousness, the scales tipped toward the land of the living.

Her eyes opened in stages of blinking. First, the lids were more closed than open; then closed and open equally; until finally they were fully open. As her wide blue eyes focused on him, a smile spread across her face.

'Morning Tim,' she whispered.

'Morning Mary,' he replied.

Her forehead furrowed as much as the natural elasticity of her 18-year-old skin allowed, as a small frown replaced the smile.

'Who's Mary?'

'You are?'

'Err no!'

'Are you sure?'

'So, I'm trying to figure out which is the most insulting. The bit where you wake up in the morning and can't remember my name, *or...*' she articulated in a slow but deliberate manner, 'the bit where you question whether I know my name.'

Tim *had* been feeling pleased with himself. As a 22-year-old struggling musician, he needed the confidence boost waking up next to a very tidy first-year student provided.

'Err, well no I just didn't know what to say. I was embarrassed. What is your name?'

'Orla. My name's Orla, but everyone calls me Lyla.'

'Lyla - like the Oasis song? Why?'

'Because that song was in the charts when I was a girl and my baby brother thought they were singing Orla, so it stuck. Ever since then I've had a soft spot for Oasis, which is why I was there last night.'

'That's a cool nickname. And I'm sorry I forgot your real name. I'm shit with names.'

She laughed. 'Don't worry about it. I was having you on, anyway. I know what this is. It's a one-night stand. Maybe it could be more, but that's what it is now. We're both young. Well, I am. Besides, we both know you're punching above your weight!'

He smiled. She was funny and pretty with good taste in music. His holy trinity. But she was right about being too young for anything other than a bit of casual. He'd been there before. It came with the territory of living in a town full of students.

'You were good last night,' she commented.

'Thank you,' he replied sheepishly.

'No, I didn't mean that! Don't get big-headed - I meant the other thing. The Oasis tribute band. I know it's just a tribute band, but you were all good - you in particular. You look a lot like Noel Gallagher. That can't be news to you. But good looking. You're a good-looking Noel Gallagher if that makes sense.'

'Definitely,' he replied.

'Definitely, maybe,' she laughed, raising her eyebrows wickedly. As she climbed on top of him, her fingernails dug into his shoulders.

Chapter 2

Tea and Toast

Tim was pleased with himself again as Lyla walked into the bedroom in his T-shirt with a plate of toast balanced on two mugs of tea.

'Do you make your own music as well as the tribute band?' she asked.

'I write and perform my own songs, but it's difficult to make a living. I do the pubs around Sheffield; the usual stuff, but the tribute band pays better than you'd think, and it's a good laugh. When I was 18, I was in a band called Prevention.'

'Prevention?'

'Yeah, it was a gimmick. The flyers used to say we were better than the Cure.'

'Funny.'

'Not really. It was lame. Once the joke wore off, we were left with a rubbish name. You could say high impact, low sustainability.'

'Do you like Oasis?'

'Yeah, I love them and if I'm honest, I don't hate looking like Noel. But that's my problem. I'm 30 years too late–I'm too retro. I should have been doing it in the nineties when this sort of music was popular. Even 10 years ago would have been better when the whole Sheffield indie thing happened with Milburn, Reverend and The Makers and the Arctic Monkeys. That was the same kind of stuff, but I'd love to have been around in the mid-nineties. My mum died when I was little, and my dad brought me up. He was into that music when he was my age. All the 90s Brit-pop, Madchester - indie stuff. He was a big Stone Roses fan back in the day. He even went to Spike Island. Have you heard of Spike Island?'

'Yeah,' she replied, 'both my parents were into all that stuff as well. And I saw the film not long back. My mum used to fancy the guy out of Shed 7. They still tour. I saw a picture of him on the internet recently; he's still quite fit for an old man. Sorry to hear about your Mum.'

He laughed. 'Your mum fancied Rick Witter and mine fancied Tim Burgess from the Charlatans. Sounds like they would have got on well. That's how I got my name, from the lead singer of a 90s indie band. They're still going as well. He has this ridiculous hairdo now. It was a long time ago when she died. I don't remember much about her. She was pretty and had black hair. She was funny and always used to sing to me while I was in bed. That's all I can remember about her. Each year I remember less.'

'But you're close to your dad. That's nice. He sounds cool.'

Tim stopped eating his toast and turned his gaze from Lyla to stare blankly toward an ash effect wardrobe next to the door. He took a couple of gulps of tea before looking at his lap. Her heart sank. She knew he was composing himself. She could guess what was coming.

'He was. He was cool, but he died 3 years ago. One minute he was here and the next he was gone.'

'How?'

'He was on a stag do with his mates on a Greek Island and they had a speedboat. One of them lost control, killing him and injuring one of the others while they were swimming. The driver had been drinking and drove it in a part of the water you weren't allowed to. He was showing off and ended up in prison, my dad in the morgue, and the other guy with one arm and loads of scars. He's out of prison already. It was a stupid way to die. Especially for someone like him. He deserved better. It's bad enough he died, but to die like that. I still get angry if I let myself think about it.'

'I'm so sorry,' she gushed, leaning forward and hugging him. 'I keep putting my foot in it, don't I?'

'It's what happened. You said nothing wrong. It always comes up. Most of the time I don't think about it but sometimes it's tough. I don't always choose to discuss it. Like when you said he sounds cool, I could have just said yes. Sometimes I do. It's easier. But it wouldn't have felt right with you. Even if - as you say - I'm just a one-night stand!'

'You're making me feel bad. I didn't mean it to sound like that, but... I don't know. I didn't expect to have such a great Tuesday night. That's one thing I love about being a student. You can enjoy yourself any night. Look at us now. If we were working, this would just be an average Wednesday. But it's not, is it?'

'I don't usually speak about it to people I've only just met, but you're different somehow. It would've been wrong to lie to you.'

'Do you have any brothers or sisters?'

'No, it's just me. But my dad set me up financially. I have a house paid for and a decent life insurance pay-out. At first, I was like – I don't want the money – but eventually, real-life kicks in and you need it. And it helps. He always wanted me to be happy and make a living from my music. That may or may not be possible, but the money gives me a few years to have a fair crack at it before I have to get a proper job.'

'And the tribute band stuff,' she reminded him, 'that pays well.'

'I exaggerated how well it pays, but it earns a few beer tokens. But it's not that. It reminds me of my dad and the music I listened to growing up. And the lads in the band. We're great mates.'

'So, who's your best mate in the band? Please tell me you don't get on with the singer. That would be brilliant.'

'No, we all get on well. The singer's called Liam, as it happens. He's a panel beater who works in Hillsborough. He's a good lad and handy if you get into trouble. Guigsy and Bonehead are Alan and Ben and both work for an insurance company in a call centre somewhere between Sheffield and Barnsley. They hate it but that's where they met, and they keep each other sane. The drummers a lad called Julian, who's training to be an architect. They're a good set of lads, and we go out a lot.'

'Who's your best friend?'

'Out of them, it's Liam. But he's not my best friend. That's a lad called Clint.'

'Clint? Is he the lad you were out with last night? I never spoke to him. What's he like?'

Tim laughed. 'That's a good question. He's a character is Clint. Put it this way. If I were writing a book about my life, this guy would get his own chapter.'

Chapter 3

A Guy called Clint

'I've known this guy all my life. He's one of the first memories I have. He's a brother from another mother and the one constant in my life.'

'That's nice.'

'He's like my brother, but also a bit like a father. He's the same age as me, but he's so smart. I don't mean he's a bit brainy; he's like a fuckin' prodigy or something. He's ridiculously clever; especially at science. Whatever room you're in, you can bet he's the smartest there. Unless you're in a room in NASA or somewhere; and even then, my money's on him. But you wouldn't know, though. He doesn't show off or anything, and the thing is, he's just like you or me. Normally, if someone's smart, they're different, even if they try to hide it. But not him.'

'You sound proud of him?' she commented.

'I suppose I am. I never really thought about it. We just like the same stuff; same music, same football team.'

'Who do you support?'

'Wednesday. There are only two clubs in this city: Wednesday and The Leadmill. I fail to acknowledge any others.'

'Fair enough,' she laughed.

'But this is what I'm on about with Clint. He's worse than me with football. When England gets knocked out of the World Cup, you'll be lucky to get more than a dozen grunts out of him for a week. I was once listening to the commentary on a Wednesday match in his back garden and we conceded a last-minute goal, so he picks up an edge trimmer and smashes it against a wall. It was brand new, cost fifty quid, and he doesn't have a violent bone in his body. It wasn't even an important game. He's one of the lads, but deep down we all know he isn't. He's destined for big, big things.'

'What does he do?'

'He went away to Cambridge University for a while, but it didn't last long. It was too easy. A waste of time. There are people there having nervous breakdowns trying to get a degree and he can't be arsed because it's too easy.'

'I bet his parents loved that!'

'His dad died when he was young, which is something else we have in common, and his mum was glad to have him back. Plus, she knows what he's like. Someone that clever will always be OK. He's too clever for education. Too much of a freethinker to be constrained by a classroom. So now he's doing some job at the university here, which is way below what he should do, but he does it to use their equipment to carry out his own research. I think it's in mathematics and theoretical physics. Or is it physics and astrophysics? Probably both knowing him.'

'You said his own research. What's that?'

Tim sat forward on the bed and put his hands on his face before sighing.

'Oh man, oh man, oh man. You're gonna love this,' he declared, laying backward with his hands behind his head. He lay there laughing and shaking his head for a while.

'Just bloody tell me then.'

'I've already told you how we grew up together and were into the same stuff. Well, we used to watch loads of films. The usual—The Goonies, Big, Independence Day, Ghostbusters, Jurassic Park, the Full Monty, Trainspotting. New stuff and old stuff—all the classics. But there was one film which we both loved more than the others. I take it you've seen Back to the Future?'

'Of course, you would have to live on the moon not to have seen it! I love it.'

'Nice,' he said, smiling, 'we used to watch all three films over and over. I've no idea how many times we saw them, but it was ridiculous. Like every kid who watched the film, we talked about how we'd love to build a time machine. Of course, normally you grow up and get a job and forget about impossible things like time travel. But this is Clint. He's convinced he can do it. More convinced now than when we were kids.'

'Wow. He really thinks he's gonna be able to figure out how to travel through time?'

'No,' Tim sighed. 'He says he's already figured it out!'

'But how?' she gasped.

'I have absolutely no idea. But it's not like in the film. It's something to do with wormholes.'

'Wormholes?'

'Yeah, he's tried to explain it to me, but I didn't get it. It's baffled the finest minds on the planet for centuries, so it's unlikely I'm gonna get it. They are tunnels that link points in space-time so you can travel through them from one point in time to the other. I don't think it's instantaneous, like in the film, but it's quick.'

'I've watched a few programs on wormholes,' she said. 'It was Albert Einstein who discovered them. There are loads of theories, but they've never been proven to exist. And even if they existed, they would be in space, so how would you find one, let alone get to one?'

'He's creating his own using electromagnetics.'

'I know you think he's clever—but do you think he's smarter than Einstein?'

'No, but he's a better mate, so I'm right behind him with all his theories and I'll help him whenever he asks me. Which reminds me. I have to get off soon to help him with his latest experiment.'

'Are you sure? I was going to bunk off today; we could spend the day in bed,' she tempted.

'Oh, believe me, I would love to, but Clint would never forgive me,' he groaned. 'You said earlier that today was just an average Wednesday. That's true to most people, but not to Clint.'

'Why, what's so special about today?'

'It's Back to the Future day. The day in the second film when he goes to the future. October 21st, 2015. It's an important day for him. He's been planning an experiment on this date for a couple of years. I can't let him down.'

Lying on her side, she alluringly peeled back the covers fully, revealing her breasts, their pertness defying gravity.

'Are you sure you can't stay?' she whispered.

'I'm sorry,' he bemoaned.

'Sure?' she asked, pushing the covers down to her feet; the power of her nubile body in plain view. Tim quickly jumped out of bed before he fell into the honey trap.

She yanked the sheets back over herself in a fit of anger, embarrassment, and frustration. Her aesthetics previously ensured rejection was an unknown quantity. But begrudgingly, she admired his resolution and the strength of friendship required to make the sacrifice. And not just the strength of the friendship, but the calibre of man willing to do it. A man who could be relied upon under such circumstances showed the character of a man worthy of getting to know. Her hostility thawed as quickly as he dressed.

'Will I see you again—and I don't mean on stage,' she asked, trying to sound the model of indifference.

'I'd like that but I wasn't sure if you wanted to,' he said weakly, his voice trailing off as he feared her reply.

She whispered, 'yes I would,' standing up naked and walking over to him, her eyes focused on his. 'I want you to have this.'

She unclasped a thin silver chain he had not noticed from around her neck and put it around his.

'Wear this for your experiment. It will bring you luck. It's very thin, so no one will know you're wearing it. Something to remind you of me. You know Tim, things will work out for you. I have a feeling. But you need to be confident. For someone who gets on stage and performs in front of people, you seem to doubt yourself. Trust me, you have a lot to be confident about.'

Without her chain, she was truly naked as she glided over to her phone on the bedside. 'Put your number in here, please.'

'I've put my landline on as well. Just in case I lose the mobile.'

'Oh, OK' she said.

She was surprised but happy. He was keen enough to plan for the unlikely event of losing his phone; nobody gave out their landlines anymore. She was thinking ahead of herself. She was young and enjoying University with no intention of starting a relationship. But some things in life can't be controlled. Putting each of her hands on his cheeks, she stood on her tiptoes and kissed him gently on the lips.

'Don't worry Tim, I *will* call you.'

Chapter 1

The Ultimate Man Cave

He had cut it fine, but it wasn't quite 3 pm. His car skidded on loose gravel as he pulled into his usual parking space. He couldn't see Clint's Red 1985 Mark 3 BMW, but the security bollard was down. It must be inside the industrial unit.

The location had always been curious to Tim. It was on the grounds of a golf course on the boundary between Sheffield and Rotherham. The entrance, from the main road, led down to the clubhouse via a private road, splitting the 1st and 18th fairway.

At the top of the track was a turning to the driving range a few hundred yards away. There were two car parks: a smaller one at the bottom of the hill next to the entrance to the range, and a large one at the top. The smaller one was big enough to accommodate customers, so it was a mystery why the larger car park existed. It had been a topic of discussion between Tim and Clint frequently, with the only explanations being the architect had overestimated the popularity of the range or he was doing a lot of LSD when it was built in the 1960s'.

Years of disuse left it overgrown except for a few spaces next to the unit. There were large concrete blocks at the entrance, to prevent unwanted cars at night, with access through the removable security bollard.

The car park had belonged to a guy called Gerald, who owned the driving range; but had given it to Clint for free. Gerry had been Clint's father's best friend before his premature death and a photo of the two of them at a wedding still hung on the wall next to the small bar in the range. The land was effectively worthless, but the gift and bar photo were both gracious gestures, appreciated by Clint, who often chatted to Gerry about his father over a drink; the two raising a whisky jar in memory of the anniversary of his death every year. Gerry also claimed to have known Tim's dad well, although his dad had never mentioned him.

'I remember your dad back in the day,' he would claim, 'he was the Pete Beale of the Leadmill—always in there. Even had his own tankard behind the bar.'

Tim never understood what he meant by that, or who the hell Pete Beale was, but it used to play well with the middle-aged men at the bar who would roar with laughter every time he regurgitated the tale.

Despite the land being worthless and the purpose of the overgrown car park remaining a mystery, Tim loved the location. There must have been close to 100 spaces and, in a world increasingly short of land and car parking, there was something perversely satisfying about being able to choose a space.

It was also a brilliant spot for a kick around with the football. Not bad for a piece of free land, anyway. The industrial unit was second-hand and been erected by mates of Gerry's for "next to nothing". It was a further act of kindness, which left Tim wondering if it was all down to friendship. His suspicious side wondered if there was something else at play. Maybe guilt? Had he ripped Clint's dad off in a business deal, or worse still slept with his wife? Maybe Gerry was Clint's real dad. Of course, he never released these thoughts into the fresh air; particularly as Gerry was one of the nicest and most sincere men he had ever met.

It was a large unit, previously used in nearby Rotherham by a steel fabrication company upgrading to a newer unit. It was battered around the edges, but roughly the size of a swimming pool and adequate for Clint's requirements.

The unit was supposed to be for Clint to carry out his experiments but had become a cornucopia of boys' toys. There were footballs, football nets, a basketball hoop, dartboard, pool table, mini bar, hot tub, fridge, shower, toilet, barbeque, patio furniture, and sofas which pulled out as beds. It wasn't unusual for the two to stay the night after drinking too much. It was the Rolls Royce of man-caves; and there was one more thing he loved about it. Parked up inside was a second-hand Delorean sports car.

There were two entrances: one large roller shutter door, which required manual opening and made a loud scraping noise, and a smaller personnel door. The smaller door had sprung open the moment the car skidding announced Tim's arrival, spewing out an uncharacteristically manic Clint.

'You're cutting it fine, aren't you?' he snapped. 'Come in. Hurry up.'

Chapter 5

The Worm Hole

'What's up with you pal, you're all over the place? You haven't stolen plutonium from dodgy terrorists, have you?'

Normally, a Back to the Future reference would have generated a better response, but Clint was preoccupied. He was dressed casually, as always, with Converse trainers and blue jeans; he was even donning a 'where we are going; we don't need roads' - Back to the Future T-shirt. But his manner was off, his usual frustratingly laid-back demeanour replaced with sweaty agitation.

'Hang on, where's the Delorean? And what on God's earth is that?' Tim noted, pointing towards a large, white cylindrical structure accessed by a timber ramp. It was huge, swallowing up more than half of the unit.

'That's the money, pal. That's what I've been working on. It's what makes it possible to access the wormholes. It's based on the string theory and the wormholes are traversable. But if you want to help me, you need to listen carefully. We don't have much time.'

'Are you serious? You think you've invented time travel?'

'Oh, trust me, pal,' announced Clint. 'I *have* invented time travel. That thing works, and it's safe. Just like we always discussed growing up. I'm going to send you back to Manchester in the 1990s. The Manchester your dad raved about. You can live there for a full week. But then you must come back. We must send you to a few years before you were born. If you're there after you're conceived, you won't exist in this reality anymore and cannot return.'

'You're serious, aren't you?'

'Of course I am. What's the problem? We've discussed this so many times. You agreed. You aren't backing out? We only discussed it last week.'

'But I never thought you were serious. Or that you could do it. Or this day would ever come.'

'Look, if you don't think it'll work, then what have you to lose? You help me out with this, and when it doesn't work, we can have a laugh about it over a few beers. I'll even get the barbeque out.'

'But isn't it dangerous? Could I die?'

'You're my best mate; sometimes the only thing keeping me sane. And you're the only person who believes in me. There's no way I would risk you unless I was sure.'

'So, what is this thing?'

'I haven't got time to explain, but the problem with wormholes is we usually consider them being gravitational, which means the internal walls attract each other and collapse. But this is based on electromagnetic field manipulation, so I have managed to prevent collapse. The closest thing I could compare it to is a giant MRI scanner. Because I create and control the electromagnetic field, I can choose when and where to place the exit to the wormhole.'

'An MRI scanner? I suppose they are safe enough,' Tim muttered.

'That's right. You don't need to know much more,' Clint continued, 'except for one thing. And this is important, so pay attention. The exit to the wormhole is vital. It must be somewhere geologically suited to work and somewhere remote, so you are not seen exiting and/ or someone doesn't accidentally walk in. To manipulate the electromagnetic field, I have coated my car in a few layers of what I refer to as "exotic matter". Without this, the interior wall will collapse. In the car's boot is a pump spray, like you might use in the garden attached to a drum with the exotic matter in. When you come back, give the car a spray a couple of hours before, just to be on the safe side, but you won't need it. But anyone or anything which wonders in will be crushed. And what's more, the hole will close, so you will be stuck where you are. You can only use a location to exit and enter once, and I can only keep it open for 5 minutes, so you *must* be ready to enter. None of this cutting it fine bollocks. If you miss your chance, you will have no way of knowing where I put the next hole. A bit like in the first film when they needed to know when lightning struck. But this isn't a film. This is real life.'

'So, I'm going in your BMW? I thought we agreed it was going to be the DeLorean. What's happened to the DeLorean?'

'The Delorean is a long story. I'll tell you when you get back. But my car is a 1985 plate so will be perfect. It will be quite new as well. Few people your age could afford these back then. I can't emphasise enough the importance of what I said before about the entrance to the wormhole. But I have built in a fail-safe. If the wormhole is not entered, I can open it up again one more time—but that's it, after that you are proper stuck. Do you understand the importance of being ready for me opening the wormhole? Not just for you to enter, but also to guard it against wrongful entry and certain death.'

'Yes. Of course. Don't worry, I have no intention of being trapped in the past. Even if they had better music back then.'

'Are you up for it then?' Clint asked.

'Are you sure it's safe?'

'It's safer than flying. The most dangerous thing about it will be your driving.'

'Will I just reappear where I set off, like in the film?'

'No. I've researched an exit in a remote area with plenty of road at the other end, although you will only be moving a few miles an hour—not 88! You won't crash and you won't need to hide the car; you can drive around in it. Don't ask, but there's ten grand cash in notes which were in circulation back then in the dash. That wasn't easy to lay my hands on! So, enjoy yourself. Oh, and there's a bag with a few toiletries in the boot.'

'But what about me changing the future? If this does work, could I do things to endanger my existence?' Tim questioned.

'No - there's no reason you should change your existence as long as you return before you were conceived. If you remain longer than your conception date, you won't exist in the present; neither will your sperm, so a different sperm will fertilise the egg. There are millions of those things. Your parents' lives will continue, but they will have a different child. Probably an upgrade at that!'

'So, it's not like the film when he disappeared from the photo?'

'No. Even if you were to accidentally kill one of your parents, you would still be alive, but you couldn't come back to the present, you would have to stay where you were until after the date you were conceived because your parents would be dead and you would never have existed. Then you could travel back to the present; but of course, you would be older—unless you then went into the future until you were the right age again. But your parents would still be dead. So if you see them, avoid them. That's the theory anyway,' Clint mused. 'The last thing I need you to remember is this. Creating a wormhole takes years. Not just the creation but the testing and location, and - once it's been used, it's gone and then I would have to go about making another to come and get you. Except I couldn't come and get you. I would need to send someone else. But who else would volunteer to go back?'

'So, the moral of the story is don't miss the fuckin wormhole,' Tim laughed.

'Yes, pal—do not miss the wormhole! Oh, and don't use your real name—especially your surname. Bauer isn't that common and the last thing you want is members of your own family asking if you're related. You don't want to draw members of your family to you; just make something up. How are you feeling?'

'I'm not sure.'

'Do you trust me?' Clint probed. 'Do you think you are going to the past?'

'I trust you, pal. I trust you not to kill me anyway, but I don't think it'll work. It just isn't possible. We'll be laughing about it later over a burger, I reckon. I've got some beer in the car. Shall I get it and put it in the fridge?'

'No Tim, you won't be needing the beer. Oh, and put your phone on the side as well. But now for the fun part. What year do you want to visit?'

'I'll leave that up to you.'

'No. You're only saying that because you don't think it'll work. But it will. You were born on 5th April 1993, so you were conceived around the 29th of June 1992. So, to add in a bit of wiggle room, let's say any time before 1992. I've done a bit of research and have come up with a few dates you may like.'

'Go on,' said Tim.

'April 21st, 1991 or August 18th, 1991.'

'Why those dates?'

'The first is the date Wednesday won the Cup, and the second is the first Oasis gig at the Boardwalk in Manchester. Or if you want to go back further, you could go to 12th August 1989, when the Roses played the Empress Ballroom in Blackpool. You once told me you'd have loved to have been there?'

'OK,' replied Tim, pausing for thought, 'for what it's worth. Send me to watch the Roses.'

'Good choice. Catch.' Clint tossed Tim a wristwatch. 'Put it on. It's a classic Casio F91-W—the watch I always wear. It was introduced in 1989, so will work chronologically. I have set the alarm to go off at 1 pm next Wednesday. TWO HOURS before the wormhole opens. There's an envelope in the dash, next to the money, confirming the time according to the dates I have set the watch by. PLEASE PLEASE PLEASE do not miss the wormhole. The concert is on Saturday 12th August 1989, but I'm sending you to Thursday 10th at 3 pm. You will return on Wednesday 16th at 3 pm. You will have a few days before and a few days after to enjoy the adventure. You will arrive on the outskirts of Manchester, so you can spend time there. Maybe go to the Hacienda. That will be open in '89.'

'You said there was a failsafe? Said you could open it up one more time?' Clint's earlier agitation had given way to his more familiar, relaxed demeanour, but this question reignited his frustration.

'Yes, yes. I have set a failsafe in. If anyone–or anything does not enter the wormhole, during the 5 minutes it's open, I will be able to open it again the following week at the same time. But this is less stable and is a last resort. Opening it up a third time would be so unstable it would be suicidal. DO NOT take the piss and decide to spend an extra week in 1989. Promise me you won't take the piss.'

'Of course not pal, what do I do?'

'This part is simple. You drive the car up the ramp and onto the platform, at which point I turn on the electromagnetic field. You edge forward until you feel the car being pulled by the electromagnets. When that happens, just turn off the engine and knock the car out of gear and this little beauty will do the rest,' Clint explained, pointing at the white cylinder.

The cylinder was huge; big enough to fit a dozen BMWs in. And worryingly the ramp entered at the midpoint; ten feet from the bottom of the huge white cylinder.

'Don't worry, you won't fall,' assured Clint, who had either taken to mind-reading or, more likely, seen his friend's concerned look as his eyes shifted from the top of the ramp to the floor. 'The electromagnets will suspend you in mid-air. It'll be cool. A bit like an anti-gravity tunnel but with magnets and in a car; so cooler.'

'What happens at the other end? How do I get out?'

'The magnets will repel the car, spewing you out into the past at about 20mph, so you will need to make sure you are out of gear and the handbrake is off. Otherwise, you will come to an abrupt stop. Make sure you have your seatbelt on.'

'But I'll be ten feet in the air when I'm puked out.'

'No, you won't; you'll only be a couple of inches. It'll be a smooth exit. Catch!' he exclaimed, throwing Tim the keys. 'Now toss me yours.'

'Why do you want my keys?'

'Because I'll be driving home in it after you've pissed off to 1989 in mine,' laughed Clint. 'You get in the car and I'll turn this bad boy on.'

The car had been thoroughly cleaned inside. Clint never cleaned his car. He was one of those absent-minded, untidy genius types. He hadn't cleaned his car so Tim would be comfortable on his journey, but to cleanse it of any traces of 2015. Tim's heart pounded. This was happening. Clint was not the guy you would bet against in any intellectual task, but Tim didn't believe he had invented time travel. Clint believed it but, for all his bromantic gestures, Tim wasn't sure if he would end up dead? He jumped as a loud crack announced the ignition of the giant white cylinder. His ears buzzed as they had at 3 am on many a Sunday morning as he staggered out of the Leadmill.

'Bollocks, this is madness. I'm gonna get killed,' Tim muttered to himself, putting his hand on the keys. The air inside the cylinder turned blue, distorted and swirled. As if hypnotised, Tim turned the ignition of the 1985 classic. 'Fuck it!' he shouted. After a deep breath, he flicked the car into gear and headed for the makeshift ramp.

The short run-up and steep angle saw the car slide back down. As embarrassing as it was for Tim's driving, Clint's inability to build a ramp shallow enough to easily access the top platform didn't bode well for the complex calculations required for traversing artificially created wormholes.

Tim reversed the car further back but was still only a few car lengths from the bottom as he accelerated. He knew the platform wasn't much bigger than two car lengths and didn't want to overrun into the cylinder. The underside of the bumper thudded against the ramp as he glided to the summit, releasing the accelerator as the front wheels met the level platform, gliding the car into the centre.

The necklace given to him that morning had liberated itself from behind his T-shirt and sat proudly on display. A blonde hair caught in one of the links reminded him of Lyla. If by some miracle he ended up in the past, at least part of her would come with him.

A frantic Clint was gesticulating at the bottom of the ramp. The buzzing was becoming louder. 'Out of gear, brake off, belt on!' he screamed.

As predicted, the car began rolling to the cylinder. Tim panicked and with the car rolling slow enough for him to jump out, he was not at the point of no return; not yet.

'Oh shit, oh shit, oh shit!' he panted as the car edged forward. Putting his hand on the door lever, he hesitated and looked up but, like holding onto a rising balloon, he had left it too late and was sucked into the electromagnetic field.

Chapter 6

The Eulogy

Inside, the cylinder was silent, like the eye of the storm; and calm, except for a feeling of gently sinking and rising. The blue aura had gone, replaced by an overwhelming sense of whiteness. He checked the car was out of gear. He checked the handbrake. He checked his seatbelt. He didn't know how long this would last. Did he have time to put the radio on? It was instinctive whenever he got into a car for even the shortest journey. It was sacrilege not to listen to music when you had the opportunity.

He chuckled. Clint had removed the fancy new radio he bought and replaced it with a battered old stereo with a tape cassette player and dials to tune the radio. Proudly emblazoned in orange letters across the top were the words 'Sanyo Entertainment Centre.' There was an audiotape protruding which he pulled out. In green letters were the words TDK C90. Handwritten on the white label were 'the Stone Roses' on side A in blue ink, blotting out the words 'Def Leppard' written in pencil. On the B Side, written in pencil, was 'The Cult–Wallflower–EP.' His heart fluttered as he took a gasp of breath. This was his dad's tape.

His father, Matt, gave the tape to him on his 18th birthday, along with an old cassette player and a Sheffield Star newspaper printed on the day of his birth. He remembered the newspaper vividly; it was a great time in his dad's life which he used to wax lyrical about after a few beers. Monday 5th April 1993's paper was a souvenir edition to celebrate the two Sheffield football teams meeting in the Semi-Final of the F.A. Cup at Wembley the previous Saturday. Despite his mother already being a week overdue, Matt still hopped on a booze coach with his mates at the local pub and went to the match. He often told Tim how it was worth it as his beloved Wednesday won the match and put one over their local rivals. 'And then two days later you were born my son,' he would proclaim, raising his glass in the air, 'what a week - the best ever!'

He would then sing, 'we've got Carlton Palmer, he smokes marijuana, Na Nah Nah Nah uh! Na Nah Nah Nah uh!'

Finally, he would stare into space in a state of extraction, the glazed smile on his face reaffirming to himself the story got better with each telling.

The tape was another story altogether. Another story he had heard many times but, like the story of Wembley, one he was never bored with; one he could recite off the top of his head; one he would give anything to hear again.

It was a warm Friday summer's evening in 1989 and his dad was out with his mates in Sheffield City Centre. Musically he was lost, describing the mid to late eighties as a musical vacuum. The Jam had split up in the early eighties, ending an era of edgy guitar-fused mod/ punk rock groups. He was approaching his teenage years when they split and felt cheated at being born 5 years too late to appreciate the scene. He couldn't get excited about the new wave of synthesized electro-pop, dominating the charts; despite being heavily influenced by his hometown. He got it; he liked it; but he didn't love it, leaving him stuck in a retro vinyl world of the Clash and the Sex Pistols, whilst sifting through the cassettes in HMV and Our Price for the next big thing.

He first went to the Leadmill in '86 to watch the Housemartins, and it had become a regular Friday night haunt. If anything were going down, musically, it would go down there; why else would he be willing to wade through an inch of piss every time he went to the toilet? It was rough around the edges back then.

Then it happened. From out of nowhere a guitar riff hung lazily in the air, followed by a hollow, echoing bass before a monotone 'can't be arsed' but somehow triumphant voice announced, 'your knuckles whiten on the wheel, the last thing that your hands will feel, your final flight can't be delaaaaaayed.....'

'Who's this?' he shouted to his friend Fozzie, who stood next to him, 'who the fuck is this?'

'It's the Stone Roses, pal. I've got it on record. Do you want me to tape it for you?'

'Yes, please pal.'

'I'll do it tomorrow.'

But Fozzie didn't do it tomorrow. Matt insisted he went back to Fozzie's that night at 3 am and had a couple of whiskies while he made him a copy.

'And that,' he would say, 'is the night the Stone Roses changed my life!'

The end of that story weighed heavy in Tim's heart because of what happened to the tape after his father's death. Matt was like his dad, brother, and friend, all rolled into one. He was like a mother, too. At his funeral, Tim planned to do a eulogy to thank him and show everybody what a great man he was. He had written a few words, followed by a specially written song. But his death hit him hard, and he was too upset to utter a single word.

After the wake in a local pub, he returned home drunk and angry at himself and the world, but mostly his dad for leaving him and the stupidity of his death. Knowing how badly this could end, he was chaperoned by Clint, who stopped the night to keep an eye on him. He ended up staying a couple of weeks. But the funeral night was the worst, with Tim smashing up the living room and even some of his dad's records. But his biggest regret was picking up the Stone Roses cassette and skimming it out of the window. The records were bad enough but could be replaced at a record fayre.

The tape was unique. He couldn't forgive himself for the tape. He thought he would never see it again. But there it was. He had skimmed it way over his fence and into open woodland behind the house. It must have taken Clint ages to find it. But why hadn't he given it to him before now, he wondered, noticing the piece of plastic he was cherishing so dearly in his hand was in the same condition and must have been retrieved soon after he launched it? Knowing Clint, he probably went out with a torch after he had fallen asleep to find it.

But why now? Perhaps because the timing was perfect? Exquisite even. What better eulogy for his father than rolling into Manchester in 1989 playing his tape?

His eyes filled as he acknowledged the enormity of the gesture and the friendship he was fortunate to have. And for the first time, not only did he believe he was heading toward 1989, he was looking forward to it.

Chapter 7

1989

With the brilliant white horizon darkening, he knew something was about to happen. How long had he been daydreaming? 5 minutes? Suddenly the car was sucked forward and, like a streak of toothpaste, ejected from the tube. Frantically, he grasped the steering wheel, dropping the tape onto the floor. The car flew into the air, only inches from the road, quickly rolling to a halt, jolting Tim forward in his seat.

'Fuck,' he shouted anxiously, jumping out of the car.

He spun around. There was no garage. No Clint. He was in front of a concrete underpass on a country lane. The underpass must be the wormhole. He was in the middle of nowhere, the underpass and road the only manmade structures he could see, but he could hear traffic above. He stepped further back to see the metal bumper rails separating the edge of the road above from the drop below.

The underpass served agricultural land and was new and rarely used. It wasn't the kind of underpass he was used to in the city. There were no lights, no drainage, and, more unusual still, no graffiti. Perfect for the wormhole. But where was he? When was he?

In the dashboard was a white envelope, and a Morrison's plastic bag, stuffed with money. The bag was squashed into the compartment; barely fitting, forcing the envelope out onto the floor. Although he needed the information in the envelope more, he wanted to see what ten grand looked like in used notes. He stuffed a few in his pocket and rammed the compartment closed.

The envelope contained several sheets of paper, mostly relating to the reappearance of the wormhole and the importance of being there on time for its re-opening. It confirmed the underpass was the wormhole. There were also recommendations for accommodation in Manchester and Blackpool. There was a map with a big red 'you are here' cross. Underneath were printed in red capital letters—DO NOT LEAVE UNTIL YOU ARE SURE YOU CAN FIND YOUR WAY BACK.

It was a good point. It was an instantly forgettable location, and he was known for forgetting where he parked his car in Meadowhall. There were no discernible landmarks to distinguish the area, so he picked up a stone and marked an x on the side of the underpass. At least he would know it was the right one when he came back. The map showed he was close to an old church near a village a few miles north of Manchester.

He got in the car and started the engine before picking up the tape. He put it into the player but before he pushed it in, he turned on the radio. He knew where he was, but maybe the Radio would tell him when he was.

The radio was more difficult to operate than it looked. There were no pre-tuned channels or digital numbers. 'How the fuck are you supposed to find a channel,' he muttered. 'And why does it keep whistling? And what's this do?'

The whistling stopped as he pressed the FM button and found a channel just before he reached 100, right at the end of the dial.

'*We always hang in a Buffalo Stance, we do the dive every time we dance, I'll give you love baby, not romance, I'll make a move nothing left to chance, so don't you get fresh with me...*'

'Happy Thursday everybody, that was Neenah Cherry, and this is Steve Wright in the Afternoon on Radio One,' announced the DJ.

'Steve Wright! I need a newspaper,' he muttered in disbelief, turning the ignition.

He passed no buildings on the small service road as he wound upwards to join the A628, which itself was narrow and winding, but much busier. He knew the road as the Woodhead Pass, linking Sheffield to Manchester; a route he had taken many times. He recognised the turning he would have to take on the way back.

He was having difficulty getting out of the junction because of the volume of traffic, but even more trouble coming to terms with the cars driving past. He still wanted to see the ink of a newspaper to confirm the date; just as Michael J. Fox did, but unless there was a 1980s car convention—and a large one at that, full of mint conditioned vehicles—he must be in '89. A flutter of butterflies swamped his stomach. The tricky clutch control required to nip in made access hard enough without him gauping at the cars. Finally, he headed toward Manchester, stopping off en route at a small petrol station.

He was in a village cruelly split in half by the bustling road. The stone cottages on either side of the carriageway, deafened and gasping for air, rued the day this stretch of tarmac was laid. He had driven through many times, feeling a natural empathy for its remaining inhabitants. But, for now, empathy was replaced with curiosity as he walked past a brand new dark blue Vauxhall Cavalier and into the kiosk.

The one person in front of him was presumably the owner of the Cavalier. He was in his thirties with brown hair, parted in the middle and unkempt sideburns which, in the sunlight, revealed a hint of ginger. In contrast to his straight brown hair, the sideburns had curled; and the more he looked at them, the more they looked like a pair of fish fingers stuck to the side of his face. He was wearing a dark grey double-breasted suit with a faint blue check, at least one size too big for him and a red kipper tie dotted with large cream circles. His swagger as he left suggested he was oblivious to how ridiculous he looked.

'Any petrol, mate?' asked the attendant.

'No, thanks. Just this,' he replied, waving a copy of the Daily Mirror in the air and putting a ten-pound note on the counter.

The attendant looked up at him in what could be described as a patented look of sarcasm before glancing at his car and smirking.

'Have you anything smaller than that?'

'How much is the paper?'

'25p'

'OK, I'll have one of these as well,' Tim responded, grabbing a copy of Viz magazine.

'£1.15 please,' came the polite response; happy his belligerence had bagged him a cool 90p extra in sales. 'Drive carefully.'

He didn't want to look at the paper in the shop, or even in the courtyard, under the gaze of the attendant, so he drove to the nearest pub and pulled into the car park.

'Ok,' he said to himself. In his heart, he knew the answer as he flipped the paper over the wheel. Thursday 10th August 1989.

It surprised him how calm he felt. He sensed he was in '89, but perhaps it was just a realistic dream from which he would awake. But now in paper print, it was real; he wasn't waking up - he was in 1989. But which was the craziest part; that he had time travelled to before he was born, or that his mum and dad were now younger than him? Or maybe it was the fish finger sideburns on the guy in the petrol station?

'There's only one thing for it,' he thought, 'book a hotel, go to the Hacienda and get tickets for Blackpool. That's my 1989 bucket list.'

Chapter 8

Whippin' Piccadilly

Tim had been to Manchester a few times courtesy of a female student he met in the Leadmill, but had not spent much time in the City Centre and had never been for a night out; so to have his first night out at the Hacienda and in 1989 was a big deal. His dad had been a student a couple of train stops away in Bolton and told him some amazing tales of nights out in the City Centre.

Driving into the centre, the size of the city and the magnitude of being in 1989 seeped into his pores. It was all-enveloping. Suddenly Sheffield in 2015 seemed distant, small and sterile. Like heroin pumping through his veins, he was hooked in an instant.

The Midland Hotel was huge, elegant and not on Clint's list. But it was straight in front of him, he was lost in a one-way system and had ten grand in the dash. Clint had told him to enjoy himself! Not fitting the hotel's upper-class demographic, he raised eyebrows when he paid in cash for six nights in a double room with an en suite. In all the excitement he accidentally used his real name.

The remainder of the money was stuffed into the black sports bag he had taken from the boot of the BMW. There wasn't much in it except for toothcare and grooming products. The only items of clothing were a light blue zip-up Levi cardigan and a few pairs of boxer shorts and socks. He would do for tonight though. He was wearing a pair of Levi jeans and a plain black t-shirt. Nothing which would look out of the ordinary in 1989.

It was 8 o'clock by the time he finished his meal in the hotel bar, casually charging it to the room as if he were used to having money to burn. Two pints of lager and a quick brandy calmed his nerves. The timeless surroundings of the Midland 1989, didn't seem any different to 2015; but he knew that would change the moment he stepped out of the lobby and into the taxi the Concierge arranged for him.

'Where are you going?' asked the driver.
'Do you know the Dry Bar?'
'Of course, pal. It's not that far. You could have walked.'

'I know,' replied Tim, 'next you'll be telling me it's not worth the twenty quid I'll be paying you either?'
'Come to think of it,' laughed the driver, 'it is too far to walk.'

If Piccadilly Square was the heart of Manchester, the roads leading to it were the veins supplying the blood. The Dry bar was situated on one of its main arteries.

It was a large rectangular-shaped room with the bar on the left and an array of seats to the right. It was busy with an eclectic range of customers dotted around; the seating area was fully occupied.

He was approached by a man in his late teens with black greasy hair, parted to one side wearing stone washed baggy jeans and a denim jacket with beige corduroy to the collar and cuffs.

'Moody wants to know if you want a lager?' he asked.

'What?'

'Moody wants to know if you want a lager but hurry up, he's at the bar. It takes ages to get served in here.'

He looked over to see a tall thin guy with blonde hair wearing an ankle-length jacket smiling and waving.

'Err OK,' replied Tim putting his thumb up to the generous stranger at the bar.

'How do you know Moody, then?' asked the greasy-haired stranger who stood way too close to him.

'I don't,' he replied.

'Why's he buying you a pint then?'

'I don't know, you asked me?'

'But why did you say yes if you didn't know him. It's not cheap in here?'

'I've never been out in Manchester before. I thought maybe the locals were friendly.'

The guy with the black hair burst into a fit of laughter which seemed to continue forever and was as annoying as it was awkward.

Eventually, he composed himself, 'You're not kidding when you said you haven't been out in Manchester before if you think people buy you drinks. Fuckin brilliant is that.'

As the two looked at each other, wondering what to say next, a pint of lager appeared magically over Tim's shoulder.

'There you go, pal. How's my favourite roadie? Have you been on tour anywhere good recently? Oh fuck, you're not him. Sorry, pal. You might as well have the pint. I thought you were someone else. You look like a mate of mine from a distance but close up you're probably better looking. But you do look like him. Nice to meet you pal. Everyone calls me Moody. Who are you?'

Tim was caught on the hop; he had still not thought of a pseudonym, regretting his reply the moment it left his lips.

'Troy,' replied Tim. 'Troy Gold.' It was a joke name he and Clint sometimes used.

'Troy Gold. What a name. I love it. You could be in a band with a name like that. So, Troy Gold – who are you out with tonight?'

'I'm on my own.'

'And what's the accent? Where are you from?'

'Sheffield.'

By now the rest of Moody's entourage had returned from the bar. Including the guy with the greasy black hair, there were eight of them.

'Sheffield. Hey lads this guy's from Yorkshire!'

'Sheep, sheep, sheep shagger, sheep, sheep, sheep, shagger!' they chanted in unison; clearly, something they had done before; probably at a football match.

'Just joking, man. It's not where you're from it's where you're at, brother. Where are you at? What are you doing here on your own on a Thursday night?'

'I've come to have a few beers around Manchester and check out the Hacienda. What I really want though is a ticket for the Roses in Blackpool.'

'The Stone Roses. Fuck me, you've heard of them in Sheffield. I thought nobody south of Crewe or east of Stockport knew about the Roses. Hey, Quinny. This guy from Sheffield has heard of the Roses.' Moody shouted to the guy with the black hair.

'Nice one. I'm Quinny by the way. I know Ian, the singer.'

Moody laughed, 'Like fuck you know Ian Brown. You saw him once walking through Warrington and you were too scared to say owt to him. And knowing you it probably wasn't even him.'

'I do know Ian Brown,' protested Quinny.

'Well, if you know him then you should be able to get our new mate Troy Gold a ticket. A gold ticket. Like Charlie and the Chocolate factory,' Moody howled with laughter.

'I will. I will get him a ticket. After I've had a piss. Hold this,' Quinny remonstrated, thrusting his pint into Tim's hand.

Moody was still laughing. 'He's a good lad Quinny, but he talks bollocks. But listen man, we need to get you a ticket for Saturday. You could come with us if you want. There's a few of my mates going. Better than going on your own?'

'Yeah, why not?' agreed Tim, 'I can drive us there?'
'What car you got?'
'BMW 320i. It's an old one though 1985.'
'A four-year-old BMW. How do you manage?' Moody howled. 'But it won't be big enough and Saturday will get messy. You won't want to be driving back the next day. The train will be better. Where are you stopping?'
'At the Midland,' he replied sheepishly, expecting a similar reaction to the BMW revelation.
'The Midland. Fuck me. THE MIDLAND. How rich are you?' Moody exclaimed.
'I'm not rich. It's an inheritance. My dad left it to me when he died.'
It was a good lie, explaining the money without making him rich, whilst discouraging further questions.
'Oh, sorry to hear that pal.'
'It's OK. He was a top bloke. He would have wanted me to spend some of it getting messed up watching the Roses,' explained Tim.
'Sounds like a top bloke. We must get you some tickets. I might know someone. I need a phone.'
Tim put his hand in his pocket and blurted out without thinking, 'here you can borrow mine.'
Clint had been thorough clearing the car and sports bag of any item not available in '89, but as people with amputated limbs claim to still feel them after their removal, Tim had been having phantom vibrations. Nevertheless, he couldn't believe what he had just said.
Moody looked at him gone out. 'You think you've got a phone in your pocket? Even the phones those yuppies have in London wouldn't fit in your pocket.'
'Err. No, just messing around. I sometimes pretend I have small things in my pocket, like phones or guitars or violins; my dad used to do it when I was a kid. It reminds me of him,' Tim scavenged in desperation, attempting to salvage the situation.
'I like it. You've only just met me and you feel comfortable enough to do that. To be fair, we've been out since 12 and I'm half pissed. Ring, ring,' he screeched taking an imaginary phone out of his pocket, putting his thumb to his ear and little finger to his mouth, 'yes. Hello. It's for you, Troy.'
'Who is it?' Tim laughed.
'It's 1981. They want their tight jeans back. Seriously brother if you want to come to Blackpool you need to do something about those. Maybe they're OK in Sheffield and stop ferrets running up your trouser leg, but not around here pal. It's all baggy baby. It has to be loose fit! I'm off until

Tuesday now. I was gonna come into town tomorrow anyway and get some clothes for the weekend. I can take you to Affleck's Palace and sort you out.'

'Yeah, sounds good.'

'Anyway Troy, I haven't introduced you to the rest of the boys, have I? You've met Quinny, he's from a place called Marple, just outside Stockport.'

Moody reeled them off one by one, 'This is Lee from Leigh, Ashy from Chorley, Ged and Gaz from Bolton and the two at the end are Mad Rhys the Lamb from Atherton and Big Neil the intellectual yob from Tyldsley. You don't wanna know how those two got their nicknames.'

Tim laughed, 'So where do you lot know each other from?'

'We're all at Salford Tech. We're not there at the minute as it's still the summer break but today was results day. They post them on the notice board, so we all take the day off work, check we have passed, and then go out on the piss. We pretend it's part of the course, so we get a free day off work.'

'You work in the summer?'

'No pal, we work all the time, it's a part-time Degree in Quantity Surveying. Day release – one day a week. Think it's Thursday next year. It's a long day 8 till 7 at night so we deserve a free day I reckon.'

'What does a Quantity Surveyor do?' Tim asked.

'You don't wanna know pal. It's even more boring than its sounds. Like an accountant but in construction. But instead of counting money, we count bricks. Had no idea what I wanted to do at school except play football or be in a band and the next thing I know I'm a fuckin quantity surveyor. No idea how?'

'I wouldn't have had you down as a brick counter.'

'Cheers,' shouted Moody raising his glass, 'that's a bigger compliment than you realise.'

Tim laughed, 'So what happened to the football and band then?'

'I'm shit at football, but I am in a band.'

'You're in a band? Cool. Me too. What sort of music do you play?' asked Tim.

'Guitar-based music. Post-punk. Like the Clash. Guitar music's making a comeback. There's loads of new bands in Manchester now. It's the Stone Roses leading the way. I play guitar. What about you?'

'I play in a tribute band mainly; singer and lead guitar.'

'A tribute band? Why? A tribute to who?'

'Err the Clash. For the money. But I'm a singer-songwriter and I do my own stuff in Sheffield.'

'Interesting. So, you don't play in a band for your stuff. Apart from the jeans, you have a good look. We'll be looking for a singer soon. Ours is leaving, but he doesn't realise it yet.'

'You're kicking him out?'

'Yes. He's a good singer and but doesn't look right for us.'

'Why?'

'Well look for yourself. It's Ged over there. You've probably forgotten which one he is; he's the giant beanpole with ginger hair. He's like Ronald McDonald. I'm sorry but have you ever seen a band with a ginger singer?'

Tim was becoming accustomed to being in the eighties and thinking chronologically before speaking, 'Mick Hucknall. Simply Red. The flame-haired minstrel of soul.' He offered with pride. As luck would have it, Mick Hucknall had featured in the Viz magazine he bought at the petrol station, where he was referred to as "the flame-haired minstrel of soul."

'You're not making the point you think you are,' laughed Moody. I just can't see a ginger frontman no matter how good he is.'

'I can imagine a ginger frontman,' defended Tim.

'Perhaps but not in an Indie band pal, it's all about image. Look at Roy Orbison. He had ginger hair and dyed it black for his cool image.'

'No, he didn't. Well, he dyed it but he wasn't ginger, he had dark brown hair like me. I saw a documentary about him after he died. Do you think I should dye my hair?' Asked Tim, who was now wondering what year the big 'O' had died. He assumed he was in the clear as there was no response from Moody.

'No, but black is a cool hair colour. Look at Quinny's - if it wasn't so greasy all the time. But your hair is good. I could see you fronting our band. Are you interested?'

'No pal, I live too far away.'

'Are you sure? The more I think about it the more sense it makes. If you can play, we could have a lead and rhythm guitar. Turn it up to eleven.'

'No, sorry. Are you lot going to the Hacienda tonight?'

'I am but I don't think many of the others will; they're already hammered and will head back to Piccadilly for the last train. Me and Ged will go. We're meeting the rest of the band. Quinny will probably go as well. He's a right piss head. Sup up, we need to make a move if we're to get in. It gets rammed on a Thursday. Hey lads - who fancies the Hacienda?'

It didn't look like a nightclub from the outside with a curved red Accrington brick façade fronting a busy road, but it had a presence befitting its legendary status. Except for the entrance doors, the full height ground floor windows were over boarded in timber with yellow and black chevrons painted onto parts of the boarding. There were three rows of windows above these, all in pairs and perfectly symmetrical with lantern lighting above the first-floor windows. There was an arrogance and swagger to the place. Tim loved it; the hairs on his neck stood up as he joined the back of the queue; which displayed the same arrogance and swagger.

As Moody had anticipated only Ged and Quinny made the trip with them across town. The days drinking session was beginning to take its toll on the two, but Moody was fine.

'Oy Moody!' shouted a man as he walked past them to the back of the queue.

'Alright man see you inside,' he shouted back, turning to Tim, 'that's Bobby, he's our bass player and the guy with him is Adam, he's the drummer. Dude, we'd be as cool as a penguin's arse if you joined.'

'Mate, I can't do it, you need to stick with Ged. He's stood right behind you. He'll hear you.'

'He won't, he's too pissed. They both are.'

'How come, you're OK? You've been out as long as they have.'

'They don't pace it, pal. And they drink strong lager – wifebeater I call it. I stick to bedwetter.'

Tim laughed, 'wifebeater or bedwetter. I love it,'

Gradually the queue edged forward until the entrance was within sight, as were the bouncers when Quinny leaned over the steel barriers and projectile vomited a couple of pints of wifebeater onto the pavement to a roar of approval from the baying queue.

'Oy you lot – out of the queue,' ordered a bouncer as he headed towards them flanked by another bouncer.

'But,' Tim protested, 'I've come from Sheffield just to come here. I'm not drunk. I hardly know him.'

'I don't give a fuck. You four out of the fuckin' queue. *Now!*' he growled.

'Come on pal,' said Moody putting his arm around Tim, 'you don't want to mess with these two they're mental. They're gagging for a fight to make themselves look good in front of the slappers in the queue. Some women are impressed with the bouncers and end up going home with them. There's a lot of slappers out here.'

'But I need to get in to see if I can get a ticket for the Roses.'

'Don't worry about that pal, Adam and Bobby are your men. We'll grab them from the back of the queue and go to the Venue.'

'The Venue?'

'Yeah, it's a club about a hundred yards down here. It's only small but it's better anyway. The Hacienda is getting too commercial these days. And it's full of pretentious pricks. And it's a bit too dancy for my liking. Don't worry Troy if you wanna go to the Hacienda there's always next week. It'll still be here.'

'For you maybe,' thought Tim, 'but my next week is in 2015, and it'll be a bunch of apartments by then.'

Chapter 9

The Day We Caught the Train

The 8:53 train to Blackpool North left the far platform at Manchester Piccadilly to a large cheer. Most of its passengers were heading to the seaside to watch the Stone Roses.

Moody's forward-thinking the previous day had secured their seats for the journey on a small regional train now packed to the rafters. He had only known Moody for a couple of days but already held him in high esteem. Booking the seats was just the latest Moody masterstroke after getting him tickets to the Roses, setting him up with the coolest threads from Affleck's Palace, and introducing him to the Venue nightclub.

Tim and Moody spent most of Friday together in Manchester, mainly in either Affleck's Palace, a compact multi-levelled indoor market full of independent stores, or the Arndale Centre, a huge shopping mall in the centre of town.

Tim bought enough clothes to see him through his remaining days in 1989, mostly from Affleck's Palace. For the Blackpool outing, he was wearing stone-washed Levi jeans and black Pony trainers from the Arndale centre and a second-hand Adidas tracksuit top, James Dean T-shirt and silver buckle belt from Affleck's palace.

He loved the tracksuit top which was navy blue with a large red, white and royal blue stripe on each shoulder. It was baggy under the arms so when he put his arms out to the side he looked like a flying squirrel. He had never seen anything like it before and would be impossible to buy in 2015. It was the perfect top to wear when the Roses played "I am the Resurrection" and everyone put their arms out in the sign of a cross.

On top of this, he had made him welcome with his mates from the band, all of whom were now on board the train.

Tim, Moody, Adam and Bobby were sat around a table with Ged sat a row in front of them in the window seat; a striking metaphor considering the conversation they had in the Hacienda queue about Tim joining their band. It was a conversation that had continued in the Venue after Ged and Quinny had hailed a taxi together.

As they could never know the real reason for him being unable to join the band, he shifted focus by showing solidarity for the incumbent Ged. This wasn't just tactical, many of the bands in 2015 thrived with uncool frontmen and he genuinely felt sorry for Ged.

He also made a big deal of the band's name. Peanut University. Who in their right mind would call a band Peanut University? Even in 2015, the name would struggle but, although they all liked it, offered to change it to anything he wanted. They hadn't heard him play or sing, or any of his material; the offer was all based on image. But for all his empathy for Ged and the impossibility of him staying, he was flattered.

Part of him wished things were different, just to see how it would pan out. Yes, he had a band in 2015. Yes, he also had a best friend in 2015, but in the short time he had known Moody they had become good friends. It was an unconditional relationship that arrived so naturally and unintended there was an air of inevitability clinging to it.

He already felt as close to the boys of Peanut University as he did his mates in the Oasis tribute band. There was a stronger bond between the boys of 1989 than the boys of 2015. Tim had put together the tribute band from word of mouth and social media to form a band of musicians to earn money playing somebody else's music.

Moody, Bobby and Adam had all grown up together, learned how to play together and created their own music and lyrics. They started the band at school with the original singer, a mate called Martin, who left when – according to Moody – he became a "girlfriend bastard", which, as far as Tim could make out meant he had a girlfriend he wanted to spend some time with. Ged had joined after meeting Moody at Salford Tech. The conversations in the nightclub included many rites of passage stories like waiting at a bus stop in the pouring rain with a drum kit because Adam's brother's van broke down.

He envied the Peanut University backstory. It was real, gritty and proper. It was how it should be? It was how he imagined bands like the Stone Roses and Oasis would have started. If Peanut University had all those backstories, imagine what a band like Oasis could tell you over a few pints.

The tribute band's backstory was tame, even embarrassing by comparison. They were a manufactured band, brought together intending to make money without risk, cynically hiding behind their instruments whilst borrowing another's creations. Perhaps, subconsciously, he had been influenced by a decade of reality TV shows which validated the manufacturing of bands to earn a quick buck. Maybe he was no more than a poor man's Simon Cowell; a thought abhorrent to him. At least the 1989 boys were not yet subjected to the sacrilege of reality TV, and when it came they would be of an age where it would fall into the category of something else to moan about.

True, he bared his soul on the solo sets around the pubs, but they were short and limited musically by his onstage solitude. He was devoid of the camaraderie and creative banter he imagined thrived at Peanut Universities' rehearsals. All they did at rehearsals for the tribute band was practice how to play, even though they could all play anyway.

As he stared out of the window at the rolling Lancashire countryside the first inner demon manifested itself. But where was it? His heart, his soul, his head, or worse still all three.

What if he stayed in 1989 for an extra week? Who would it hurt? He could go to a band rehearsal and see what it was like. He could go to the Hacienda but without Quinny this time. He had plenty of money and Clint had built in a failsafe.

But if he delayed it a week the wormhole would be less stable; the risks would be increased. And if he went to rehearsals, he would be jeopardising Ged's place in the band. He had agreed to stay in 1989 for a week. It was a privilege he must respect. Most importantly he made a promise to Clint. The manifestation was new and small; embryonic even. It could still be controlled. He had to go back before it became too much for him to resist.

He had only been in 1989 for two days but was already making comparisons about the relationships he had with his new friends and his friendships in 2015. His mind wandered to his favourite Beatles song "In My Life". Tim interpreted the lyrics to mean you could fall in love and form new relationships without diminishing existing ones but had never experienced such emotions at first hand. But that was crazy, he had known one set of friends for years and the others for days.

But then he had never done anything like this with his other friends. He was on a packed train going to a gig and stopping overnight with nothing but the clothes on his back and the money in his pocket. In 2015 he would have gone in his car with a boot full of clothes and stopped in a Travelodge. Blackpool accommodation had been booked up for weeks and Moody had booked four places in some apartments. It wasn't a proper hotel, or even a Bed and Breakfast.

'Where did you say we were staying?' Tim asked.

'It's a place called The Grand Hotel Apartments. I've stopped before, it's OK. Plus, there isn't a proper reception or anything. We just pick up the keys from a deposit box I have the combination for and then we go in and out as we please. If it were a B & B, they would probably notice there's one too many of us. There's a games room downstairs with a pool room and jukebox. You'll love it. Besides, we won't be there much. One of us can sleep on the floor, or one of us might pull anyway. Don't worry about it, pal. It's all good.'

Tim wished he could get his phone out and google the place.

The Grand Hotel Apartments in Blackpool had nothing to do with the Grand Hotel itself and was situated at the opposite side of the resort to both the train station and the Empress Ballroom. It took over half an hour to walk there via the less scenic route through the back streets of Blackpool, a journey which would have been 15 minutes longer down the seafront. But this was a minor inconvenience, according to Moody, as they started in the perfect location to pub crawl down the front to the Empress Ballroom.

The apartments themselves, although basic, were a pleasant surprise and clean and modern. They had two rooms on the ground floor, both with double beds; something which seemed to phase nobody except Tim.

'We can get three in one of the beds if we go top to toe,' Moody announced to widespread indifference.

They visited a shop across the road and bought two crates of a lager called Royal Dutch Post Horn, which Moody assured tasted better than it sounded. It would have to be as there was no fridge in the shop and was at room temperature. He had noticed the lack of chilled drinks in 1989, even the lager in pubs wasn't as cold as he was used to. Balancing out the purchase Moody popped 5 toothbrushes and a tube of toothpaste on top of the lager. 'We're not animals,' he laughed.

Down a flight of stairs in the basement was a games room dominated by a pool table in the centre with a snack vending machine, dartboard and jukebox along a wall.

'It's got some good tunes on it this jukebox,' claimed Adam. 'There's no Roses but there's some other stuff. What's that song you like Bobby?'

'I don't know which one you mean.'

'You do, we always play it when we come here. We come here a lot Troy and they never change the jukebox. But I don't mind, we have a playlist. You know Ads it's that sophsti-pop one.'

'Oh, it's by the Kane Gang. Not sure what it's called.'

'That's it. It's his guilty pleasure. We all have one on here. I usually put on "Alone" by Heart and Moody – get this – loves T'Pau. Seriously T'Pau. Can you believe that?'

'Wow, really T'Pau?' Tim laughed. He had never heard of any of the bands.

'Don't forget Quinny,' interrupted Moody. 'He usually comes, and his song is "Boxerbeat" by The JoBoxers. We all like that one. I'm gonna put that one on as well. It's five for a quid. You pick one Troy, I'll give T'Pau a miss today.'

Scrolling down the list, Tim didn't recognise any of the songs, so he picked one at random. "Sometimes" by Erasure.'

'So, Troy, my boy, have you ever played the triangle game?' asked Adam.

'No. What is it?'

'We leave the triangle on the table and only use the cue ball. This way we can all play and it doesn't cost anything,' explained Bobby. 'And you get three shots to get the ball around the triangle and back into the D without hitting a cushion. Like this. If you don't do it, you have to chuck 10p in the triangle. If you do it, you take the pot. I once won a tenner. Here, have a go.'

'It's not as easy as it looks; it can take ages for anyone to do it,' laughed Bobby, 'especially when we started to get pissed.'

Chapter 10

The Brown Mile

The triangle game descended into a drunken farce with no victor, leaving a pile of change in the middle of the pool table; at least what was left after dipping into the winnings to feed the jukebox. By the point the first crate of lukewarm Royal Dutch Post Horn had been polished off nobody could concentrate on the frustrating game, instead opting for a jukebox karaoke.

Boxer beat by the JoBoxers was the most played song and, despite not having heard it before, Tim now knew most of the catchy lyrics which bounced around in his head as the five headed out of the apartments towards the seafront.

Tim was fascinated with the music on the jukebox which contained music mainly from the early to mid-eighties. His dad used to say the mid-eighties were a musical vacuum and the jukebox told a tale of a decade trying to find its identity; waiting for something to happen. By the look of the jukebox, the Roses had arrived just in time. He was living his dad's life. He had never felt so close to him.

'Have you been to Blackpool before, Troy?' Moody asked.

'Never.'

'Your first trip to the brown mile,' Moody laughed. 'you're in for a treat. The tourist board calls the seafront between the two piers the golden mile, but when you look at the sea, you'll see why we call it the brown mile. We're right at the top and will pub crawl down to the Empress Ballroom at the other end. A mile of pubs, amusements and fast-food heaven. We'll need some food to soak up the beer. I've got a pocket full of change from the triangle game nobody won. There's six quid here, so just enough for 5 lagers.'

The side street adjoined the main road opposite the South pier. To the left, he could see a rollercoaster which must be part of the pleasure beach Moody had talked about on the train, but they turned right, heading towards the world-famous tower he could see faintly in the distance. As they walked down the right-side of the promenade he was surprised how far away the sea was. There was a main road, a couple of tram tracks, open grassland and the sea way in the distance. He couldn't see the beach but there were metal railings beyond the grass suggesting there was a drop-down to it.

It was a warm day, but the sea breeze blew sharply in their faces forcing their noses to ingest the fast-food odours further down the promenade. After a few hundred yards they came to a large detached red-brick pub with a large chimney on either side, next to a fish and chip shop. At the front of the pub were picnic tables full of people washing down their fish and chips with lager.

'So, here's the plan,' announced Moody. 'Troy, you go with Adam to the chippy, Ged you come in the pub with me – they can see you a mile off - and Bobby you grab that table over there.'

'We've got the best deal,' said Adam as they joined the back of the queue. 'The pub will be rammed but there's only a couple of people in front of us.'

'We didn't ask them what they wanted,' Tim pointed out.

'Peas or Curry?'

'What?'

'Which do you prefer Troy, peas or curry?'

'Curry.'

'That's 5 fish and chips with salt and vinegar, 3 curry and 2 peas. You OK with that?'

'Yeah.'

Adam was right. It was at least 20 minutes before Moody and Ged joined them outside with Moody fuming to the point he could barely hold the two pints in his hands without spilling them.

'They did it to me again boys. Those fuckers ripped me off again.'

'But how?' asked Adam, 'You had a pocket full of change.'

'I know, I know. So, I had the right money - six quid - and I put it on the bar, and he counts it up, puts it in the till and tells me there were only five pounds there. I watched him count it, the bastard. Then he says we can't have the last two pints unless I give him another quid and there's this big queue and he shouts, "who wants these lagers?" so I had to give him the quid.'

Adam laughed, 'you see Troy we come to this pub a lot and the bar staff rip us off all the time. They give you a quid less in your change and when you argue they say they gave you the right money and you've put the money in your pocket. That's if you notice. Most people are either that pissed they don't notice or that glad they finally got served they don't care. They must make a fortune. They do it all the time. Tossers.'

'And he was no use, that lanky streak of piss,' Moody shouted, nodding at Ged. 'He just stood there laughing.'

'Yeah, but it was as funny as fuck. You ought to have seen his face,' Ged sniggered. 'And on the bright side, Quinny is in the bar. He got a ticket off a bloke he knows this morning and hitchhiked his way over. He knew we'd start here, so he's been in a while. He's finishing his pint with the boys he hitched with and coming with us.'

'As soon as we've had our food we'll sup up and move on. I'm not stopping here,' announced Moody scoffing his food just as Quinny walked out of the pub, his arms held aloft.

'Hey boys, I'm here. Who's ready to have a laugh?'

Quinny was in a good mood and looked the part with blue Adidas trainers, a gold-colored long-sleeved top with an imprint of black flowers and baggy black jeans. To mark the occasion, he had even washed his hair. Tim had seen the top in a stall in Affleck's Palace.

'Hey, Quinny. Good to see you, pal. We'll be ready to party when we get out of this dump.'

'What do you mean? They've not ripped you off again? You use the right money in here. You should know that by now.'

'I did Quinny, but he put it in the till and said I was a quid down.'

'Right boys. I'm fed up with this every time we come here. Are we all done?' Quinny growled.

'Yeah,' replied Moody despite only being halfway through his food and lager, 'what are you gonna do?'

'Just get ready to run. That's all you need to know.' Quinny grabbed Moody's half-empty pint pot and headed back towards the pub shouting, 'the fuckers will rue the day!'

Tim's heart pounded as he ran behind Adam with the other 4 close behind. He had watched through the window as Quinny stormed in with the pint pot before hesitating and putting it on a table. Tim breathed a sigh of relief only to see Quinny pick up an empty bottle of Newcastle Brown from a shelf before shouting "chiselling bastards" and launching the bottle toward the back bar. Tim was on his heels and down the road before it landed but he heard an almighty crash and a loud echoing cheer from the pub.

He felt sick. Maybe it was the run, or the lager and fish and chips sat heavily on his stomach, but more likely it was the sheer panic bouncing around his head. Adam was having no such problem, his athletic 6-foot frame gliding along and his tight black permed hair bouncing as he howled with laughter. His hair didn't fit in with the rest of the band but then Roger Daltrey had his hair tightly permed during the 'Tommy' stage.

Tim was afraid to look back but could hear Quinny screaming 'the fuckers will rue the day' repeatedly to the amusement of the others.

Adam swung right down a side street before heading into a crowded pub.

'Take your tracky top off and tie it round your waist, Troy. And grab one of these,' ordered Adam thrusting an almost empty pint pot from a nearby table into his hand.

The others followed with Quinny quickly covering his distinctive top with Moody's denim jacket, before donning a ridiculous "damn seagulls" bucket hat he stole en route. They split up and Quinny started a conversation with two strangers who looked uncomfortable as he put his arms around them.

'You're no good at this, are you? Just laugh for a bit and pretend we've been here a while. They'll be gone soon.'

'Who?'

'The bouncers. There's a couple of them in here. They're behind you. Play it cool?'

Tim's heart skipped, his worse fear realised as a hand firmly gripped his shoulder; a gruff voice announcing, 'come outside son. I want a word with you.'

'You'd best go pal. He's serious. I'll wait in here for you.' Adam stuttered, for once shaken. Tim looked back at him for support. He couldn't believe he'd been thrown under the bus.

The howls of laughter revealed it was Ged's hand on his shoulder.

'Oh man, you ought to see your face. You wouldn't hold up under interrogation,' Adam noted.

'So, they aren't after us?'

'No,' laughed Quinny, 'those fat fucks won't come after us, they're too lazy. They didn't last time.'

'Last time? Are you serious?'

'Yeah,' confirmed Quinny, 'I did it the last time they ripped us off.'

'You've done that before? In the same pub? And you went back in?'

'Yeah.'

'Weren't you scared they'd recognise you?'

'Well, no,' shrugged Quinny, 'what can they do about it anyway? They couldn't prove it. It was a few months back. I doubt they'd recognise me. Although they didn't try to rip me off so maybe they did recognise me and didn't want another smashed mirror. But they got one anyway.'

Tim sighed. He was happy the ordeal was over but worried what the rest of the evening may bring, but for the moment a wave of relief washed over him causing him to forget the pint in his hand was not his but somebody else's dregs. Adam grabbed his wrist with the drink inches away from his mouth.

'Careful pal, that's not yours. You don't wanna catch AIDS.'

'Cheers. I forgot it wasn't mine. You can't catch AIDS from a pint pot though.'

'You might be able to. Nobody knows, but I've heard you can catch it from somebodies' spit,' suggested Adam.

'Me too,' said Ged.

'I've heard you can't,' countered Bobby.

'Of course, you can't,' said Tim.

'Yeah, you can,' weighed in Quinny.

'Well, that's 3-2. What do you think Moody?' Asked Adam.

'I've heard different things, but it is a bodily fluid so probably, yeah.'

'There you go, Troy. That's 4-2. You can catch it from a pint pot,' Adam announced victoriously.

'That's not how you decide if something is contagious or not, but I wasn't going to drink it anyway,' Tim conceded.

'You've no idea who had that pint before you. What if it was some bummer's pint? You do know AIDS is a gay disease?' Quinny added.

'Bummers? Are you for real? You can't say stuff like that.' Tim protested.

'Why not?' asked Quinny puzzled, 'what am I supposed to call them?'

'Gay,' Tim said with exasperation,' You can't say "bummers" it's homophobic.'

'What the fuck? Have you swallowed a dictionary or something? Is that even a real word? Has anyone else heard that word?' Quinny asked, looking around to a sea of blank faces.

'It is a real word,' Tim defended, 'everyone uses it where I come from.'

'Well, none of us have heard of it. It sounds like a gay robot to me. Homorobotic, what a load of bollocks.'

'Quinny you fuckin plank, he said homophobic, not homorobotic,' corrected Moody.

'Whatever. I get it. I'll not say bummers anymore. I've nothing against them it's just what people call them where I live. It must be much posher where you come from. But then you drive a BMW and can afford to stay at the Midland.'

'Oy Quinny leave it there,' ordered Moody.

'Well, Troy,' Adam interrupted, 'sounds like I've just saved your life, so by my reckoning, it's your shout. Lagers all around? Come on pal, I'll give you a hand at the bar.'

It was obvious Moody and Adam had deliberately extracted him to avoid further confrontation but the three-deep queue at the bar gave him time to stew over Quinny's comments. 1989 didn't sound that long ago but the narrative Quinny had used not just to describe gay men but also to blame them for a worldwide epidemic was from the dark ages. He could see Moody and Quinny squabbling. Adam put his hand on his shoulder.

'Don't worry about Quinny, he's OK but he's not the sharpest tool in the box. We all have friends who say things without thinking. The sort of things you would never say yourself and if you heard someone else say you'd be pissed off; but when it's a mate you let it slide for some reason. You must have one of those back in Sheffield?' Adam asked.

'Yes of course. I have a couple.'

He was lying. He couldn't think of any. Maybe this was because he always spoke out when he needed to. He possessed a moral centre and would defend what he believed to be right, even when it was difficult, a trait he was respected for.

This was all very well in 2015, but he was in a different time altogether. He had got in the BMW to grab a taste of the late 1980s but had only been thinking about the music. The conversation with Quinny made him realise just how far he was from home culturally. His dad told him how music in the eighties reflected difficult social and political times. The first single his dad ever bought – and the first one Tim had smashed after his funeral - was Ghost Town by the Specials. His dad always proclaimed if any song summed up the '80's; that was it.

There was resentment and jealously in Quinny's comment about him staying in the Midland and driving a BMW. 1989 was less affluent than 2015, but the people were just as happy and more content with less.

Perhaps somewhere during the subsequent 25 years society had developed too fast and over evolved. He missed some technology from 2015, but not others. He was beginning to realise how over-reliant he had become on technology. Sure, a mobile phone would have come in handy to meet up with Quinny, who had been lucky they turned up at the first pub and not changed plans. If the routine had been broken he would have been left on his own. But was that part of the fun? Nevertheless, being able to contact each other was a technology he missed.

The lack of a smartphone, on the other hand, summed up his theory on over evolution. He had been unable to check out the apartments which had been the only occasion he had missed his phone. But the benefits had been total engagement with his friends with no digital distraction. There was a window of time between 1989 and 2015 when mobile phones were just phones and the internet could only be accessed by a computer. Was this the perfect balance?

The were no repercussions when he returned to the gang with the drinks, the incident was seemingly forgotten. The door to the pub flew open and in burst a group of lads, one of them carrying a portable stereo on his shoulder playing Made of Stone at full blast. As the song reached the chorus the cheers reached a crescendo as groups of young people with arms around each other's shoulders bounced around the pub chanting the lyrics. But they weren't lyrics anymore they had morphed into an incantation announcing the arrival of a magical time. Not everyone understood the sorcery, but those who did were spellbound.

As Tim soaked up the atmosphere, he fought back the tears welling up in his eyes. It was his dad's favourite song and a timely reminder of why he was there.

Chapter 11

Ebenezer Goode

The empress ballroom was fed by a rabbit warren of corridors full of young people queueing for the bar and toilets. Both queues were huge and as they passed a guy was punched in the face for trying to jump the toilet queue. Some had decided it was too long to wait in and too dangerous to jump so pissed in the corridor instead.
'Fuckin scrubbers,' Quinny commented.
'Fuck you,' came the scouse reply, much to his annoyance.
Quinny didn't like scousers. Outside the Ballroom, a tout with a Liverpool accent had tried to sell them a ticket. Rather than just ignore him Quinny told him to fuck off.
'I'll give you a call if I need a car stereo pal,' he shouted before turning to the rest of the gang, 'I fuckin hate scousers, I do.'
'Yes Quinny,' said Moody, 'we know.'

The more discerning scrubbers were trying to piss into an empty plastic pint pot which they either missed or the high-pressure liquid knocked over: but most of them just pissed straight onto the carpet. Quinny was spot on. It was disgusting. Tim couldn't believe his eyes; he had never seen anything like it before. Where was security? There's no way you would get away with that in 2015, he thought.

The main hall was big and ornately decorated, it's vaulted ceiling exuberantly stealing the show. The beauty and intricacy of the internal decorations made the pissing antics even more annoying. What little of the timber floor which could still be seen amongst the sea of people was already covered in squashed plastic pint pots.
'I can see a few of those being launched during the gig,' Quinny commented.
'A few what?' asked Tim.
'Pint pots of piss, pal. You must have been hit by a pot of piss in your time?' he laughed.

'Is he serious?' Tim thought before replying, 'yeah, a few.'

'Boys come over here a minute, where it's quieter,' Quinny said pointing toward an empty corner. As they approached a pile of sick revealed why the corner was deserted.

'Last week I visited the E corner and got us all a little present.'

'The E corner?' quizzed Ged.

'It's in the Hacienda,' Moody jumped in immediately to show how cool he was. 'It's next to that big speaker at the back. It's where everyone gets their drugs.'

'That's right,' Quinny confirmed. 'But not any old drug. This is ecstasy. Fuck acid, fuck speed – they are all so 1980's. But these bad boys are the next generation. Everyone will be taking these in the 1990s.'

'Even the Queen and Thatcher?' laughed Adam.

'Especially the Queen and Thatcher. If anyone needs one of these chill pills, it's definitely that bitch Thatcher.'

'Are they safe?' Ged enquired, 'have they been tested?'

'Yes,' confirmed Quinny 'they've been tested by the Queen's physician himself and there's a number in the bag to call if we have any problems.'

'Oh, that's good,' said Ged.

'Of course, they're not tested you daft twat,' snapped Quinny, 'and there's no Ecstasy Ombudsman either if you're not 100% satisfied. Or a money-back guarantee. They're illegal drugs for fucks sake. Are you saying you don't want one?'

'No, I want one.'

'So why ask?'

'Just wondered.'

'So, don't ask moronic questions then,' Quinny bemoaned, 'these are top grade man. It's got a little dove on the front. Only get the ones with the doves on the front, the others are shit. That's what I was told by the drug dealer and he wouldn't lie! Only kidding but I've heard from a few people the doves are the best ones. This guy's a mate of mine who works for a band and he brings them over from Spain. I can't tell you who the band is though, it's top-secret.'

'It's the Happy Mondays,' announced Moody.

'I can't say.' Confirmed Quinny.

'I wasn't asking, I was saying. It's the Happy Mondays. Everyone knows. It's the worst kept secret in Manchester. But it's not even the band, just some people who know them and everyone in Manchester knows them. So that could be anyone in Manchester under the age of 25. We've met them so it could be us.'

'Shut up,' Quinny snapped. 'Who wants one?'

Tim didn't know what to do. He had never taken recreational drugs, although he did smoke a bit of blow. But then he had never travelled back in time before and he would be the only one not having one. What happens in 1989 stays in 1989 – right?

'I'm in,' Tim confirmed.

'Nice one, Troy my boy. Ged keep an eye out for security. If there is any,' Quinny said taking a plastic bag out of his pocket and removing 6 small white tablets imprinted with a picture of a dove.

'You first Troy.'

Tim stood there as Quinny carefully placed the Ecstasy on the centre of his tongue like a communion wafer.

'Troy my boy – do you feel loved up?'

'I feel loved up, doved up, 22, psycho for sex and glue,' Tim rattled out before realising he had quoted lyrics for a song that hadn't been written yet.

'What?' said Quinny.

'Err. Song lyrics. They're lyrics to a song I'm working on,' He lied.

'Fuck me, Troy, I like it,' said Moody.

'Right lads – down the hatch,' ordered Quinny passing around the rest of the tablets.

'I've never done this before. How long does it take to work?' asked Ged.

'Really, you do surprise me Ged,' laughed Moody. 'It'll just happen gradually. You won't even notice. But keep an eye on Quinny. When he turns into a lizard, you'll know it's happening.'

'A lizard what do you mean?'

'He does this thing with his tongue like a lizard. He sticks it in and out like this.' Moody demonstrated by rapidly sticking his tongue in and out between his lips, 'like a crazy iguana.'

'No, I don't,' denied Quinny.

'Yes, you do,' disagreed Bobby, 'every time. It's mental. It's how I know the drugs are working.'

'We need to push to the front now if we're gonna get a good view. They'll be on soon,' Moody pointed out.

The Roses were the main event, but the crowd was entertaining to Tim, who had seen pictures of the gig and had watched a DVD with his dad; but this was different gravy. The DVD was grainy and didn't communicate the eclectic gathering dressed in crazy get-ups. There were bog-standard indie mixed in with goths, post-punk revivalists and acid house heads all crammed as close to the stage as they could. It was a sea of baggy jeans, mohair jumpers and smiley face t-shirts.

'Do you feel it?' shouted Moody.

'Feel what?'

'This! It's the start of something big. I know it is!'

Tim knew Moody's gut feeling was true. Plastic pint pots of what he hoped were lager flew with increasing regularity. These were poorer times than he was used to, and he couldn't imagine many people being frivolous with their expensive lager. On his way to the front, he saw a guy pissing into a pint pot surrounded by people, but none of them batted an eyelid. He feared the worse, but it was a small price to pay.

The cheers and projectile piss pots reached a crescendo as the band walked on stage, the lead singer wearing his famous money T-Shirt, one which Tim had seen students wear at the nineties themed nights in the Leadmill back in 2015. As Ian Brown bounced a yo-yo on stage and the first bass notes to the opening song echoed around the Ballroom, Tim was in ecstasy. Literally.

Chapter 12

Hallelujah!

Hundreds of sweat-drenched youths spewed onto the promenade as the concert ended. A combination of people who would never again be in the same place at the same time disbursed in different directions. The concert had been triumphant for the Stone Roses and a mouth-watering benchmark for aspiring musician Moody who ran up behind Tim, jumping on his back to force a surprise piggyback. He fell back to the pavement as Tim failed to grab his legs. Moody put his arm around him.
'Sorry about that pal. Just excited. Wasn't trying to be homo robotic or anything,' he laughed. 'But seriously Troy, that was life-affirming. Life-changing. This is what I want to do. This is what I have to do. This is what I am gonna do. But I need you Troy, my boy. We, the Undergraduates of Peanut University, need you. Troy Gold the Yorkshire troubadour, who thinks he has a tiny phone in his pocket. I don't know what it is about you, but I know you are the missing piece of the jigsaw. What did you think to the Roses?'
'Fuckin awesome!' he shouted throwing one arm around Moody and the other around the nearest person, which happened to be Adam. He couldn't stop smiling. His face was like an acid house T Shirt.
'Is everyone here?' Moody asked. 'Shout out if you're not here.'
'We're all here,' Ged confirmed. 'But where are we going?'
'A mate of mine from Stockport is a DJ in a club here.' Moody revealed, 'it's a trendy club usually full of townies. You know the type where you have to wear shoes and a shirt. But he's talked the owner into doing an indie night tonight because the Roses are in town. It's called the Palace Nightclub. It's down here somewhere, up a ramp, I think. We walked past it on the way down. It'll be rammed but I've put us on the guest list. I didn't know Quinny was coming so we've only got 5 places. We'll have to move around a bit to confuse the bouncers, but it'll be OK.'
A large neon light beckoned the boys up the ramp towards the entrance, trailing out of which was a large queue patrolled by a bouncer. A couple of

barely dressed girls with peroxide blonde hair marched angrily away from the club.

'It's disgusting. We come here every week and now they're telling us they're letting all these scrubbers go in tonight. I'm done with this place I'm never coming here again!' one proclaimed. No doubt she went back the following week anyway.

'We're on the guestlist pal,' Moody announced with authority. 'The DJ Adam has put us on. I'm Moody.'

The bouncer laughed as he looked down at his clipboard. 'So's my wife pal. So's my wife. Go on in.'

The bouncer was so pleased with his pun he neglected to count them as all six sailed into the club.

Inside was so full it was hard to imagine many of the people standing in the queue would get in; but another thing Tim had noticed was that everywhere seemed busier than in 2015, especially the pubs.

There were a lot of familiar faces from the concert and they had already spotted the pissing Scouser, seemingly doing very well with a brunette.

'Fuck me,' scowled Quinny, 'If that dirty scouse fucker can pull, even you might get your end away Ged.'

'You'll not wind me up tonight pal, I feel awesome,' Ged replied, leaning forward and kissing Quinny on the forehead.

'Give over you daft get,' said Quinny, trying not to laugh, 'look at your pupils, they're like dust bin lids; you look like a lanky owl. You all do. Them doves are a flapping.'

'I love this song. It's the new Monday's song. Hasn't even been released yet,' Adam screamed, running to the dance floor waving his arms like a 4-year-old child.

Soon they were united in the middle of the dancefloor; a circle of friends; five twentieth-century conquistadors and a time tourist. The night was young. And so were they.

Hallelujah was the perfect song to frame the moment.

Chapter 13

Foul Play

'Who's got the key?' Adam asked.
They left the Palace over an hour ago but had only just found the Grand Hotel apartments. It was 3.30 am.
'I've got one,' announced Moody. 'Ged's got the other one. Does anyone know what happened to him?'
Tim was worried about Ged. He was the only one of the gang who had not met up outside the club on what had turned out to be a long and meandering stagger home.
'No, I'm a bit worried about him, to be honest,' he confessed.
'Why?' asked Adam.
'Because he's had to come home on his own. It's not safe at this time of night.'
Quinny laughed. 'Fuck me Troy, you must have staggered home on your own from the boozer in the middle of the night when you're pissed. I've done it loads and so has Ged. The thing with Ged is he can't take his beer, so he sneaks off early without telling anyone. He does it all the time. Sometimes I wonder about you, Troy. You really are as soft as shite.'
Quinny was right, he had walked home on his home from pubs and clubs but always had his phone with him. Same with his mates. Whenever they left, they sent a text. It reaffirmed what he had thought earlier about needing phones for emergency contact. But these guys had never known such technology. He was embarrassed about being called soft, but he couldn't defend himself.
'He's just showing concern you fuckin neanderthal that's all,' Adam defended to Tim's relief and surprise. 'Maybe he's pulled?'
Quinny laughed again. 'Nice one pal, I love it. That lanky streak of piss?'
The streets off the promenade looked similar and they had repeatedly wandered down side streets, before realising their error and turning around.

They had also been delayed by singing Stone Roses songs and bumping into friends of Moody's. This guy knew everyone in the Northwest of England under the age of 25.

'Anyway,' continued Adam, 'talking of lanky streaks of piss, who was that guy we bumped into outside the club?'

'Which one?'

'The really lanky skinny one with big white trainers and a Castrol GTX jacket. Kept dancing around like a lunatic. He was off his tits.'

'Oh him. Yeah, he's always off his tits he is. He's called Gizmo.'

'Where do you know him from?'

'I don't really but he's from Salford and is always in one of those two pubs over the bridge from the 'Tech. The first time I met him was in the Woolpack.'

'Is that the one at the bottom of the tower block?' Adam asked.

'No that's the Sports Bar, but he's always in there as well. Anyway, he comes up and starts talking like he knows me. Just like he was today, big fuckin owl eyes. I can't get a word in and while he's rattling on, he buys me a pint. So now I feel rude if I say I don't know him. You know that feeling don't you Troy? So, then he starts talking about his brother Lee and how I went to school with him. I don't know his brother Lee, but I can't bring myself to tell him. It's funny, I suppose, but what if he's in the pub one day and this Lee comes in and says he doesn't know me? What then – I've had a pint off him under false pretences? He doesn't look stable. And he's got this mate, a small stocky bloke, who's even more mental. Probably get my head put back.'

'Nah he's another one who's as soft as shite,' said Quinny.

'You're probably right. He kept saying Troy was a spaceman from the future.'

'Yeah, because you were taking the piss and telling him I had a tiny phone in my pocket. He was well out of it.'

'Listen guys,' said Moody, 'Ged's got the only key to your room, so you'll have to wake the fucker up, otherwise you two are sleeping on the pool table. See you in the morn...'

'Sssshhh,' said Quinny, 'I can hear someone in the pool room.'

The apartments were occupied by a young clientele, so it was no surprise someone was down there, but as the noises got louder it was clear what was happening.

'Someone's shagging down there!' Quinny grinned, 'let's go down and catch them at it.'

Tim didn't want to go down. He wanted to leave them alone, but as he had already been called soft by Quinny he didn't want to make his reputation worse, although why he valued Quinny's opinion was a mystery.

Tim was at the back and the only one not sniggering as they crept down the shallow flight of stairs before assembling like a naughty set of schoolboys on the landing next to the door. The sex noises were louder to the delight of the other four, hardly able to contain their amusement.

'BUSTED!' shouted Quinny bursting through the door, the smile on his face morphing into bewilderment at the site of Ged standing opposite him, thrusting against a naked girl bent over the pool table.

'Alright lads,' he said, removing his hands from her butt cheeks and putting them behind his head, slowly gyrating his pelvis as if attempting to emulate a 1970's porn star. He was fully clothed except for the jeans around his ankles. 'This is Annette.'

Annette didn't look up as her head gently rocked backward and forward. Each of her ample breasts rested on separate pool balls which rolled slightly forward and backward in time with Ged. It was too precise to have been planned and synced perfectly with her shoulder-length black hair swaying in mid-air.

After what seemed like an eternity Quinny spoke.

'Err, do you have the key to our room pal?'

'Yeah, it's in my pocket, just grab it.'

'Are you serious they're wrapped around your fuckin ankles? I'm not coming over there.'

Putting his hand back on her butt cheeks he clumsily pulled his shoes through his trousers before kicking them to Quinny, sliding halfway on the wooden floor before stopping. As Quinny approached the trousers Ged was already back in action.

'Can you piss off now please lads, I'm a little busy here?' Ged requested, the novelty of gaining a few lad points having worn off.

'Fuck me this is grim,' winced Quinny, bending down to pick up the trousers, turning away his head in disgust to avoid staring at the crunched-up boxer shorts nestled in the middle. Grabbing the trousers and standing up quickly he realised, to his horror, he had grabbed the boxer shorts accidentally.

'OH NO! – they're his fuckin undercrackers!' he screamed throwing the boxer shorts across the room and picking up the trousers. Even Tim was in hysterics as Quinny quickly rifled through Ged's pockets, grabbing the key and throwing the trousers in the direction of the boxers.

By the time Tim, Adam, Bobby and Moody got back to the room Quinny was already consoling himself with a lukewarm can of Royal Dutch Post Horn.

'That was the worst thing that's ever happened to me. Ever. I've just spent the last hour washing my hand,' he exaggerated, 'if I had an axe, I swear to God I would chop that hand off. There were skid marks all over the place. It was like the fuckin M62 in there.'

'That was brilliant,' Adam spluttered gasping for breath as he laughed, 'not just the undercrackers but how she just stayed there bent over the pool table when we walked in. She never flinched!'

'And what the fuck was Ged doing with his hands behind his head. Who does he think he is? Studley Moore?' continued Bobby. 'Did you see his eyes? They were bulging so much I thought they were gonna pop out of his head. You're not the only one with mental scars Quinny. I can never unsee the look in his eyes.'

Quinny's head was out of his hands now as he lay on the bed laughing, 'Cheer's lads, I feel better knowing I'm not the only one who was freaked out.'

'She was surprisingly fit though. I mean for Ged. She had a great pair of tits. But she must be a bit of a slapper just to carry on like that. Or pissed. Or both,' observed Moody.

'Not half,' exclaimed Quinny, 'I hope he was wearing a nodder or he could have AIDS by now. He could be dead in 6 months.'

'It that how long it takes to kill you?' asked Adam.

'Yeah, a mate of mines sister goes out with a bloke who's training to be a doctor and that's what he says.'

'Fuck me,' replied a stony-faced Adam.

'Poor Ged?' laughed Tim, 'It's a bit of a stretch to assume he's gonna die in 6 months because he's had sex.'

'Fuck me, Troy. Haven't you seen the adverts with the big gravestones falling over? You have sex with a bird who has it you're dead in 6 months, I'm telling you. I hope it's not that nurse my mate was telling me about.'

'Which nurse?' asked Moody.

'The doctor I was telling you about earlier. There was a nurse on his ward who caught AIDS from a patient.'

'How?'

'Can't remember, think he spit in her face; but she got it and now she goes around deliberately infecting men. She takes them to a hotel room and in the morning when they wake up, she's gone; but when they go to the bathroom, she leaves a message on the mirror in lipstick,' Quinny baited.

'What? What does it say?' obliged Adam.

'Welcome to the AIDS club.'

Tim couldn't believe his ears. How was no one calling bullshit on this story? Did they really think you could catch AIDS if somebody spat in your face? Maybe they hadn't been properly educated about the disease, but it was clearly an urban myth. A few hours ago it was a gay disease, now a killer nurse was roaming the streets of England infecting men with a deadly virus. It made him angry. He was dying to say something but was beginning to realise when to bite his lip. Clint had told him not to stand out in the past. So, instead, he opted for humour.

'Couldn't you see if he was wearing a nodder, Quinny? You were stood close enough?'

'Don't remind me, Troy,' he groaned. 'I'm knackered lads I've got to sleep. It's nearly 4.'

The room was small with an en suite toilet to the left of the entrance door with a double bed in the middle of the room and an armchair in the corner near the window. Quinny was laying with his head at the foot of the bed with Bobby next to him spun the other way, already asleep.

'I'm gonna sleep here,' Adam said, 'If Ged comes back, I'll send him next door to sleep on your armchair, but I doubt he'll be back anytime soon.'

The room next door was identical as Tim and Moody adopted a similar top-to-toe position as the door swung open to reveal a beaming Ged and remorseful-looking Annette.

'Hey, boys me and Annette are gonna have a stroll up the front. The other way, past the Pleasure Beach towards St. Anne's. I used to go there when I was a kid. It's a mild night so we will watch the sunrise. I know a really beautiful spot.'

'That's nice,' Tim commented. 'Make sure you get back in time for the train, pal.'

'Don't worry about me Troy, I might catch a later one, or stop here another night with this beauty. Which reminds me Moody; I've decided to quit the band.'

'What?' Moody exclaimed. 'You've just watched the gig of your life, one which should inspire you to greater things, but you're going the other way?'

'Yeah, but that's me. When everyone heads towards Blackpool, I go the other way to St Anne's. It's just the way I am. Me and Annette have been talking. We're gonna go travelling somewhere. See the world. There's more to life than Manchester. Besides, I can't see Peanut University taking off. And all this Manchester stuff will be over in a few weeks. This was the pinnacle, this gig tonight. Why don't you ask Troy to join? Anyway, boys see you around. You'll probably not get any sleep with Bobby and Quinny next door. Sounded like they were having a snoring competition.'

'Sounds about right,' Moody added.' I bet Adam's pissed off about that.'

'He's not there, it's just them two. Ciao boys.'

As the door closed behind them Moody began laughing.

'Troy, have you ever seen the film, "This is Spinal Tap"?'

'Yeah.'

'Well, you know how they always have to replace their drummer when he spontaneously combusts.'

'Yeah.'

'Well, that's what we are like with our singers. Except instead of spontaneously combusting, they meet a girl and turn into girlfriend bastards. He's only met her tonight and he's quit the band.'

'Maybe he's in love. Anyway, I thought you wanted him out of the band?'

'I do,' said Moody, 'but he isn't in love, he's just not thinking straight because he got his end away. But you must see this is a sign.'

'A sign of what?'

'Stop pissing around Troy. Me buying you a pint by accident and then us all getting on so well. Then Ged leaving the band, and all this in a few days. It's meant to be. You look the part and I just know you can put lyrics together. What was that you said earlier about being loved up and doved up?'

'Oh, you mean loved up, doved up 22, psycho for sex and glue, lost it to Bostick, yeah?'

'That's fuckin' brilliant – and you've added a bit to the end. We need you pal. We've got a rehearsal on Thursday and I won't shut up until I've talked you into coming. I'll keep on all night if I have to,' he claimed, closing his eyes and drifting off to sleep.

Tim wasn't tired. How could he be? He could hear talking outside and peering through the curtains saw Adam smoking a cigarette whilst talking to Ged and Annette. There was little chance of him sleeping any time soon, so he decided to join them.

By the time he joined Adam outside the others were disappearing down the street toward the promenade; two glowing cigarettes happily fading into the distance.

'Can't sleep either?' asked Adam.

'Not really. It's been some night.'

'Want a cancer stick?'

Tim didn't smoke. He vaped sometimes but never smoked. None of his friends smoked either, but in 1989 everyone smoked, especially in pubs;

even the smallest pubs and even if people were eating. He found the concept of smoking abhorrent and his education meant he had no excuse. He could only assume his 1989 friends were as well educated about the perils of smoking as they were about how AIDS was transmitted. But despite not having had a cigarette he still stunk like an ashtray and had passively smoked at least 20 during the day.

He didn't take drugs either but had still dropped an 'E' earlier. He was only in 1989 for a week; why not give the ball a kick? After all, what happens in 1989, stays in 1989.

'Cheers,' he said taking a cigarette out of the packet, noticing the blue stripe down the box, 'are they Regal?'

There was a picture of Tim's dad on his way to Wembley holding a packet of Regal cigarettes. He told Tim he smoked Regal because they were blue and white stripes and spelled lager backward.

'Yeah, I always smoke Regal. I didn't think you smoked?'

'Yeah, but I don't smoke much. I always smoke Regal though, they've got blue and white stripes like Wednesday and Regal spells lager backward,' he plagiarised.

'Cool, I'll have to remember that. Not the Wednesday bit obviously. I'm a Bolton fan. But, yeah, it does spell lager backward. I hadn't noticed that before,' Adam mused.

'Have you got a light, please?'

'Of course,' Adam replied. It was a shiny Zippo lighter which he held aloft in front of Tim's face. 'I got a shiny one for when we play cards, so I can see the reflection of the cards passed over it.'

'Does it work?'

'No, but I do have a marked deck I play with sometimes. That works, but don't tell any of them lot.' He was holding the lighter in his right hand with his thumb on the bottom and his two forefingers on the lid at the top. As he applied pressure the lid flipped open with a 'dink' his two fingers and thumb now holding the base of the opened lighter. Tim could smell the petrol as Adam's thumb hovered on the flint. But rather than spinning it, he stopped, suspended in time, staring at the lighter before lowering it and, with his left arm took the cigarette from Tim's mouth.

He leaned toward Tim.

'What are you doing?' Tim snapped, recoiling backward. 'You tried to kiss me?'

'I'm sorry, I'm so sorry.' Adam was distraught. His panic-stricken apologies and welled-up eyes changed Tim's demeanour.

'Sorry pal, I didn't mean to react like that. I was just surprised, that's all. I'm not bothered, it's flattering.'

It wasn't the first time a man had come onto him. It wasn't even the first time that week. He was on the dance floor in the Leadmill with Clint in 2015, when he heard a man screaming at the top of his voice. To be heard over the sound system was an achievement so he turned around to see what the fuss was about. Stood behind him was a man in his mid-20's with short-cropped blond hair, who he had been talking to earlier in the night. He was pointing at Tim and screaming.

'YOU. YOU. I WANT YOU!'

Clint was bent over in hysterics.

It was a strange experience. Why would someone behave like that? Clint made a joke of it and took him for a double Southern Comfort.

But this was more awkward. More unexpected. He didn't have to deal with the shouting guy; he simply walked past him on his way to the bar. It was the night he met Lyla. He had forgotten all about it until now.

'Please don't tell the others,' Adam begged. 'They don't know.'

'How could they, it only just happened?'

'No, I mean.... You know?'

'That you're gay? So what? It's not a big deal?'

'Not a big deal? That's easy for you to say. Well, they all think you're gay.'

Tim laughed, 'Do they? Why?'

'Because of what you said in the bar to Quinny.'

'So, what if they think I'm gay? Who cares?'

Adam paused, taking a long drag on his cigarette. 'Do you still want a fag?'

'Yes please.'

Tim took the cigarette as Adam opened the lighter without the previous protocol, no longer feeling the need to impress.

'You know what I don't understand?' Adam said.

'Quantum physics,' Tim joked.

'No,' replied Adam looking puzzled, 'you.'

'Me? What about me, I'm Mr. Average.'

'No, you aren't Troy. There's something about you. You're somehow... I don't know.... enlightened.'

'Enlightened?'

'Yeah, and I don't get it. My brother's at University in Sheffield and I've asked him what it's like. He says it's just like Manchester, but smaller. Just as much of a working-class shit hole and the people are pretty much the same. But then here you are, super tolerant and understanding, using big words no one has heard of. It's like the guy with the Castrol GTX jacket said. Maybe you are from the future? Or perhaps you're from a different planet.'

Tim didn't know if it was the cigarette or Adam's comment but suddenly, he felt sick and his head was spinning.

Adam laughed, 'But that's just the drugs talking, man. It would be great if you were from the future though. Can you imagine that? I guess you're just a nice bloke Troy, my boy. Which is just as well now you know my secret.'

Tim wasn't sick anymore, but he was still lightheaded. He coughed.

'You OK with that fag?' Adam asked.

'Yeah, I don't smoke much. I feel lightheaded.'

'That's normal when you aren't used to it. Are your ears still buzzing from the gig?'

'Yeah. Fuck me it was loud in there,' Tim said. He paused before continuing, 'why don't you just tell everyone? I think they would be cool with it. It isn't a big deal.'

'I've thought about telling Bobby. He's the nicest person you'll ever meet. Totally sincere, kind and I know he'd be fine with it, like you.'

'So why didn't you?'

'Him and Quinny are best mates. They grew up together. It's a mystery to me how they've stayed friends, being so different. I wouldn't want Bobby to say something to him by accident when he's pissed. Can you imagine Quinny's response? You heard him today. The guy's a fuckin neanderthal. Do you know once we were in the Beer Keller in Manchester for his birthday and we met some lads at the next table from somewhere in Yorkshire? I think they were from Sheffield. Anyway, we ended up having a War of the Roses arm wrestling competition.'

'Who won?'

'Yorkshire. But only because they had this one lad who was good. Anyway, we're drinking steins which were 4 quid a go. 4 fuckin quid. What a rip-off. Anyway, when Quinny went to the toilet I spotted one of the Yorkshire lads pissing in his stein, the dirty bastard. When he gets back, I told him, expecting him to go mad, but he just laughs and says – it's only piss. And drinks it anyway. That's what he's like.'

'So, if he's such an idiot then why are you bothered what he thinks? Why be concerned about what someone who knowingly drinks piss thinks of you! I wouldn't be.' Tim knew the hypocrisy of his comment. Only moments ago, he had gone to the pool room, against his better judgment, to avoid further criticism from Quinny. He did seem to have a strange influence on people.

'I'd never thought of it like that. Fuck it. I'm off to bed. Are you coming? I don't mean to bed with me, I mean are you coming back in?'

'I know what you meant. Don't apologise. Don't ever apologise. You can come to our room to avoid the snoring if you like? And you can have the bed. I'm fine on the armchair. I'm not that tired.'

'I was right about you, Troy my boy. You are a good bloke.'

Chapter 14

Wormhole 1

WEDNESDAY 16 AUGUST 1989 - 2.45 PM.

Finding the underpass was easy, and the cross on the wall confirmed he was in the right place. It was too easy. He had given himself extra time but found it with such ease he arrived over an hour and a half early. Despite the isolated location, the last thing he needed was to draw attention to the underpass which, although innocuous enough now, would soon be lit up like a Christmas tree. To kill time, he headed back into the village sliced in half by the relentless bypass. He considered a bite to eat and a quick pint in the local pub, but paranoia overcame him. What if he drank too much and lost track of time or worse still got pulled by a passing policeman and breathalysed?

Instead, he set up camp in a local café and ordered a bacon butty instead of his usual full English, nerves had taken the edge from his appetite. It was a wise choice and the crispy bacon with tomato dip did the dual task of settling his nerves and soaking up the remainder of last night's beer. He had been hungover the entire week in 1989.

He had been out every night since Blackpool with Moody and the gang, who were complete beer pigs. The drinking culture was vastly different from what he was used to back home. For a start he wasn't allowed to drink what he wanted – it had to be a pint of something. If your drink was smaller than a pint then you were a 'poof'. Despite the ridiculous volume of liquid being consumed, you could not skip a round. If you did you were a 'poof'. The pubs made the problem worse by closing at the same time – 10.30 during the week and 11 o clock at the weekend. To get around this they ordered 2 pints at last orders despite only having 20 minutes to drink them. If you didn't get 2 pints at last orders you were a 'poof'. No wonder Adam didn't want to come out.

He had never drunk so much but loved it despite the beer bullying, instigated mainly by Quinny who, despite being the least intelligent managed to control it with his own brand of psychological judo, intimidating the others into timid submission.

He arrived back at the underpass with 15 minutes to spare, but the nerves had resurfaced. He feared the presence of a passer-by when the underpass was doing its party trick. It would be difficult having to explain what was happening; worse still if natural curiosity resulted in the unfortunate person being sucked into oblivion.

Clint had a plan to deal with such an eventuality but to Tim, the plan itself was more unimaginable than the consequences. In the boot of the car, hidden in the spare tyre, was a small plastic travel bag containing 5 swabs and 5 syringes, each with enough chloroform to knock out an average-sized adult for 30 minutes. The thought of having to do this terrified Tim, but he was struggling to think of a more appropriate solution. The only alternative, he could think of, was to knock them out with a punch, but this would be worse than the chloroform. Besides, Tim was no good at fighting and from what he had seen the 1989 cohort was tougher than its 2015 counterparts and it would be more likely him who got knocked out. But the wormhole was only open for 5 minutes and, with just a few minutes to go, there was no one within eyesight so the syringe and swab remained in the tyre well.

Also in the boot was a round white tin with a purple lid complete with a picture of an old-fashioned soldier in a bright red jacket with gold decorative shoulder lapels stood next to a Mary Poppins-esque old fashioned lady with a blue umbrella. Blazoned across the front of the tin were the words Mackintosh's Quality Street – Chocolate and Toffees. There were no chocolates or toffees in the tin – they had been emptied onto the back seat of the BMW. Tim had bought the chocolates for its container which would act as a vessel to transmit a message to Clint. The message was that he wasn't coming home until next week.

He picked up the tin which he had sprayed with the exotic matter. It felt greasy. He hoped it would stop the tin from getting crushed in transit. He could imagine Clint's reaction at the news he wasn't coming home despite having promised he would. He would probably smash the tin to pieces with the nearest blunt trauma object. Maybe he wouldn't react so badly if I left the chocolates in, he laughed to himself. Either way, the prognosis for the tin wasn't good.

He knew going back a week later was less stable and riskier but wasn't it all ridiculously risky in the first place? How could he even be sure the wormhole would open again today? And if it did, what's to say it would be any more stable now than it would be next week?

The alarm on his Casio beeped to indicate a new hour was upon him, as it had every single hour since he arrived in 1989. He didn't dare turn it off in case he reset the time and fell out of sync with Clint.

A buzzing sound began to escalate giving way to a solitary crack so loud the tin nearly flew out of his hands. Had there been any chocolate in the tin he would have shaken them out of their wrappers. Frantically, he looked around, but nobody was there.

The underpass was eerily quiet transcending into a brilliant white, cloud-like distortion.

'Shit,' he muttered. Part of him hoped it wouldn't work so his betrayal would not be required, but Clint had delivered as promised. He always did, which made Tim even guiltier for his frivolity in ignoring the plan just to live it up for another week. He looked at his Casio. 3.01. Only a minute had passed as he looked around again for intruders.

'Oh, fuck it,' he thought. 'I'll stick some chocolates in.' He wanted a distraction, so he opened the tin and stuffed in a few handfuls before putting the note at the top and snapping the lid in place.

He walked over to the edge of the underpass and threw the tin into the centre of the swirling vortex. It hovered in the middle, gently swaying up and down without imploding. It was peaceful; almost hypnotic, before another loud crack and it was gone.

Chapter 15

Somebody's knockin' at the door.

SATURDAY, OCTOBER 31ST, 2015

Thud. Treble twenty. Thud. Treble twenty. Thud. The final dart drifted into the treble one.

'Bollocks,' Clint mumbled. He had told himself he couldn't stop until he scored at least one hundred and forty. He could have played safe when the first two landed in the treble and gone higher where there was more space; but what kind of person doesn't go for the treble twenty with their last dart? The kind of person who would be sat down relaxing now. He had been hammering the darts in for over an hour and his legs were beginning to ache. He was alone, so what did it matter if he got the maximum, or even one hundred and forty? It mattered to him. Everything mattered to him, so he continued.

He needed a distraction. His glorious man cave was empty without his best mate but it was still better than risking having to deal with trick or treaters at home.

3 days ago, a metal tin of chocolates had been repelled from his back to the future machine instead of the expected mark 3 BMW. He had been stood at the back of the room wearing eighties wrap-around shades to help his eyes cope with the brilliant swirl and to welcome his friend back from the decade. At first, he feared the worst as the small metal object landed at the top of the ramp with a clank, believing the BMW had been crushed into a small metal square, his despair turning to anger as he opened the tin and read the note. It was the most unwanted and disappointing of gifts, even by Quality Street's standards.

Thud. Treble twenty. Thud. Treble twenty.

BANG.BANG. BANG.

Clint jumped as somebody banged heavily on the door. He glanced at the clock on the wall. It was a novelty Elvis Presley clock Tim had given him as a gift in full Rock 'n' Roll pose with his pendulum legs swinging from side to side. It was 3 'o'clock. It couldn't be trick or treaters; it was too early and who would come here? Who could it be? The only person who ever knocked on the door was Tim, and he was living it up in the eighties. Unless he had made it back another way. It couldn't be him, could it?

BANG.BANG. BANG.

'Open the door!'

It was a woman's voice.

He stood there, rooted to the spot.

'I know you're in there, your cars outside. Now stop pissing around and open this fuckin door. NOW!'

Could it be an errant lover who has tracked him down after he loved and left her, but never called? In his dreams! But really, who could it be?

'Open,' BANG, 'the,' BANG, 'Fuckin,' BANG, 'Door.'

The dart was still in his hand. For once he played it safe, throwing it above the others, almost overdoing it as it landed in the double twenty. 'Mmm, one sixty,' he thought as he walked to the door.

She was 18 years old with shoulder-length blond hair, her pretty face shrouded with disappointment upon seeing him. She wore skin-tight light blue jeans and a plain white T-Shirt which accentuated her figure and breasts. Clint was a big fan of literature and had a curious habit of comparing women's breasts to great authors and their seminal works. It was something he never shared with anyone, not even Tim. He knew women would be offended and men would find it weird; but if he kept it to himself, what harm was he doing? The PC police couldn't read his brain just yet. These are a pair of Dostoyevsky's, he thought. Maybe not a Brothers Karamazov, but definitely a Crime and Punishment.

'It'd be grand if you stopped staring at my tits and let me in. Bejesus, it's freezing out here,' she proclaimed, her Irish accent becoming obvious. 'And what has Dostoyevsky got to do with anything?'

'What?' he exclaimed, 'I said that out loud? Did I say anything else?'

'No,' she said, suddenly realising she was in the middle of nowhere with a guy who randomly whispered Russian authors' names whilst looking at her tits. Her taxi had gone, and she hadn't even picked her bloody coat up. From his appearance, she assumed and prayed he was Tim's best mate, Clint, not the potential serial killer he projected. She vaguely recognised him from the night she met Tim.

'You look frozen. Do you want a cup of tea, or a whisky? I have a few tracky tops on that rack over there if you want to put one on. That grey one is a winter one. It's got fur on the inside.'

'Thanks. Can I have a whisky, please? Neat.'

He had somewhat redeemed himself inquiring about her welfare before asking who she was.

'So, who are you? And how did you find me? The only person who knows about this place is Tim, so you must know him, but he would never tell anyone about it. I'm not trying to get you drunk, just leave what you don't want.'

'Thanks.'

There was a lot in the glass, for sure, but she was Irish and wasn't about to start leaving whisky. It was deep brown, with an equally deep, but slightly sweet taste.

'That's not bad. Is it a scotch, somewhere in the middle of Scotland as it's not too peaty?' she enquired.

'It's bourbon, actually,' he replied, trying not to laugh, or dent her confidence. 'I can see what you mean though it is much more like a mid-range scotch than some of the lighter Irish Whiskeys you are probably used to. Bourbon is underrated though. I blame Jack Daniels for that.'

She appreciated his candour and thoughtfulness in washing over her mistake.

'I'm sorry to push, but you never answered me,' he continued, passing her the grey zip-up hoodie. 'You can keep that. Who are you? I don't know you, but you're pretty and know about this place, so you must be a friend of Tim's?'

'Does he know many pretty girls, Tim?'

'One or two. They're drawn to him. I don't know why, he's not that good looking or anything; I think he looks like an ugly Noel Gallagher, but there's something about him girls like. It's a mystery to me, but not to you, or you wouldn't be here.'

'Oh. I only met him the other night. I'm Lyla. You must be Clint?'

'Yes, I am. How do you know my name and what are you doing here?'

'I met Tim in the Leadmill a couple of weeks ago. You were in, but we didn't speak, I think you were in the other bar, but I did see you.'

'I don't remember you.'

'It was the night he played in the Oasis tribute band at the Royal Standard, with the Velcro Teddy Bears. It was a great night, and I went down to the Leddy with my mates after and bumped into him at the bar. He said he'd just been chatted up by a bloke on the dancefloor and had come into the small bar to get away from him. You were there at first but left him at the bar on his own. I recognised him and went over.'

'When was this?'

'It was a Tuesday night. The day before Back to the Future day.'

Clint looked shocked, 'Back to the Future day. Are you a fan as well? You must be to have known it was Back to the Future day the next Day.'

'I like the films, but I didn't know about that. Tim told me about it the following day. He stopped at my place that night,' she added coyly.

'Oh, I see; he told you it was Back to the Future day, did he? That explains it.'

'He told me what an important day it was for you both.'

'Yeah, we used to watch it all the time as kids and wondered what we would be doing on that day. Strange to think that a day that seemed so far into the future has been and gone. I suppose it was an important day for us both to look back on the past and reflect on the future.'

'Yeah, I guess that's why it was important for you to carry out your experiment on that particular day.'

'*What!*'

His scream was loud and unexpected, causing the usually calm and unflappable Lyla to jump, her heart pounding through the fleecy lining of her new hoodie.

'He told you about the experiment? The stupid fucker told you about the experiment?'

Clint paced around frantically with his left hand on his forehead, 'Great Scott!' he exclaimed.

Chapter 16

Braveheart

Lyla was born and raised in a small town 40 miles north of Dublin and was the fifth of 7 children, with 3 sisters and 3 brothers.

Part of the film Braveheart had been filmed in the town back in the nineties, a subject which although exhausted, was still discussed in the local pubs. It was impossible to have a conversation with anyone past the age of 40 without being reminded of the town's claim to fame or subjected to a laboured story of how they were an extra in the film. One of her many Uncles used to tell her how he fought in a battle scene, wearing a silver Casio watch which could be seen on his dead body as he lay slain in a field. It was a great story, at least the first time around, except that despite having watched the film many times she had never managed to spot either him, or the watch.

It was a picturesque little town with the River Boyne marauding rampantly through the centre on its meandering journey to the Irish sea. It was home to one of the largest Norman Castles in Ireland, a backdrop to the film, ensuring a steady flow of tourists throughout the summer.

She enjoyed a happy childhood in beautiful surroundings and was close to her siblings and parents. But, despite this, she longed to move away and head to England as soon as she was old enough. She had extended family throughout England, including relatives who ran a small florist shop in Sheffield. She had visited many times and they offered her a job if she ever came to live in the city.

She arrived in Sheffield in the spring of 2015, although the term didn't start until early September. It appeared to those around her she must be unhappy in her life to be so desperate to get away to the big city. But she wasn't unhappy, just keen to move forward. Being part of a large sibling group came with many challenges and with the stretched household finances meant luxuries were exactly that. But she didn't care about the finer things in life or having to wear hand-me-downs, which being the fifth child and second daughter were the norm rather than the exception. Her siblings competed for anything from food to a share of their parent's attention, but she was happy just to be part of a large family. She enjoyed the support, laughter, and most of all the anonymity.

Her best friend was an only child and Lyla found the attention lavished upon her and the expectations which came with it stifling. Not only was she part of a large family, but she also wasn't what she thought of as a 'key' child. She wasn't the first or last girl, let alone child, her positioning in the clan languishing towards the back of the field, a position which suited her fine. The fifth child can fly under the radar with low expectations safe in the knowledge there was a whole bunch of siblings called upon before her in a crisis. So, she could head to England three months early, with the minor ripples caused dissipating into the pond of siblings. Had her best friend attempted such a feat there would have been one mighty splash. With this freedom, she settled into city life quickly without much thought, or contact, with her previous life.

It was no surprise to her she had been the youngest to leave home and had detached herself so easily. Growing up she was always the toughest of the bunch and was a difficult person to upset or unsettle so was agitated that Clint's earlier scream had caused her to jump, particularly as the offending sentence terminated with the words "Great Scott." Clint seemed a nice bloke but there was clearly more than a little geekiness in there and he was ultimately standing in the way of her purpose. She decided it was time the dynamics of the room were swung in her favour.

'Yes, of course, he told me about the experiment. He told me everything. We were pretty tight me and Tim,' she proffered with confidence.

'You were pretty tight? So how come he never mentioned you to me then?'

She didn't let him see how the remark cut her as she countered, 'So, where is he then? Is he here? Is he hiding?'

'Hiding? Why would he be hiding from you if you were so tight?'

'Do you know where he is?'

'I don't believe he told you about this place. How did you find it?'

She paused. 'OK, he wasn't answering my calls, so I knew something was wrong, so I tracked his I phone.'

'Whoa, are you a stalker?'

'No,' she snapped,' I'm looking out for him. Something must be wrong. He hasn't returned my calls or messages.'

'Have you ever thought he just isn't that into you?'

'No! He is. Something's wrong, I can sense it, and it's got something to do with you.'

'Think about it. I'm his best mate and he never told me about you. Besides, if you met him the night before the experiment then you could only have known him for one night.'

'What do you mean I could only have known him for one night? That was nearly 2 weeks ago. How do you know I haven't seen him since then?'

A hot flush washed over Clint's head. How could he have been so stupid?

'I didn't know, I was guessing.'

'I don't believe you. Why is his phone here if he isn't? Tell me where he is before I lose my temper.'

'Who the fuck do you think you are, coming to my property and demanding things? Who the fuck are you? What kind of weirdo stalks a bloke after one night? He's *my* best mate who I've known my entire life. You've known him for 2 minutes and yet you come around here shouting at me. I want you to leave. He never mentioned you. Doesn't that tell you anything?'

She was fuming inside. 'Who the fuck am I! Who the fuck are you to say that to me?' she thought. There was no doubt in her mind she was right about Tim. She was as surprised as anyone about what happened that night. She always had love at first sight down to weak-willed losers who needed other people to complete themselves. She wasn't incomplete. She was the whole package. It wasn't her intention to move to Sheffield and within a few months fall head over heels with some local she met in a nightclub, but it happened, and she was here to do something about it. But, as angry as she was with Clint, he was the one with all the answers, so she needed to adopt a different approach.

'Ok, I'm sorry I didn't mean to lose my temper, I'm just worried about him. I know I only met him that one night, but something clicked. Trust me I'm not one of those girls who fall in love at the drop of a hat. I've never been in love before and for all I know this might not even be love. I'm confused. I don't normally go off like this, I'm usually calm. But I've not been sleeping or eating well. I might be coming down with something. Please don't throw me out. At the very least I need you to phone me a taxi.'

THUD. THUD. THUD.

Clint was back at the dartboard. Unlike before he had not set himself a target, which was just as well considering they were no longer peppering the treble twenty.

THUD. THUD. THUD.
THUD. THUD. THUD.

As a person usually in control she couldn't have been more frustrated, especially as he clearly couldn't play. She could tell he was deliberating, deciding his next move. From what she knew he was extremely intelligent and, in her experience, intelligent people take forever to make their minds up without a nudge. Patience was a virtue she had in small measures.

'Fancy a game?' she asked. 'Around the board, but in the doubles and stay on until you miss. Nearest the bull to start.'

He said nothing and, without eye contact passed her a dart which, without a practice throw, she landed in the inner bull. Unable to beat her, he surrendered all the darts as the game began.

She was on the double 5 before he was handed back the darts. There was a dartboard in the games room back home and she was the best player. She could beat most of them with her left hand, which meant nobody wanted to play against her. There was just something about being beaten by a girl with her left hand which grated on her brothers. Double 5 wasn't a great start by her standards, but it was enough to send a message.

Clint wasn't expecting her to be so good, but it was a nice distraction to have company, especially one so pleasing to the eye. There was something sublime about the way she played, giving extra concentration on her final dart, jerking forward as she released. With her perfectly conditioned blonde hair and a body that looked as though it had been poured into her clothes, Clint cursed Tim. Tim always landed the girls he fancied without even trying, despite not being particularly good-looking. As she released the final dart her breasts moved slightly prompting an epiphany for Clint. He needed to learn the guitar. Physics is great and comes in useful for many things, but it doesn't loosen the knicker elastic.

Despite the defeat, he enjoyed the company. She was Tim's girlfriend, but there was no harm surreptitiously admiring her whilst her concentration was on the game.

'Can you tell me where he is, please?'

'I think he's gone to visit family, but I'm not 100% sure and I can't ring him because his phone is here.'

'I should have toyed with you a little longer, Clint, before finishing you off. Perhaps you would have been able to come up with something better than that. You're his best mate and he hasn't been in touch for nearly two weeks? He could have emailed you or messaged you on Facebook or anything.'

'I'm not on Facebook.'

'That I believe, but nothing else. I don't understand why you're lying, but just to play along with the charade – what family exactly? From what he told me you are as close to family he has since his dad died.'

'He told you about his dad?' Clint muttered as if to himself. 'On the first night.'

'Yes, he said he doesn't normally mention it.'

'He never mentions it. I don't know anyone he's told. The only people who know are those who were around at the time. I had to tell the lads in the band and make them promise not to tell him I had told them. He hates talking about it.'

Lyla sensed Clint's demeanour towards her soften, a feeling reciprocated as she felt Clint's kinship towards Tim.

'Has this got anything to do with the experiment he left me for? He told me you think you've invented time travel.'

'Jesus, did he tell you his PIN as well?'

'No, but he told me yours,' she laughed. 'He also told me you're a super genius who makes Stephen Hawkins look like David Beckham. He believed in you. That's why he rushed off even though he was on a big promise if you know what I mean? So, come on tell me the truth. I need to know if I'm wasting my time having feelings for this guy.'

'You couldn't handle the truth.'

'You watch too many films.'

'I'll give you that, but if I told you – you wouldn't believe me.'

'Try me, Clint. I'm open-minded.'

'Would you believe me if I told you, I sent him back to 1989 to watch the Stone Roses?'

'I'd prefer to believe that than he shagged me then dumped me?'

Chapter 17

The Final Wormhole

WEDNESDAY 4ᵀᴴ NOVEMBER 2015 - 3.00 PM.

The fireworks began a day early for Clint and Lyla as they stood at the bottom of the ramp gazing upon the surreal spectacle of the 2015 end of the wormhole, the distorted blue air inside the cylinder swirling, occasionally dropping a few shades. A loud buzzing punctuated with sharp cracks made conversation impossible, but there was nothing left to say.

The dart game had spilled into the oversized glass of whisky and continued onto several more tongue looseners, with both convinced by the end of the evening they were better friends than they were. But they found common ground, not all of which revolved around Tim with Clint amazed someone he barely knew believed in him. She found time travel hard to believe but was so desperate to find Tim she was willing to try anything and against her better judgment agreed to accompany Clint on what he referred to as the final wormhole. But, as the blue air turned brilliant white and the bumper of an old, red BMW protruded out, she was converted. They looked at each other with delight as the car exited the swirl with a loud crack, making its way down the ramp.

'Brakes, brakes!' shouted Clint as the BMW sped down the ramp without slowing, crashing heavily into a steel column.

'Tim, Tim!' Lyla screamed as she sprinted over and yanked the door open. 'He's not there.'

'What?' gasped Clint staring at the empty driver's seat. 'What the fuck, Tim? Where are you? How can the car have made it back without you?'

'What's that?' asked Lyla, still screaming, pointing into the driver's side footwell.

Tim leaned forward, pulling out a 45 Vinyl record in a plain white sleeve. It was 'In My Life' by the Beatles. As he turned over the record there was a note.

Play this and you will understand. I'm sorry. Tim.

'You selfish fuckin knobhead,' Clint cried, snapping the record in two.

It had been 10 minutes since the empty BMW thudded to a halt against the steel column. After five minutes of screaming Lyla was sat silently on the sofa staring blankly at the Beatles record she held; half in each hand.

Clint was inspecting the damage to the front end of the car, which he had moved away from the post. The two silver squares at the front, above the bumper, which looked like steel were plastic and had snapped off. The bonnet had sprung open and wouldn't close properly. He noticed a metal bracket in the bonnet opening catch, carefully picking it out with his fingers. It must have been part of the fixing device for the now-defunct plastic decorative feature to the front radiator grill, he assumed. Click. The bonnet closed.

'Oh, it's not as bad as I thought.'

'What?' she snapped.

'I thought the bonnet was bent and that's why it wouldn't shut, but it was just a clip stuck in the bonnet catch; even the bumper looks OK. It's just that plastic bit at the front which is knackered and I can get one of those from a scrapyard. There's one near where the old ski village used to be,' he announced with an air of relief.

'Are you serious?'

'Yes, at least that's some good news.'

'No, I mean *are you fuckin serious?* After what you've done, all you are bothered about is that fuckin shit heap.'

'Shit heap? It's a classic. And what do you mean what I've done? It's not my fault the selfish twat decided not to come back.'

'No, Clint, this is your fault. You did this. This is your contraption.'

'It's alright you being pissed off with him not coming back, but what did you expect? You've known him for 2 minutes. I've known him all my life.'

'I don't care. Me and him were good together. I know he felt it too. You said so yourself. He told me things he never told anyone before. Personal things. Secret things.'

'Yeah, you were close, but I've lost my best mate.'

'Lost him? So that's it, you're just gonna give up?'

'I'm not giving up but there's nothing I can do. He's stuck in the past. The wormhole has gone. It won't come back. That's it. Goodnight Vienna.'

'You're not even going to try? I thought he was your best mate. I wouldn't give up on my best mate that easy.'

'You cheeky bitch. I've not given up, but there's nothing I can do. You've no idea what I've lost. You're only a kid. You'll have another bloke hanging out of you in no time. But I won't get another friend like him. He's more than a best friend. He keeps me sane. He's the only one who knows about all this. The only one I can talk to,' Clint snapped back his voice deteriorating from aggression to despair.

Lyla was furious at being called a cheeky bitch and the crude accusation she would have another bloke 'hanging out of her' left her seething. 'Hanging out of her' like she was a common slapper. He was good at insults, she had to give him that. But he was the right amount of upset. Her fury at the car diagnostics had withered away. He was distracting himself from the inevitable consequences hurtling towards him. And again, what was the point upsetting him? If there was a door to the past, Clint held the key.

'He's not the only one you can talk to. I know about it all. You can talk to me, now,' she reassured.

'Thanks. That means a lot.'

'But there is one thing I don't understand, Clint.'

'What?'

'Why have you given up on him?'

'What? He gave up on me. On us!'

'Did he, or did he get carried away in the moment? He had to make a big decision in an instant. You know how much he loved Oasis. He told me his music would have been successful if he was born in the nineties, this is his chance to prove it.'

'You're right. He used to say all the time how he'd loved to live in the nineties. It was one of the reasons I invented this thing, so we could go back in time and watch our favourite bands. But only one of us could go back at once. The machine needed setting up, and only I know how to use it. Maybe one day I could have taught him and I could have gone back. But now he's ruined it.'

'He's made a mistake, that's all. He *will* regret his decision sooner or later, maybe not at first but sooner or later, he *will* want to come back.'

'Do you think so?'

'Yes, definitely.'

Lyla wasn't sure, it was just a hunch, but she possessed an air of confidence that was impossible not to be swept away in.

'Even if you're right. It's too late now.'

'This is what I don't understand. Why do you say it's too late. Why don't you just go back to the past and rescue him? Give him a few months and then go back and see if he has made a mistake; and if he has, bring him back.'

'It's not that easy. You've no idea how long it took to create that wormhole. And to create the exit to come out at an exact location and an exact time.'

'But if you've done it once, you can do it again.'

'It isn't that simple. I wish it was. Besides now he's gone I can't do it on my own. I can't operate this thing *and* go back in time.'

'What have I just said to you? I'm here now. I can help. I'll go back in time.'

Clint looked at her, 'Seriously you'd do that for him.'

'Yes, without hesitation.'

'But I'd still have to figure out a new wormhole and that could take years, even if it is possible. And each day which passes here passes in the past for Tim. And when we go past his conception date he no longer exists and everyone, including us, will forget about him.'

'When is that?'

'I can work out how many days from when he was sent back, including the days which have passed, there are until his conception date. Then I can add that many number of days on from here and I'll know how many days I have to puzzle out a new wormhole.'

'So, what are you waiting for? Get puzzling.'

'Are you sure about this Lyla? It could take years and you will have your life on hold?'

'I'm sure.'

'And if you get there, how will you even find him? And what if he doesn't want to come back? What if he has a new girlfriend and you've done all this for nothing?'

'You let me worry about that and I'll let you worry about the brainiac stuff.'

'OK,' enthused Clint, rejuvenated at the prospect of seeing his friend, and the dawn of a new challenge. 'I'll get my notebook.'

Chapter 18

A Mad Ferret is Born

NOVEMBER 1989

He was a fully paid-up smoker now as he spun the Sheffield Wednesday striped, lager spelled backwards cigarettes in his hand. It was his father's brand; at least until he realised the stupidity of smoking and stopped. It was unlikely he would have wanted his son to follow in his smoky footsteps. But stopping hadn't helped him in the long run, Tim thought. Maybe if he still smoked, he wouldn't have had the accident. Maybe he'd have been on the boat having a fag instead of being killed. Perhaps he'd have died prematurely of a smoking-related illness with Tim amongst the loved ones moaning at him for his self-accelerated demise, blissfully unaware the King-size Regals had by happenstance bought him more time. He was overthinking things again. He threw the box on the table next to the Zippo lighter which, if he knew beforehand how often you had to put lighter fuel in, wouldn't have invested a small part of his dwindling fortune on.

They met in the café often on a Saturday morning. Sometimes they would go to the match. He was an honorary Man City fan now he lived on the dark side of the Pennines. They were much worse than Sheffield Wednesday, but he loved going to the match with his new mates. If like today, there wasn't a match they would do a bit of shopping and have a few cheeky scoops before heading back to an outbuilding next to a pub in Marple, for band practice.

The Wimpy Café, in the Arndale Centre in Manchester, was an ideally located meeting point for the band members. It was a bit like the McDonald's he was used to but the food was better and came with waitress service. What he found weird was being able to smoke in a restaurant, a nuance he was still not used to, as he flipped the Zippo 'Adam style' and lit another coffin nail. The Arndale Centre was a large ugly building plonked in the town centre clad hideously in the kind of cream-colored ceramic tiles you would normally associate with a public toilet. So, 10 o'clock at Wimpy's in the big toilet had become a tradition for the members of Peanut University.

'Are we still changing the name of the band then?' asked Moody, also smoking a cigarette. He smoked Embassy Filters, which were in the same red striped packet as the Embassy Number one Bobby smoked but smaller. He claimed the smaller cigarettes were better for him because he was smoking less quantity per cigarette, although because he used to finish them so quickly, he seemed to end up smoking more during the day. For an intelligent man, he was prone to saying stupid things.

'OK, so we said we would all come up with one name,' he continued.

'Yes,' replied Adam, 'Troy's right. Peanut University is stupid. I think we should call ourselves the Northern Monkeys, but spelled N-O-R-V-E-R-N- M-U-N-K-I-S. What do you reckon?'

'I like it,' said Bobby.

'Me too,' added Moody. 'I'm going for Football Chicken. I know it's stupid, but I like it.'

'I'm going for ED-209. Like the robot in Robocop. The one at the beginning which goes a bit crazy. You don't have to tell me what you think immediately, you have 10 seconds to comply,' joked Bobby.

'What about you Troy?' laughed Moody.

Another thing he had become accustomed to was his new name.

'Mad for It.'

'Mad Ferret. I like it.' said Adam.

'Me too.' Agreed Moody and Bobby in unison.

'No, Mad for It, not Mad Ferret.'

'But that doesn't make sense,' Adam commented. 'Mad Ferret is much better. It reminds me of Quinny. You know when he drops an E and he looks like a crazy iguana. But instead of a crazy iguana, it's a mad ferret. I love it. It fits in with the acid house club scene in Manchester. Mad Ferret. It's perfect.'

Despite his protests, Tim was outvoted. Mad Ferret was born.

Chapter 19

The Beautiful Ones

It was a tough decision not to go back. A decision that haunted him every time he allowed himself to think about it. The guilt was mainly Clint shaped. He betrayed him because he fancied living in a time where his music would more likely be appreciated. Aside from Clint, he had little to go back for. Except for Lyla who, for some reason, played on his mind more than a brief liaison should. Fortunately, he hadn't had much time to dwell on his decision. The band took up a lot of his time, but his main distraction had been adjusting to life in 1989.

He returned the BMW because it didn't belong to him. It was Clint's, as much as he would love to have kept it. He just hoped it had got back in one piece and had not rolled down the ramp and smashed into a column, or something. Besides, he was beginning to discover nuances of living in the past he had not considered before. What if another version of the car existed in 1989? It would look like he had cloned the plates or something equally dodgy. He needed to fly under the radar until he found his feet. The last thing he wanted was a visit from the police. How could he have insured or sorted an MOT if he didn't even have a logbook? Not officially having been born yet he had as little documentation as the car. There were lots of similar questions he wished he could have asked Clint before he left. He felt Clint had sent him out unprepared, but then he wasn't expecting Tim to do the double-cross. If only there was a time travel compendium. If only the internet existed.

He still had a substantial amount of the money Clint sent him with, but it was disappearing, fast. And here was another problem of time travel. He couldn't open a bank account. Fortunately, cash was king in 1989, with everyone under the age of 40 using it. Credit was the domain of the middle-aged. But he still had to keep it safe.

After making the big decision to stay he wasted no time in reducing his overheads by moving into a room at Moody's. Moody had quit his job as a Quantity Surveyor to study full time. He chose a degree in Construction which he figured covered all the bases as he was still moving in the right direction but being full-time, could spend more time focussing on the band. He enrolled at Bolton Institute of Higher Education which; although sounding like a mental asylum had a growing reputation and was close to Manchester. Better still Moody's Uncle was a property investor who had bought a couple next to the rapidly expanding Institute to rent out to students. One of them was a five-bedroomed property above a car repair shop. He agreed Moody could stay in one of the rooms for free if he made sure the other students did not trash the place.

Moody offered Tim one of the rooms, agreeing to chip in half as he did not have to pay for his room. Tim questioned whether this was OK and would not put him into too much debt with his tuition fees only to be met with the same blank expression he got whenever he spoke in 2015 lingo by accident. His expression was equally blank as Moody explained, not only did he not have to pay tuition fees, but most people received free grants to study. If he had any form of identification, he would have boarded that gravy train. Instead, he satisfied himself with a cash in hand job as a barman at the Derby Arms, a pub in between the flat and the Institute to supplement his dwindling savings, which he hid under a piece of floorboard in the corner of his room like a character from a Charles Dickins novel.

Moody would have paid the whole of Tim's rent just to have him live under the same roof. He loved his company and was desperate to give the band a good go and get a few songs under their belt. Every Saturday may have been band practice, but every day the two would write songs and jam together. Moody used to say that this was probably how Lennon and McCartney got started and there would be a national trust notice outside the flats one day to commemorate where it all started.

The day turned into a quick shuffle around Affleck's Palace followed by the obligatory homage to Piccadilly Records, before deciding the Dry Bar was a good idea.

The Dry Bar was always packed on Saturday with Manchester's a la mode. They had seen Shaun Ryder, Bez and most of the gang from the Happy Mondays a few times before. They had a record deal and already had a couple of albums out but only Tim knew their next album would send them to the next level. He wasn't sure exactly when, but his dad used to tell him how the Happy Mondays and the Stone Roses appeared together on Top of the Pops, describing it as the day the nighties began. They were only a few weeks away from the end of the decade and Tim could sense the aura around Manchester, and the pubs around Piccadilly, was palpable.

Moody made a beeline for the Mondays whenever they were in to chat about all thing's music. It couldn't do any harm to rub shoulders with a signed band. Tim was overawed at times, particularly when chatting to Shaun on one occasion about his next album Pills, Thrills and Bellyaches.

The surrealistic nature of his existence threatened his sanity as much being in the past threatened his mortal existence. Except it wasn't a threat to his mortal existence, it was a yawning inevitability drawing closer with every day, every pint of lager, every new Happy Monday's album. He knew when the clock ticked past his conception date he would no longer exist in the memory of those who knew him in 2015. He was already a refugee of time, but passing his conception date would be the official stamp of permanence.

Speaking to one of his musical hero's just months before releasing his seminal work had loosened his grip on reality. He had spells when he believed he was dreaming, trying to wake from his slumber. But he wasn't dreaming. He really was in 1989. It was awesome, unbelievable and dangerous. He was losing his mind but couldn't speak to anyone. He was surrounded by more friends than he had ever had but was the loneliest he had ever been. He hadn't seen Shaun today but spotted Tim Burgess from the Charlatans standing in the corner of the bar. He loved the Charlatans but wasn't sure if they were famous yet. He didn't seem to be drawing much attention, and none of his friends said anything. He decided not to speak to him. He was still coming to terms with meeting the Happy Mondays.

And then there was his mum. This is the guy she used to fancy, the guy he was named after. He didn't look much skulking in a dark corner of a Manchester pub, a skinny kid with a floppy fringe, but the connection to his mum tipped him over the edge. He was hot and faint as the room spun in unison with his stomach, he staggered outside, slumping on the kerb.

'Get a grip, get a grip,' he muttered, 'this is what you wanted. It's real, so deal with it.'

Adam had been the one to notice him leave and went to check on him. He told Adam he needed a breather, and the day session was catching up with him. Adam's calm manner soothed the temporary insanity as they sat on the kerb, smoking in silence. When they went back in, Tim Burgess was gone.

As they arrived at the pub in Marple all eyes focussed on Tim. Moody was a great guitarist but for all his efforts showed little aptitude for songwriting.

None of the band did. Although it had never been officially agreed, Tim was the songwriter.

The outbuilding to the rear of the pub was far enough away to not be disturbed but close enough to nip in for a pint. They were already half-cut. The drink in the Dry Bar had turned into what Moody called a 'Leo Sayer'; rhyming slang for an all-dayer.

Tim had a few songs in his back catalogue – or rather future catalogue – which they had been working on. He had always assumed the reason for his songs' lack of success was because they were in the wrong era and were chronologically out of time. But here he was, in a band full of accomplished musicians at the beginning of the 1990s. This was *his* era. This was *his* music. But it wasn't working. Something was missing. The few gigs they had played were flat. He focussed on nailing a signature tune. One which would define their music, get them noticed and start a platform to build upon. A breakthrough song.

He had been working on a song called 'Time Waits for No One' which he had written since arriving in 1989. It was an in-joke about his situation, which was probably why he was the only one who seemed to appreciate it.

When the band voted to drop the song, he brought out the big guns. His most popular song from the future was called Money and had always gone down well at gigs when he was in Prevention. It was a sermon on the evils of money with a stirring chorus proclaiming, 'money's to blame.' He felt sure this song would resonate even more in the 1980's Thatcherite backdrop. It was their strongest song which they would open with to a good reception. But there was still something missing.

'Let's get started on Money. See if we can push it over the line.'

A uniform hush around the room followed by shoegazing was halted by Moody.

'Look pal, we've been talking. Money is a strong song and we've got it tight man but we're wasting time improving it. It's a middle of the set song. We need a banger and that's not it.'

'You've been talking behind my back? Having a reyt laugh,' he spurted in an untypically Yorkshire sprawl. 'Well, that's fine. Come on then let's hear it. I assume if you're saying Money's crap then you've written a better song because so far I'm the one doing all the work.'

'Jeez man,' yawned Bobby, 'If you want to be in a band, you're gonna have to learn to take criticism. You know we haven't written anything. Were musicians. You're the brains. Moody sees something in you. That's why he wanted you in the band. We all do. We've been at this long enough to know we're shit at writing songs. Ged used to write most of the songs for Peanut University and they were bobbins.'

'He's right, man. If this thing happens you need thicker skin than that. Don't take the song thing personally. We've gone as far as we can. We need a new one. What about that one you told me about in Blackpool?' added Moody.

'What do you mean?'

'You know, loved up, doved up, 22 psycho for sex and glue. It stuck in my brain. It's irreverent, cool and now. If the rest of the song is anything like that it'll be ace.'

It was one of many slips of the tongue committed during his time in 1989. It was impossible not to, but he was surprised Moody remembered it considering the state they were in at the time. He hadn't realised yet, but this was the moment which changed his life, even more than getting in the BMW.

It was 1 am when they finished. Quinny, who lived in Marple and introduced them to the rehearsal area, had turned up at midnight. He knew the landlord who was still serving.

'This is the one,' Moody proclaimed, waving a piece of paper in his hand. 'This is the one we've waited for pal. "Here They Come" is our new show opener. It's fuckin brilliant. And I never realised until tonight just how good you are on guitar as well. But that song you wrote. Just like that. You have a couple of lines in your head and you make the rest of it up in less than an hour. And what a song. I'm buzzin man. I'm fuckin buzzin. This must be how the Roses felt when they wrote Resurrection, or the Clash when they wrote... I don't know... all of their songs. What's wrong with you? Why aren't you more excited?'

'It's been a long day. A proper Leo Sayer.'

'Yeah,' he laughed. 'The Leo Sayer to top all Leo Sayers. Shame we didn't see anyone famous in the Dry Bar, but with this bad boy, it'll be us people want to talk to. I knew today was gonna be good when I started the day with a double flusher. Like my brother always says – start the day with a double flusher and you can't do anything wrong.'

'That was you? It woke me up.'

'Yeah – you could say I started and finished the day with a piece of paper in my hand. What a day.'

Tim wasn't tired, and despite the late hour and being awoken by Moody's toilet antics, he didn't think he would ever sleep again. He was remorseful. What had come over him? How could he live with what he had done? It was bad enough choosing not to go back to his own time but now he had stolen a song from the future. He knew he had to be careful not to bring attention to himself and not to change the future. It was ok for him to make his mark on his new era, but with his material. But if he steals other people's songs, he changes their future. And worse still. What if the song had been written years before? It could already exist. It was like the BMW. You can't have two versions of the same thing existing at the same time.

His mood turned from remorse to panic. The song he stole was "Beautiful Ones" by Suede. It was from an album his dad had on vinyl called "Coming Up" which had a bright green sleeve. He didn't know how many albums they had done but this wasn't the first. It was the second or possibly third and was nearer the back end of the nineties than the beginning, so it couldn't have been written yet.

He swung back to his old friend remorse, with panic still in hot pursuit. He consoled himself that the song was not identical to the original, selectively omitting the part where this was memory, not integrity-based. He changed the lyrics through necessity, but the arrangement was altered for a more anthemic feel by removing the low pedal note which accompanied the original melody. This was a well-polished song he needed to rough up a bit and unsmooth the edges – make it sound more like the Jam than T-Rex.

He had done a good job with his petty larceny. The melodic la-la-la chorus ending was replaced with an anthemic whoa – whoa -whoa chant and some of the lyrics had been changed on purpose to add edge. By the time they staggered from the outbuilding and headed back to Quinny's flat, they had the finished lyrics down on a sheet of paper which, if you wanted, you would have to kill Moody and prise it from his dead fingers.

'HERE THEY COME'
BY MAD FERRET

High on diesel and gasoline, psycho for drum machine
shaking their tits to the hits,
Drag acts, drug acts, suicides, in your tattoos you hide
screaming my name again,
Loved up, doved up, 22, psycho for sex and glue
lost it to Bostik, yeah,
Shaved heads, rave heads, on the pill, got too much time to kill
get into birds and bands,

Oh, here they come, the beautiful ones, the beautiful ones
  Whoa! Whoa! Whoa! Whoa!
  (REPEAT)

Loved up, doved up, hung around, stoned in a lonely town
shaking their meat to the beat,
High on diesel and gasoline, psycho for drum machine
shaking their tits to the hits,

Oh, here they come, the beautiful ones, the beautiful ones
  Whoa! Whoa! Whoa! Whoa!
  (REPEAT)

You don't think about it,
You can't do without it,
because we're beautiful,

And if you think that I'm going crazy
It's you that made me,
Whoa! Whoa! Whoa! Whoa!
  (REPEAT)

Chapter 20

The Angel of Death

The flat was only a 10-minute walk from the pub, but Quinny insisted they got a pint to walk back with. As soon as they walked through the door Adam and Bobby ran toward a black mock leather executive office chair. They sat on it at the same time and started pushing each other.
'Get off. I was here first.'
'No, I was.'
'Fuck me, lads,' said Quinny, 'You get on my bastard tits with this. It's every time you come here. It's just a fuckin chair.'
'It's more than just a chair. It's the best seat in the house,' claimed Bobby.
'And it has access to the CD player. Whoever sits here gets to choose the music for the night,' added Adam.
'Well, you still get on my tits. It's like having a couple of kids. Can't you just take turns or something?'
'It's my turn,' said Adam, 'You sat here last time.'
'No, I didn't, you did. It's my turn.'
'Fuck me that's enough, both of you get out of the chair. Troy's sitting there. It's his first time here so he gets dibs on the chair. And no jumping in it when he goes for a piss. No chair crimes allowed for fucks sake.'
The two skulked away, sitting on a large pine Futon settee bed with blue covers.
'It's me next time,' whispered Bobby in a squeaky childlike voice, to howls of laughter.
Moody had been carefully skinning up a joint which they passed around as Quinny opened a large bottle of Diamond White cider, pouring the contents into the 5-pint pots they had walked back with.
'Whoa,' Bobby said,' I've still got some lager left in that.'
'It's a snake bite now. I need to get rid of the cider. I need the plastic bottle.'
He returned from the kitchen with a bucket half full of water, a serrated knife and a roll of tinfoil.
'What are you up to?' asked Bobby.

'It's a bucket bong man. You'll love it. Gets you stoned quicker.'

'Do we need to get stoned quicker?' asked Adam.

'Probably not, but it'll be a laugh.'

He cut the end off the plastic bottle and loosely wrapped the top in silver foil before punching small holes in with a knife pushing it into the neck of the bottle, filling it with cannabis leaves.

'Right, who's first?'

'Alright, I'll do it,' Bobby said.

'I'm gonna light this and lift the bottle till it's full of smoke. Then, when I take off the silver foil you have to suck up all the smoke in the bottle. Don't leave any in there or it's a waste of gear and this stuff is expensive. You'd know that if you ever bought any, you tight fucker. Suck it all in until the water gets up to the neck. Just imagine you're sucking Moody's cock. Again.'

'Funny. Get on with it.'

One by one they did the bong with Quinny finishing off proceedings with a double helping.

It wasn't long before the bong did its job.

'Fuck me,' said Bobby sinking into the sofa. 'I am so stoned. Put some tunes on Troy, while I get a few tinnies if I can get my arse off this chair.'

Tim was completely stoned. He felt the cool mock leather chair suck him in as a big, pointless smile took over his face. He tried to play it cool as his arms gripped the arms of the chair pushing his lead-like body to stand up, but his arms buckled as he slumped back.

'Fuck me, Troy. You're stoned. I'm so stoned. That bucket is the shit. Just spin the chair around man.'

Tim spun the chair around, but the arm caught on a large potted plant preventing it from spinning all the way around. Leaning over the other chair arm he could reach the CD player but couldn't figure out how to use it so he pressed a triangle button which he assumed must be play. The Stone Roses came on.

'Oy Troy,' said Bobby, putting two packs of 4 cans of Royal Dutch Post Horn on the table, 'to the side of the player there's a blank CD with LA written on it. A mate of mine gave it to me. It's from a Liverpool band called the La's. They've got a record deal and finished recording their first album this week. It's not getting released for ages, but he burned me a dodgy copy. Stick that bad boy on so we can see what the opposition is up to.'

Tim reluctantly began looking for the CD. He just wanted to sit back in the chair. His head was gone. Who said this was the best seat? He saw a blank CD sitting under a spherical glass paperweight containing a photograph of

Quinny holding a magnifying glass to his mouth amplifying his smile, with the glass in the paperweight further increasing the gargantuan grin. It was the last thing his head needed as he leaned further, overreaching and falling forward, the chair tipping over trapping him underneath. The room erupted.

'Help me then,' he said in a barely audible whisper, his face pushed into the carpet by his own weight, his arms trapped by the chair. He couldn't move. Nobody came to help. As he lay there, he noticed a pile of videos next to his face. He had only ever seen them in car boot sales back home, never in anyone's house before. His neck wouldn't move and he could only see the bottom two, 'Withnail and I 'and 'Back to the Future'. It was like the gods were taunting him, his stoned brain unable to resist the irony, he burst into laughter. His stomach hurt he laughed so much, gasping more air to fuel more laughter. Still, nobody came just the laughter growing louder and louder. Five adult men were unable to move because one had tipped over in his chair. The laughter continued as Tim tried to roll over. 'I'm like a tortoise on its's back,' he thought, laughing even more.

'I can't move,' screamed Adam.

'I'm coming,' Moody gasped, crawling along the floor to rescue his fellow tortoise, collapsing beside him. They lay face to face screaming in hysterics. Moody rolled onto his back, still gasping for breath kicking up at the chair, missing before connecting, releasing Tim onto the floor in a heap, taking down the leaning tower of VHS on his way to crushing Moody. By the time they got up and Tim sat back on his chair, the album was done.

'Troy, my boy,' said Bobby, 'I've never laughed so much. That was fuckin awesome. Do you have any more party tricks like that?'

'Fuck, fuck, fuck,' shouted Quinny, grabbing his head, his mood suddenly turning to panic, 'does anyone else see that?' He was pointing above Tim's head.

'What you on about, Quinny?' asked Bobby.

'Something is floating above his head. It's like the angel of death or something.'

'There's nothing there, pal.' Bobby reassured, holding his friend's hand. 'You've got stoned too quick. You're chucking a whitey again. Remember when you had that mega bong at that party last year and you had an out-of-body experience. Reckoned you watched yourself walk home.'

Bobby's sat on the chair arm hugging Quinny.

'He gets like this sometimes. He overdoes it. He had twice as much as us. We once went to this club in town. It was a right shit hole. Not even a proper club and we got talking to these blokes who were proper dodgy.

Part of the club was outside, so we went out with them for a smoke. I didn't want too I thought they would kick the fuck out of us but Quinny insisted. They were alright as it happened but still dodgy. Anyway, they had this massive joint. Made the Camberwell carrot look like a cocktail stick. Fuck knows what was in it, but it was so strong and I reckon it was laced with something. These fuckers had mad eyes. Their metabolism was shot. I reckon they could have taken anything. I took it easy, but Quinny proper goes for it. When we go back in the club it's hot and stuffy and he starts getting paranoid, so I bring him back here and I doss on the settee. Next thing I hear this noise in the kitchen and when I go in, guess what he's doing?'

'What?' asked Moody.

'He's wallpapering the speakers to his stereo. Even got the little decorating table out. He'd been doing a bit of decorating at the time, so all the stuff was in the house, but nevertheless, he got the little table out and mixed the paste. They looked a right bollocks when he'd finished but, you know what Quinny's like, when I asked him what he was doing he was so enthusiastic about it I nearly helped him."

'Jesus.'

'I've known this lad all my life and there's never a dull moment. Come on pal, let's take you for a little walk outside in the fresh air. You'll probably puke up but when we get back the angel of death will be gone and I'll put you to bed.'

As Bobby took his friend for a walk, the sound of beer cans opening signalled the night was only over for some.

Chapter 21

Putting on the Ritzy

The Ritzy Nightclub in Bolton reminded Tim of the fancy club they went to in Blackpool. It was a strange venue for newly renamed Indie wannabies Mad Ferret to play their first gig. Located on the edge of the Town Centre with a curved frontage, from the outside it wasn't a million miles away from the Hacienda, but the similarity stopped inside which was as glitzy as the name suggested, the interior decoration a sea of mirror cladding, brass handrails and neon lighting. The elevated stage sat in front of a timber dance floor above which hung a huge lighting rig. Behind the stage was a half-height mirror-clad wall with a walkway leading to a bar with four rows of four TV monitors behind.

The large dancefloor was surrounded by a scattering of more half-height mirror-clad walls with drinks shelves and barstools, behind which was a seating area leading to two curved staircases, serving a first-floor viewing gallery wrapping around three sides of the building. There was a second, larger bar to the left, in front of the main entrance.

As Tim stood on the stage the view over the empty dancefloor was bigger than he expected. The wrap-around viewing gallery looked as impressive as it was daunting. It was the biggest venue he had played with any of his previous incarnations. The soundcheck was complete and the butterflies were starting to arrive.

Ritzy was Bolton's biggest nightclub and always packed on Thursday, Friday and Saturday night. One thing Tim found odd about 1989 Bolton was the lack of variety in the nightlife at the weekend. Most of the Clubs and Pubs operated a strict dress code which included trousers and shoes as a prerequisite for admission. The Ritzy was one such club and would usually be populated with well-dressed young people. Student night on Tuesday was one of the few places the emerging student population could go in their normal clothes.

Tonight was going to be packed as alongside the band was a promotion for Labatt's – a new Canadian lager. Well, new to everyone except Tim. For £2.50 entry, it was 50p a pint with product giveaways. The band had been given two boxes, the contents of which they were to throw into the crowd during the gig. Tim wasn't keen on the idea, but the ever-pragmatic Moody pointed out they were getting 25p for each ticket sold. One box was full of blue mesh Velcro fastened wallets emblazoned with the Labatt's logo and Canadian maple leaf, as was the blue mesh-backed baseball caps in the other box. Moody took one of each to put in his scrap box to auction off in years to come when he was old and had blown his fortune on riotous living. They had got the gig as the guy who run the Ritzy was mates with the manager of the student union bar who in turn was mates with Moody.

'You alright man?' asked Moody, standing at the back of the stage.
'Of course.'
'You realise this place will be rammed later. At 50p a pint it'll be full of beer pigs. If you're not nervous, you should be!'
'I am a bit. You?'
'Yeah, but I'll be alright as long as I have this.'
'What?' Tim asked, turning around.
'This bad boy,' he said pointing at the Labatt's baseball cap.
'You can take that fucker off!' he laughed.

The table, in the VIP area, was full of pints of lager. At 50p a pint they just kept coming. It was cheap to those who'd bought a ticket but for free to the band. But the boys in the band didn't need to use their free allocation of Canada's finest. People were falling over themselves to buy them a pint. What hadn't been drunk was dripping off the table onto the Art Deco patterned carpet. The only dry area was the overflowing ashtray.

If there was cheap beer, Quinny was usually somewhere around. He had turned up halfway through the set but now had his proverbial feet under the table and was the unofficial fifth member, wolfing down the free beer.

Tim and Moody cast a glance at each other across the table, breaking out into knowing grins. This had been the moment they clicked. And they knew it. 'Here They Come' had been such a triumph they played it twice with 'Money' as an encore.

Tim was buzzing. He had never been this high before. And it was a natural high. He had never played to a crowd that size and got such a reception either. When they left the stage, they were the centre of attention and ushered to a booth by a bouncer, who formed a VIP area with red rope. According to Moody, it was something they did at the weekend for Yuppies trying to impress their girlfriends and were charged 50 quid for the privilege. But they did not need to pay 50 quid to sit there to impress the ladies. It was free and the ladies already seemed impressed, with or without the brass-trimmed red twisted rope barrier.

Her name was Giovanna, and she was a student at the Institute. She told him twice what she studied, but he had forgotten and thought it rude to ask again. Her hair was black with either a natural curl or demi wave complimenting her smooth olive skin which as she leaned forward to speak slid forward over her breasts. She wasn't his usual type, but he was hopelessly drawn to her despite the club being full of his usual type. Maybe that was why.

She was dressed smartly in tight black trousers with a mottled two-tone pattern and a classic white shirt buttoned exactly right to draw the eye towards her cleavage. She was the smartest dressed person within eyesight and looked more like the band's publicist or accountant than a fan. Tim couldn't take his eyes off her only breaking contact with her panda brown eyes to sneak a glimpse at her breasts. A slight smile revealed she was onto his antics but didn't mind. Didn't mind – she was enjoying it as much as him. Almost.

He had not been with a woman since arriving in 1989, not since Lyla. He thought about her a lot but had not given sex a second thought. The band and the stress of his decision to stay and its implications on Clint weighed heavy on him. He had drunk a lot of alcohol in 1989 but instead of relaxing him acted as a depressant. He had stopped smoking cannabis with the rest of the band as this just made him ill; he was fed up throwing whiteys. Suddenly he was relaxed. The pure rush of the amazing and successful gig had put him back where he used to be. Maybe it was an endorphin rush.

Everything was back, including his sex drive. He remembered women existed. All he could think of was her on top, straddling him with her huge tits bouncing in front of his eyes. He couldn't get the image out of his head. But it was a risky strategy. She was beautiful and classy. She didn't seem the type who would go for a one-night stand.

The club was full of sure things. Girls he could easily get back to his place. Guaranteed sex and dirty deeds. If he wanted sex, Giovanna was a big risk. Perhaps too big. But he could not get the bouncing tits image out of his head.

He had to make this happen.

Chapter 22

Common People

'Wow,' uttered Tim as the taxi stopped outside the entrance gates to Giovanna's house. 'This is beautiful. Are we still in Bolton?'

'Yeah. Welcome to Lostock,' Moody replied, equally as impressed. 'It's different to Deane, don't you think? We'll have a place like this if you write more songs like "Here they come", pal.'

'Follow me,' laughed Giovanna tapping the keycode into the pad on the stone gatepost. 'It's a bit of a walk to the house but I didn't want the taxi driver to see the key code or the house. You can never be too careful,' she explained as the gravel on the meandering driveway crunched beneath their feet. 'My parents are away on business, so we have the old place to ourselves.'

'How many bedrooms has it got?' asked Tim.

'Six double bedrooms, all with en-suites, six reception rooms, home office and gymnasium,' explained a smiling Sarah. 'I'm training to be an estate agent.'

Sarah was Giovanna's best friend and equally as pretty and impeccably dressed, although her tits were significantly smaller, which in Tim's current mindset made her invisible. When he realised her name was Sarah, Moody insisted on singing the chorus of "Sarah" by Bob Dylan, proving beyond any doubt only Bob Dylan himself was equipped to carry off the lyrics. Still, it must have worked to a degree as they crunched their way up the driveway hand in hand.

One leaf of the arched double doorway swung open to reveal a large hallway and timber stairway leading to the largest open plan kitchen and dining area Tim had ever seen. The decoration was traditional and obvious with pastel shades and mahogany woodwork. It seemed old-fashioned to him, but then everything was old-fashioned by his standards. He was in 1989.

'Grab a couple of these,' said Giovanna as she passed him two large green bottles. It was Grolsch lager, with a pot swing top lid with a pink rubber stopper attached to a thick wire device wrapped around the neck of the bottle. It seemed over-elaborate for a bottle of lager.

'You like the tops? If I catch you tying them to your shoelaces, I'll disown you!' she laughed.

'Why would I do that?'

'To be like Bros.'

'Bros? Who are they?'

'Come on pal, you must know who Bros are. Even you aren't that cool. Everyone knows who Bros are,' laughed Moody.

'Oh yeah, Bros,' he laughed in ignorance.

'I'm a bit of a Brosette' said Giovanna.

'Me too,' agreed Sarah.

'We'll take them upstairs with us. Are you OK in the guest room Sarah?'

'Well, the ensuite is a bit small for my liking, but it will have to do,' she teased.

Giovanna smiled and held out her hand to Tim, 'Walk this way, Matt.'

Sarah giggled and grabbed Moody, 'We're this way, Luke.'

Giovanna's room was the first right at the top of the stairs. It was huge and with the far end of the room sloping in the direction of the hipped roof, was full of character. Between two roof lights in the sloping ceiling was her bed.

'Make yourself comfortable, I'm going to powder my nose,' she added, nodding at the bed as she headed for the ensuite.

He took his shoes off and lay on the bed. What did she mean to make himself comfy? Did she mean get naked? Quinny told him a story once where he got back to a girl's house and when she went to the toilet, he got into the bed naked only for her to come back fully dressed. She told him to put his clothes back on and leave. But what if she came out naked and he was fully clothed. That would be less embarrassing he thought, popping open a bottle of Grolsch.

'Don't open the other one,' she said walking towards him, 'they are both for you.'

She was stood at the end of the bed in a powder blue silk dressing gown which, as she threw off, revealed a black laced floral teddy with a plunging neckline. She climbed on the bed and crawled towards him like a lion stalking prey.

'Now, let's get this party started.'

Her nose twitched as she began to stir, whilst he lay on his side watching her sleep. He studied her face as he had Lyla's. It was round and tanned with a flawless complexion. There was no small pockmark on her face like Lyla's, her visage was perfect, her eyelashes and eyelids so much so they must be groomed regularly. As she awoke, he continued to draw comparisons between the two. It was pointless, as he would never see Lyla again. Maybe he could look her up when he reached 2015, but she wouldn't remember him. After his conception date, he would no longer exist in the future and by then would be in his fifties. He imagined the horror on her beautiful face as a fifty-year-old man tried to explain they were lovers in an alternative time parallel. Creepy. Even Pepe le Pew couldn't pull that off.

They were both beautiful. Giovanna was of Greek origin and oozed traditional and obvious beauty laced with Mediterranean allure. She had an air of mystery and unattainability about her which made his current situation even more unlikely. How did a scrawny Yorkshireman manage to pull this off? She wasn't bothered about the gig and never mentioned the band. He took a chance on her and it somehow paid off.

Lyla was different. It made sense they spent the night together. It was as obvious as his rendezvous with Giovanna was baffling. Her beauty was also natural but with little make-up and effort, her skin slightly flawed and by comparison, transparently pale. There was no mystery to Lyla. Her appearance and personality explained themselves.

'Are you staring at me, weirdo?' she asked, snapping him from his early morning daydream.

'Just feasting on your beauty,' he replied, sliding his hand under the sheets and onto her right breast.

'Oy cheeky,' she laughed pushing his hand away, 'didn't you get enough last night?'

But he hadn't. They had sex once, his breast fixation ensuring it wasn't a marathon session.

'Yes, of course,' he lied, trying to hide his disappointment, 'I just thought you might want a bit of morning glory?'

'Morning glory. What are you talking about?' Her full-on laugh annoyed him. 'But I would love a drink of water. You wouldn't mind getting me one, would you?' she asked rhetorically.

'Of course,' he replied, jumping out of bed and heading to the ensuite in the boxer shorts she had made him put back on immediately after sex. 'Where are the cups?'

'You were going to get me tap water?' she said, 'Oh, you're so funny.'
He said, 'Yeah.'
'I'm not drinking tap water. There are bottles of Evian and Perrier in the fridge. I'll have either, I'm not fussy,' she claimed, unaware of the irony. 'You can put my nightgown on if you want.'
He stomped down the elaborate staircase like a petulant teenager in the powder blue silk dressing gown chuntering to himself about what a princess she was. But that wasn't his real problem. He would have skipped down the stairs had his morning glory plan worked out.
As he walked into the huge kitchen the door at the other end swung open revealing a smiling Moody dressed in just his boxer shorts.
'What the fuck are you wearing?' he whispered loudly. 'You look a right twat.'
'Yeah, well perhaps you should have put one on you scrawny get.'
'So how did it go, Troy my boy? Did you get your end away?'
'Yeah. You?'
'Yeah. Just finished round 2 and she's sent me out for a bottle of water. Apparently, water from the tap isn't good enough. So, they have it in bottles in the fridge for fucks sake. They must be proper minted if they can afford to buy water in bottles. Have you ever heard anything so ridiculous? Still, I'm not going to upset her, am I? I might get round 3 in before I go if I'm lucky.'
'Yeah, I'm on water duty too.'
'So, what was she like then? I noticed she's got huge tits. Bet you had some fun with them?'
'It was OK but, I don't know, it was a bit weird afterward. She made me go straight to the ensuite, have a body shower, and put my boxers back on before I got back in bed.'
'Me too.'
'Don't you think it's weird?'
'Yeah, but it's this AIDS thing that's spooking everyone.'
'But you can't catch it from lying next to someone in bed.'
'You never know. Nobody knows. I read somewhere in 50 years half of the world will be dead with AIDS. It's a virus so it's impossible to cure. Look at the common cold. That's a virus and there's no cure.'
'Who wrote that rubbish,' laughed Tim.
'I don't know. Some scientists somewhere. Anyway, how do you know it's rubbish. You can't see into the future?'

'No, I can't,' Tim backtracked, 'it just sounds unlikely to me. But anyway, the gig last night. I want more of that, so I've been writing another song in my head whilst I was in bed.'

'Yes. Yes. That's it, Troy my boy. What's it go like?'

'Well, the first verse goes like this. She came from Greece she was quite astute, she studied at Bolton Institute, that's where I, caught her eye.'

'Mmm,' pondered Moody, now drinking the bottle of water he was supposed to be fetching before screwing his face, 'tastes like tap water to me. I'm not sure about the lyrics. They sound clumsy. Like you're trying to fit too many words in. Maybe I can help with that.'

'No mate, they're fine. The song's called "Common People" and it's a banger. Trust me.'

Chapter 23

The Hallamshire Hotel

DECEMBER 1989

'Have you heard of the Hallamshire Hotel?' shouted Moody from the front room to Tim in the kitchen, who was shallow frying a panful of pork chops, 'It's in Sheffield City Centre. You must have heard of it. Adam's brother is at Sheffield Polytechnic and his mate is on the phone and he has two gigs for us in Sheffield.'

Tim knew the Hallamshire Hotel in 2015, but it wasn't a pub he went in. It was just another town centre pub differentiated by a beautifully ornate and intricate brown terracotta frontage and his dad's stories of its glory days back in the eighties and 90's. He used to go there with his mates to watch local bands. He couldn't pass the pub without shaking his head and bemoaning how the once legendary pub/ gig venue had become a townie pub. "We used to go from here down to the Limit. Then when that shut down it was the Leadmill." According to him, Pulp played there for years before becoming famous so it would be an ironic venue for the debut of Mad Ferrets 'new' song "Common People". A shiver meandered down his spine as he dwelled on his time travelling plagiarism. He comforted himself that he had only nicked a couple of songs from already established bands. It wouldn't affect their careers. Would it?

'Yeah, I've heard of it. It's a good venue. Where's the other place?'

'The Nelson Mandela Building. It's the Student Union at the Polytechnic. That's the bigger gig. We do the Hallamshire next Thursday and if they like us, they cancel the DJ and put us in the Student Union on Friday. It'll be packed. If that goes well, we might even get the Leadmill one night.'

'Do it!' shouted Tim.

'I just did,' said an excited Moody walking into the kitchen. 'We owe Adam's bro a pint, bro.'

The gig room at the Hallamshire did not scream the legendary status described by his dad. The long narrow room papered in green flock wallpaper had a small stage at one end with fixed seating running along one wall below half a dozen windows hidden behind thin orange and green paisley curtains. It had taken an age to get the kit up the narrow flight of stairs, in the middle of the pub, leading to the unlikely venue. Had it not been for his dad's rave reviews he would have had reservations. They were the only band on and had set up early due to Tim constantly badgering Moody of the gig's importance. But that wasn't the reason. He wanted to get there early and have a wander around Sheffield in 1989. So far, the impact of his time travel had been diminished by him living in a city he wasn't familiar with, but this was different. He knew this part of Sheffield like the back of his hand. The Hallamshire was on West Street and parallel to Division Street – both areas he went out drinking in regularly.

'We've got some time to kill before the gig. Shall we have a wander?' asked Moody, his question confirming Tim's plan was complete.

It was about 5 pm as they stepped outside into the cold night, a splattering of Christmas decorations stretching across West Street confirming the approach of festivities. It didn't look that different from how he remembered it from the future except there were more Pubs and fewer takeaways. But something was missing. The pair of shiny steel tram lines running in parallel down each side of the road, so iconic they had spawned an entire music festival in his era, were gone.

'Come on Troy, stop staring at the road like a freak and point us in the direction of a decent pub. You're supposed to be from Sheffield, aren't you?'

'Yeah, I'm from Sheffield!' he boomed with pride. 'You're in my backyard now lads.'

But this wasn't his backyard. Or was it?

'Where's a good pub then, knobhead. It's fuckin' freezin' out here?' Moody added.

Which of the pubs he knew would have been around in '89? The Frog and Parrot probably, but definitely the Washington.

'There's a good one down here called the Washington,' he announced heading for a side road.

As they headed up the street, he noticed most of the pubs were still there but had different names and were much fuller than they would have been in 2015.

'What about this one?' said Moody.

'It's not the Washington.'

'I don't care. It looks like a big ship inside and it's packed and there's a few birds in.'

'Yeah, let's go in, it looks alright eh Troy?' asked Bobby.

'Yeah, yeah, I go in all the time,' he lied. It didn't exist in 2015.

The pub was small, busy and full of smoke. The bar was decorated like a galleon ship, complete with frayed twisted rope handrails. At the back was a raised area that looked like the deck of a ship and the tables and seats made from planks and barrels to complete the nautical illusion.

'Ey, I like it in here,' Adam said,' I feel like Captain Pugwash.'

'More like Seaman Stains,' laughed Bobby.

It was a nice pub. Warm and welcome in a way they weren't in 2015. He didn't know why but he preferred the pubs in 1989. As he looked around at the happy, smiling faces a thought occurred to him. He was in Sheffield. It was 1989. Were any of the smiling faces his parents?

Despite the ground floor of the Hallamshire being packed only a handful made it upstairs to see the band and the gig could at best claim to have been sparsely populated. But it hadn't put them off and the unveiling of Common People, along with Here They Come and Money, had gone down well with the lucky few fortunate enough to have seen it. Amongst those coming to offer plaudits afterward was a tall, skinny bespectacled man in his mid-twenties wearing a suit jacket top and shirt which could have been cut straight from the curtains. He had spotted his distinctive fluffy mushroom haircut at the back of the room during the gig, but it wasn't until he spoke to Tim, he realised it was Jarvis Cocker. He was younger but didn't look much different from when his dad had taken him to see Pulp a few years ago. There was no doubt it was him. Despite his slim frame, he had no problem pushing to the front of the small crowd to congratulate him.

'Ey up mate. Good set,' he said holding his hand out.

'Thanks, pal,' squealed Tim with enough unexpected enthusiasm for those around to look in mild astonishment. Calm down you idiot he thought. Nobody else knows who this is.

'Errr yeah, anyway my name's Jarvis. I'm in a band as well.'

'Oh yeah, what you called?' quizzed a recomposed Tim.

'Pulp. We've played here a few times. You got more than us and you're from Manchester.'

'The band are. I'm from Sheffield, but I live in Manchester. Well, Bolton. They're both the wrong side of the Pennines anyhow.'
'Whereabouts in Sheffield are you from? What's your name?'
'Ti... Troy. I'm from Grenoside.'
'Troy, that's an unusual name for 'round here. I've got a mate who lives up Greno. Well, more a mate of a mate.'
'Cool, have you any gigs lined up in here, or anywhere for that matter with – what are you called – Pulp?'
'No pal, we're on a sabbatical now. I'm studying in London. I've just come up today for Christmas. I'm still writing though. Should have a few ready for when we start again. Who writes your songs?'
The familiar judder ran up his spine again, like a naughty schoolboy about to be caught copying on his maths exam by the teacher.
'Me.' Tim whimpered.
'Who?'
'Me.'
'You're a good writer pal. That one you sang at the end.'
'Here They Come?'
'Yeah, that one. That's a good song. Brilliant lyrics. Abstract, but relevant and so now. But completely different to that other one I liked.'
The judder began to concertina around his body. 'Which one?'
'You know, the one with the posh Greek bird, who wanted to be common?'
'Common People?'
'Yeah, that's it. Completely different writing style from the other. It's more like an amusing story than a song. That's how I write. In fact, it's weird. The story reminds me of something which happened to me in London. I met a rich Greek girl who seemed to want to be poor for some reason. If you changed the Bolton Institute line to St Martin's College and made it rhyme that could have been written by me. But to write two songs so varied is different class, pal,' he mused.
'Well, it was me who wrote it. Me and Moody got off with these girls last week and mine was Greek and she was loaded and she had this massive house in a posh part of Bolton. Ask him if you don't believe me,' he spluttered, pointing at Moody.
'Yeah,' said Jarvis looking shocked, 'I believe you. I know you wrote it; I just heard you sing it. Don't worry I'm not planning on nicking it. Honour amongst songwriters, an all that!'
'I'm sorry,' Tim apologised, 'I don't know why I said that.'

'Don't worry pal. You have to be nuts to be in a band. They're both social commentaries, but Common People is an amusing anecdote, whereas the other is an inditement of today's youth or society or both. Not many can switch between the two. They sound like they have been written by two different people. It's a talent. Listen if me and my mate Richard help you get your stuff down, do you fancy coming for a few pints with us – probably end up at the Leadmill. You can store your stuff here and move it down to the Students Union for tomorrow night.'

'I'm not sure if we're playing tomorrow yet.'

'Trust me, pal. After that set, you're playing.'

No trip to 1989 would have been complete without visiting the Leadmill, but to be stood inside with Jarvis Cocker and his mate, who turned out to be Richard Hawley, was the gravy on the Yorkshire pudding. In 2015 these two were Sheffield royalty and would have caused quite a stir, but in today's currency were just another couple of rock star wannabees.

His favourite haunt looked just the same outside in the dark evening, but inside was different. The bar where he met Lyla was gone, replaced by the most disgusting toilet he had seen, even by 1989 standards. It was an inch deep in piss and too small for the size of the club. The queue for the urinals was trumped by the queue for the bar which was ten deep all the way along. But there was a small hut next to the dance floor selling cans of Red Stripe straight from a chest freezer, which was the go too solution for the three remaining musketeers, the rest of Mad Ferret having headed back to the hotel. Moody protested at Tim carrying on the night with his two new buddies with an important gig the following evening. But his words landed on deaf ears; there was no way he was going to miss an evening that was about to turn from amazing to surreal.

'Oy Richard,' shouted Jarvis, 'Isn't that your mate from Grenoside at the can bar? I bet Troy knows him. He's from Greno, as well.'

The judder man paid Tim another visit. Grenoside is a small place, how could he explain how they had never met. How could you not know someone called Troy Gold in a small village? He must tell people less about himself. It would make his fake life easier.

'Matt! Matt!' Richard shouted, his friend responding with a smile and a wave as he headed over.

Matt? It couldn't be. Tim thought, turning around in slow motion, the flashing lights blurring and the music fading. His knees buckled as he rocked forward, steadied by Jarvis.

'You alright mate?' Jarvis asked.

'Yeah, yeah, fine,' Tim assured regaining his bearings, 'been drinking on an empty stomach. I'm alright now,'

But it wasn't the lack of food that threw him. It was the approach of his 19-year-old Dad.

'Ey up pal', his dad said nodding. 'I hear you're from Greno. You must live at the bottom end. What team do you support?'

'Wednesday.'

'Nice one. I hear you're in a band. What sort of music do you play?'

'Indie. Sort of stuff you'd hear in here. I'd like to play the Leadmill one day.'

'From what Rich tells me you're good, and he knows his stuff. Stick with it, pal.'

And that was it; he was mates with his dad. As the four of them bounced up and down on the dancefloor to the latest indie anthem, it was the best night of his life; one he thought he would never top.

Chapter 24

Miss Marple

3 February 1990

Tim was aware of the existence of Marple before going back in time. The train from Sheffield passed through it at speed, if he caught the direct one to Manchester, or stopped if he caught the slow one. He would not have remembered it except for the fictional Agatha Christie detective of the same name, but in 1989 the small borough just south of Stockport became the crux of his new world with the band. He had grown attached to its picturesque rivers and canals, and the many pubs they would go in before, or after practice. Bobby and Quinny grew up there and still lived in the area. It was Quinny's settee they slept on to avoid the taxi fare back to Bolton.

On the back of recent gigs, they dared to dream bigger. There was much to look forward to and a lot to thank Marple for. They were always made to feel welcome and treated local gigs as hometown gigs. It was the place they practiced and where the breakthrough song 'Here They Come' was written. The local shop was where the flyers were printed out on the photocopier. It was the spiritual home of the band. It was the scene of many of their triumphs and rites of passage stories to be told way in the future to generations yet to be born. But today it was the venue for Bobby's funeral.

The small village church was packed to the rafters for the service. It was the first time Tim had been to a burial. Many of those attending were under 25 and shuffled around solemnly in dark coloured baggy double-breasted suits. It looked like they had borrowed their dad's cast-offs, but this was the fashion. Every item of clothing in 1990 was two sizes too big. It reminded him of the guy in the petrol station the first day he arrived. The guy with the fish finger sideburns. But he didn't feel like laughing today.

The remaining band members had formed a micro-group to help them cope with the proceedings. A triptych fort to repel the continued emotional attack. There was even a small group of teenage girls gathered outside the churchyard wearing Mad Ferret T-shirts. Bobby would have loved it, but it did nothing to relieve the despair of the remaining Ferrets.

Quinny was there. Quinny was always there. But he was different on *that* day. He was taking care of business; making sure his mate got the send-off he deserved. They had known each other since nursery and although they seemed different in all the ways you could be, they were so close. He knew all Bobby's family and friends how only a lifelong friend could. He was a link to his past and present, his family and his friends. He was the keeper of many of his friend's memories and secrets. He knew the family side and the friend side. They stood beside each other in this very church at 8 years old in the school play dressed as little Christmas trees in brown corduroy trousers and green mohair jumpers. He stood beside him in the Empress Ballroom when they dropped their first 'E'. He didn't share as many memories as his family, but they were broader in range. More recent.

Tim hadn't realised but Adam and Quinny were keen cyclists and belonged to a club, most of which had turned up on their bike in full cycling gear. Something else he would have loved. The only one of his mates not there was Ged who was interrailing across Europe with Annette.

Being so young he was survived by much of his family including his two sisters, parents and 4 grandparents, all taking turns in breaking down and offering support. Only Quinny was able to keep it together, offering condolences and support to the different groups of family and friends. He hadn't had a drink since Bobby's death. He needed to make sure everything was planned how Bobby would have wanted. It kept him busy, diverting his attention from the oncoming reality. He wasn't gone until he was buried. He hadn't had time to blame himself yet. It wasn't his fault, but he would anyway.

Tim, Moody and Adam hadn't been distracted by the preparations and were already blaming themselves. They were all there the night he died, so they all blamed themselves. Quinny's guilt was in the post with a first-class stamp on it. Tim was burdened with the added responsibility of being a time bandit. If he had stayed in his own time, this wouldn't have happened. That was for sure.

The five of them had gone for a night out in Manchester and ended up in the Hacienda. It was the beginning of a new decade and the buzz around Manchester was building into a youth-fuelled cultural crescendo with the Cities music scene at the forefront of a new optimism sweeping the entire nation. Everything was changing in a good way. Guitar bands were fusing with acid house and dance music and it was exploding onto the Hacienda dancefloor. Anything was possible. Creativity was everywhere. The city was unstoppable and so was Mad Ferret.

1989 felt like the transition from the end of something bad, into a glorious new dawn. Tim hadn't been there long enough to understand the social and political undercurrent for this, but he had been there long enough to feel it. He was swept along with everyone else. Whether or not he should be there, or even deserved to be there, he was in the eye of the storm.

In December they followed up their gig at the Nelson Mandela building with another at the Leadmill. When they returned over the Pennines, they had traction. People were talking about them as Manchester warriors returning home after conquering Sheffield. They were part of the scene and played dozens of gigs around Manchester in a couple of months. They weren't big names yet, but they were out there. Big enough for some people to recognise them but small enough for most people not to. They still had the anonymity they would later crave. Tim was in the queue at the cloakroom at the beginning of the evening when the guy behind tapped him on the shoulder.

'Excuse me, pal.'

'Yes,'

'That guy in front of you. Is that him out of Northside?'

Manchester had a way of keeping your feet on the ground.

It was a brilliant night. It was impossible to have a bad night out in Manchester in 1990, especially in the Hacienda. If you could get in that is. But Mad Ferret could get in now. Without queuing and even with Quinny.

Bobby was the first to pull. He needed no help attracting the ladies, but the bonus of minor notoriety with the band made him more desirable.

Tim was standing next to him when a stunning young girl flanked by three friends approached him, 'I don't know what it is about you tonight, but you're irresistible to women.'

It was sickening how much girls liked him. He didn't even have to provide his own chat-up lines. It was no surprise when he left the club with the prettiest of the bunch on his arm. As he turned around, Quinny shouted, 'Go on Lad!'

He moved his fist in front of his face, pushing his cheek in and out with his tongue, his trademark fake blowjob innuendo, whilst the others cheered like baying wolves. That was the last time they saw him alive.

Despite Quinny's gesture, Bobby's intentions were pure. He walked her back to Victoria Train Station to make sure she was safe before making his way to the Ramada Hotel where they had ordered a taxi to meet them at 3 am to take them back to Marple, where they would all doss at Quinny's place. The train was late making Bobby's timeline tight to get to the Ramada. If he was five minutes late the lads would assume he had gone home with her and he would be stuck in the centre of Manchester on his own.

Running through the dark streets, he lost his bearings and couldn't remember how to get to the hotel. In a state of rushed confusion, he hurdled a knee-high wall to take a shortcut through a car park. But he was disorientated with things not as they appeared. The car park he saw was further in the distance and on the other side of the wall was a twenty-foot drop onto a lower level of the car park. Had he jumped 3 metres earlier he would have hurtled into the Manchester Canal, 3 metres later he would have landed on a grass verge next to the car park. But he didn't. He landed on a metal railing separating the two, impaling his leg.

The post-mortem ruled he survived the fall with relatively minor injuries, considering the height he fell. The cause of death was exsanguination. He bled to death after pulling himself off the railing.

Unaware of the tragedy his four friends waited in earnest, at the meeting point, for the taxi which never turned up. They all presumed Bobby had gone home with the girl he left the Hacienda with, maybe using their taxi; although that wasn't the kind of thing Bobby would do. After considerable effort wandering around Manchester flagging down taxi's which invariably sped past, full or not, they eventually arrived at Quinny's just before 5 am.

Tim, Moody and Adam left Quinny in a café near to his flat after a full English to soak up the previous night's booze. As usual, Moody had driven to Quinny's the day before and dropped Bobby off at the station, en route back to Bolton. After a couple of hours rattling around the flat on his own, Quinny decided to have a wander over to Bobby's to discuss the previous night's events over a couple of pints as the football results came in. With a bit of luck, they would bump into a few more of the Marple massive and take it through to last orders.

Although Bobby spent much of his time at Quinny's he still lived at the family home and as Quinny approached he saw Bobby's dad heading toward the car.

'Hello, Mr. Harris!" he shouted across the street.

Mr. Harris ran frantically towards him, out of character for the usually laid-back middle-aged man. It was as he spotted Bobby's mum already sitting in the car crying, he began to panic. He knew something bad had happened.

'Why weren't you there with him? Why was my boy on his own?'

The next part was a blur. He couldn't remember any of the words, or the order they came in. The next thing he knew he was kneeling in the road crying, holding up the traffic.

But now he stood upright on the ornately decorated gothic pulpit delivering an assured eulogy for his best friend. Bobby's father's brief accusatory words were dismissed as the desperate lashing out they were. They didn't blame him. It was a stupid tragedy. All that mattered now was getting this right. Articulating the influence his beautiful friend bestowed upon him whilst assuring the congregation he would *never* be forgotten, occasionally drifting into best man's speech territory. There was a brief respite from the pain when he explained how his prowess with the opposite sex earned him the nickname "Shagger Harris".

It was perfect. He did himself proud. He did his family and friends proud. But most importantly, he did Bobby proud.

Chapter 25

The Cool Before the Warm

MARCH 1990

Three weeks after the funeral, the future of the band was uncertain. Moody wanted to take his mind off the pain but wasn't sure if it was too soon to look for a new bass player. Adam was the one who wanted to continue the most. He was conflicted and unhappy before the accident and the band was his pressure release valve. Without it he was festering in self-doubt, his inner demons eating away at him.

They were all taking Bobby's death badly, but none more than Tim. There were pangs of guilt. Could they have done more? But just as Bobby's dad realised it wasn't anyone's fault, they all came to the same conclusion in their own time. For all they knew he was sowing his oats with the best-looking woman in the club. They had no way of knowing the tragedy had occurred.

Nobody could understand why Tim blamed himself so much, but then nobody knew his time travelling back story. If he had stayed in the future this wouldn't have happened, and that was a fact. He couldn't share his pain. For the first time, he wanted to go home. He wanted to go back to the future. But he couldn't. He was stuck in 1990 and all the reasons which had motivated him to defy both Clint and nature did not seem important anymore.

Before the accident, he was a fluid songwriting machine and had the bones to several new songs of his own awaiting their musical flesh. But his creativity was now as arid as the Sahara Desert. He sensed Moody and Adam were ready to start the band back up; or at least talk about it. He was angry they were ready to leave Bobby behind and jealous they could. He hadn't been turning up to his shifts at the Derby Arms and had been sacked. With Moody at lectures, he borrowed his car and drove over to Marple to see Quinny.

Quinny was also off work. Once the adrenaline rush of helping with the funeral subsided, he became depressed and couldn't face leaving the house. Quinny was suffering as much as Tim. It seemed the only place to go.

'Ey up Troy,' chirped Quinny as he opened the door, his brief smile of appreciation diminishing with guilt. How disrespectful it was to allow himself to smile. He always said 'ey up' to Tim in his best Yorkshire accent. It was either a piss-take or mark of respect, it was difficult to say with Quinny but even this seemed frivolous now.

'Ey up pal,' replied Tim, flopping into the black mock leather executive chair.

'Do you remember the last time you sat in that chair?'

'The angel of death night?'

'Yeah, and you fell off the chair and trapped yourself under it. I've never seen him laugh as much and I've known him all my life.'

'Yeah, we were unbelievably stoned. You took a bad turn.'

'It was weird. I was laughing and then I saw this thing floating above you. It wasn't the angel of death more a guardian angel.'

'You saw your guardian angel?'

'No, pal. It was yours and it didn't look happy.'

'What!' Tim exclaimed. He didn't believe in the spiritual world and even if he had leanings that way, he wasn't going to be swayed by Quinny, let alone after a double bucket; but the hairs on the back of his neck hadn't read the memo. 'What makes you think he was mine and why wasn't he happy?'

'It was just floating there looking at you like you shouldn't be there. You know what it means, don't you?'

'No,' croaked Tim.

'It means you should never double dip on buckets. One will get you there, but two is goodnight Vienna.'

'You know we laughed all the way through the Roses album. That must be nearly an hour just laughing. Never did get to listen to that other album by the band your mate knows.'

'The La's. Shame it's a good album. It's in the machine, you can take it with you if you want?'

'Thanks. Might listen to it on the way back. Does Moody's car have a CD player?'

'A CD player in a car. Who do you think he is Richard fuckin Branson?'

'I miss him you know?' said Tim.

'Of course, you do brother, he was the best of all of us. I can't believe he died before me. The number of scrapes we got into when we were younger. And it was always him getting me out of the shit. I bet he's saved my life dozens of times. Who's gonna look out for me now?' Quinny's voice cracked as it tailed off.
'We'll look after each other.'
'You're a good lad Troy. Odd, but a good lad.'
'Odd?'
'The CD player in the car is the latest, but there's a new one every time I see you. Like the homophobic comment and the tiny phone in your pocket. I have a theory on it.'
'What theory?'
'I think you're from a rich, middle-class family and you're ashamed of it. That's what the song Common People is about. You're the rich kid trying to slum it for a bit. You probably do have a CD player in your car or hang around with people who do. That's what I reckon.'
'I'm not rich, I just say things without thinking sometimes. And the homophobic thing — I just think you need to be respectful of people's feelings.'
'That's what Bobby said. He was a good judge of people and he thought you were OK. And since he died I've had a lot of time to think about things, like the words I use. Life is short and people are fragile, emotionally and physically. Why waste the little time we have being mean to each other? I didn't mean to be offensive it's what people say where I live. But, you were right and I've stopped using that word. Knowing you has made me a better person. It's weird. I don't know what it is. I can't put my finger on it. It's not that you're cleverer than me. I mean you might be but it's not that. It's something else. I don't know what though.'
Tim was uncomfortable and desperate to move the conversation away from himself, 'You must really miss him; you were at school together?'
'I know what people think. They think we were two completely different people and couldn't understand why he would hang around with a doofus like me. But it wasn't like that. We were twins. We liked all the same things. Football, cycling, running, cricket, music. Everything. Did you know we learned to play the guitar together? I'm just as good as him; better maybe. He read somewhere that Lennon and McCartney learned to play the guitar opposite each other which is why one of them plays left-handed.'
'Is that true?'
'Dunno, but that's what Bobby used to say. I was the left-handed one, even had to buy a left-handed guitar and bass to practice with him.'

'How come you aren't in a band then?'

'I used to be at school with Bobby. We were called Clandestine. More of a rock bank with bandanas and all that stuff. We used to take it in turns to play lead or bass. We were shit though. Only played at school at Christmas assemblies and the odd discos. Of course, he used to pull all the birds, even back then. He loved it and carried on, but I wasn't as bothered. I didn't see a future in it. I love what you guys do. Did? What's happening with the band? You carrying on?'

'We've not spoken about it, but I think the other two do. Especially Adam, but I'm not sure. Doesn't seem right.'

'I'll tell you what's not right.'

'What?'

'Quitting. Bobby would hate that. And so would his family. I had his parents around here yesterday. They've never been here before. Fortunately, the place was tidy and there were no bongs or buckets or shit knocking around. They wanted to thank me for the eulogy and Mr. Harris wanted to apologise for blaming me when he found out. But he didn't have to, he didn't really blame me. He was upset. I've known him all my life. Since I can remember anything, he's been there. And one thing he mentioned was the band. He kept an eye on it and he knew you were making a mark. He went to a couple of gigs and he spotted the difference. Like the rest of us. It's hard not to.'

'Difference?'

'Since you joined everything seems possible. That's the difference. Before it was just a hobby. Something fun to pass the time, like playing football at school. I was one of the best players but when I went on trials I was playing against the best in the city and knew I wasn't good enough, so I started to look for the next thing. Before you came along Peanut University were looking for the next thing. They knew it wasn't happening and were settling. Look at Moody, he'd resigned himself to becoming a Quantity Surveyor, like me. A fuckin brick counter! You turn up, he quits to focus on music. You've got a lot to answer for. You can't just waltz in here and then quit. I get it. It's a fuckin tragedy, but not carrying on the band would be another tragedy. Mr. Harris told me to tell you guys to continue in Bobby's name. Finish off what you started. He was a founder member.'

'Oh. I see.'

'You know me and the guys talk about you a lot.'

'Really?'

'Yes, really. You turn up in the Dry Bar on your own at the exact time the band was about to break up. Moody loved you from day one. And Bobby too. Not so much me or Adam.'

'You and Adam don't like me?'

'I didn't say we don't like you. We just weren't sure about you.'

'Why?'

'I'm not sure about Adam. Did you have words in Blackpool? Ever since we got back from watching the Roses he hasn't seemed that keen on you. But I wouldn't worry about that, he likes me much less. But I've always felt there was something off about you. Something odd, like I said earlier. But over the last couple of months, I've come to the conclusion you are odd, but in a good way. A creative way. That's probably why you write such good songs. Money's not bad but Here They Come and Common People are ace. I mean top drawer, so rather than question why you are different why not embrace the difference. And in this case, the way you are different is songwriting. The others look the part, and can play but trust me, they couldn't write their way out of a paper bag, even if it were wet.'

'Well, that's candid of you.'

'That's what I mean. Who says candid? But if you stuck that in one of your songs it would probably work. Anyway, you need to start the band up again.'

'You don't think it's too soon? You think everyone will be alright with it?'

'Alright with it. Haven't you been listening to me? People are counting on it. It's the only thing that makes sense right now and the only way to salvage anything from this mess. You need to do it for Bobby. Everyone around here knows who Mad Ferret are. If you put an advert out there, you'll get a new bass player, easy.'

'Why do we need to?' asked Tim.

'Because the fuckin bass won't play itself, obviously.'

'I mean why advertise when you could do it. You could take his place. He'd love that and so would Mr. Harris, by the sound of things. It'd be perfect.'

'The thought had crossed my mind but I'm not sure.'

'About what?'

'I wasn't sure if it was weird and if you three would want me in.'

'I do and Moody will agree with me, I think we both know that.'

'What about Adam. I've told you he doesn't like me.'

'It's a democracy and he's outvoted. If you can play as well as you say you can, you're in as far as I'm concerned.'

'Ok,' mused Quinny, 'Let me think about it.'

Chapter 26

This Time Next Year Rodney!

JUNE 1990

The lounge area of the flats was a large open plan layout with an equally generous kitchen. Tim was sprawled on one of the two large maroon Chesterfield settees. Every time the landlord visited, he mentioned how lucky they were to have Chesterfield settees, claiming they were the only students in Bolton to have them. But nobody cared, they were just settees. If he loved them so much, why weren't they in his house? They weren't even that comfortable. The bidet in the bathroom was far more unusual for student accommodation, but he never mentioned that.

All the band were there with a few of Moody's friends from the Institute. Tim was sitting on one of the Chesterfields watching Only Fools and Horses on the TV. Behind were a couple of Moody's mates throwing a mini basketball at a tiny plastic hoop, arguing who had eaten the last tin of Heinz beans and replaced them with a tin of Quik Save beans.

It was the episode where Rodney won a painting competition in the under 15 category and became a member of the Groovy Gang. It was a classic episode. He had watched them all with his dad and this was one of his favourites. But in 1990 it was a recent episode and this was the first time it had been repeated, so the Chesterfields were full of those who hadn't seen it the first time around but heard how good it was.

Tim was consistently surprised by the nuances of the era. This kind of excitement for the repeat of a TV would never have happened in 2015. There was much more variety of TV shows and channels, diluting the impact of any one show. And then there was streaming and access to shows. If you missed an episode you had to wait months to watch it again unless you taped it on a video recorder which although only carried out the simplest of functions was surprisingly difficult to set. Tim hated the Video Recorder and never bothered setting it. What was the point, he had seen most of the stuff before anyway? A Video Recorder was also an unusual possession for students. He couldn't believe a basic and cumbersome piece of electronics was held in such high esteem? He hated the pride Moody took in the machine amongst his student friends. Whenever he mentioned he had a video, without fail the response would be 'have you got a video?' in a fake accent. It was a line in another sitcom, The Young Ones. He cringed every time it came up, whilst everyone else rolled around in hysterics.

He did like the camaraderie created by the repeated TV show, more than singular people sat in dark bedrooms binge-watching an entire series in one day. There was an appreciation for the creative outlet he didn't feel in 2015. His dad used to sit him down in front of the TV as a kid and say, 'Watch this – it's a national institution.' He understood what he meant now. They settled for less but appreciated it more.

As was often the case, Quinny was the fly in the ointment, having watched the episode before he couldn't resist saying, 'watch this bit, Troy!' before the funny bits. It would have been annoying even had he not already watched it a dozen times. But for once his irritation wasn't Quinny shaped. It was something Del Boy had said earlier in the episode which resonated with his own decision-making process. In the episode, he had entered one of Rodney's paintings into a competition for a holiday and won. When it came to light Rodney was too old, Del Boy had the opportunity to come clean but didn't, he lied and said with a smirk on his face, 'I don't know why I said it,' to laughter from the audience. Tim had said something he should not have, and he didn't know why. But nobody was laughing and now it was too late.

As the final credits rolled up the screen Tim went to talk to Moody who was on his own outside. In the middle of the far wall was a patio door which led to a large flat roof over part of the car mechanics covered in loose white chippings, another idiosyncrasy more worthy of note than the Chesterfields. Around the perimeter of the roof was a small parapet wall about a foot high with no railings to prevent falling over the edge. He couldn't believe this was legal for student accommodation but then this was 1990, it was just another health and safety misdemeanour. It was amazing humanity hadn't become extinct before he was born. Or maybe the bitter middle-aged men at the pub who talked about the snowflake generation were right? Perhaps he worried too much?

'Ey up Moods. Don't you like Only Fools and Horses then?'

'What? Of course. Everybody likes Fools and Horses. But it's hard to concentrate with this bad boy burning a hole in my pocket,' he replied tapping the back pocket of his jeans, rattling the Maxell C90 cassette.

Tim's heart thumped inside his chest as he felt nauseous. Why had he done it? Dell Boy's antics had hilarious consequences but his were real, not played out in a fictitious sitcom.

Maybe it was the pressure he had been feeling. Since the band reformed, with Quinny on bass, they were expected to seamlessly continue their journey to stardom on the back of the songs he started before the accident. But the songs hadn't worked out. Before, he was on an effortless roll, but now he was forcing songs to a conclusion, discovering the hard way you can't force creativity. The expectation weighed him down. From the band, from Bobby's family, but most of all from himself. In his mind he was responsible for Bobby's death – there was no doubt about it. Had he gone back when he should Bobby would be alive in 2015. He would have a wife and family, perhaps even grandkids. A man like Bobby was guaranteed a bright future, a future which he had taken away from him. All he could do now was to repay his family and create a legacy for his dead friend.

The self-doubt crept into his mind, multiplying like a virus. He always believed he hadn't made it as a musician because he was born in the wrong era, but now he was where he should be, he was still unsuccessful. Maybe he just wasn't talented? There's no maybe about it. He had tried twice in two different timelines and was still a failure. But he couldn't afford to be a failure after what he had done. He hadn't just killed Bobby; he had betrayed Clint and couldn't get Lyla out of his mind. If he had met her a few weeks before he would have known that staying in 1989 was a mistake. But he didn't realise he had fallen in love with her until it was too late. He was confused, lonely and angry with himself, but it didn't excuse what he had done.

He was under pressure and google didn't exist. The internet didn't exist, never mind Google. If it had he wouldn't be in this mess, he would have cherry-picked a few songs from different artists, like he had the Suede and Pulp songs. Nobody would have known. But he couldn't be sure what year a song was written. The panic attack during his opening conversation with Jarvis Cocker, when he thought he was claiming credit for Common People, was forgotten in the kick-ass night he subsequently spent with Jarvis, Richard Hawley and his dad. But that moment had scared the living hell out of him. He couldn't risk walking down that street.

He went to the library to research his problem. After a discussion with the Librarian, she proudly presented him with a CD-ROM full of all the latest news and current affairs. He took it gratefully so as not to offend her and in the desperate hope it would be better than he imagined. It was slow, clumsy and held little information about popular music or culture. He would have learned more about 1990 by looking out of the window. But there was this thing lurking at the back of his mind. It was easy to ignore at first, laugh off even, but it stopped lurking at the back, muscling its way to the front until he could ignore it no longer. There was one band he knew all about. He knew when they formed, what year all their albums were and the lyrics and chords to their greatest hits.

Oasis's first gig was on August 18[th,] 1991 at the Boardwalk in Manchester. It was one of the optional dates given to him by Clint to visit. Noel was not a band member yet and it was more than two years before they were signed. If he had chosen to visit that date – and he nearly did – this unforgivable treachery would not have been possible. It was almost a year and a half until the debut gig and he knew from a documentary he watched the only song they played from the first album around that time was Columbia. He also knew that one of his favourite Oasis songs *Whatever* never appeared on an album. He thought he was clever, although devious was a more apt description.

The rest of the album remained the same, although he changed some of the lyrics on Shakermaker from "Mr. Clean and Mr. Benn are living in my loft" to "Mr. Sheen and Mr. Benn are both dead in my loft." He thought this, with a faster tempo, gave the song an edge. Whether it did or not was irrelevant as he was the only person to hear both versions.

Sat in the back pocket of a delighted Moody was a live debut demo album by Manchester upstarts Mad Ferret.

DEFINITELY, MAYBE
BY MAD FERRET

Rock 'n' Roll Star
Shakermaker
Live Forever
Up in the Sky
Whatever
Supersonic
Bring it on Down
Cigarettes and Alcohol
Digsy's Dinner
Slide Away

Married with Children

'He would have been proud of this demo tape, you know?' said Moody walking across the roof to the back of the flats.
'Who?'
'Bobby, of course.'
The rear of the flat was like the opening scene to Coronation Street, populated with two up two down back-to-back brick terraced housing with small outhouses at the bottom of the gardens. All that was missing was the ginger tabby cat running along the roof. One of the students who lived there said the opening scenes were shot behind the flats, but Tim didn't believe him.
'Mmm,' he replied.
'I don't get you sometimes Troy. You wrote this album in a couple of weeks and you stand there like all you've created is a slice of toast. This is genius pal. Genius. And the timing couldn't be better.'
'What do you mean?'
'Music isn't just about talent and songwriting. That's part of it, but it's also about timing. What's going on at the time. The Pistols, the Clash, the Jam would have been no good in the 1960s, same as the Beatles wouldn't have the same impact now. Yes, the times influence the music, but great music influences the times as well. It becomes a soundtrack for the era; for a generation. Music has been shit for a while; since the punks back in the late '70s and early eighties. But that's about to change. Everything is changing. Just because a new decade starts doesn't necessarily mean that times change with it, but that's what's happening now. The eighties were a depressing mess, and this new decade is full of hope and at the centre of it is the music and Manchester is the epicentre. You must be able to feel it?'
Of course he could feel it. It was impossible not to.

Chapter 27

Dodging a Silver Bullet!

The problem with the demo tape – apart from having murdered his favourite band before they were conceived, was it was exactly that – a *demo* tape. He knew all about the legendary gig in King Tut's club in Glasgow when Alan Mghee signed Oasis for Creation records. He had read everything about it back in the days when the internet existed. Alan Mghee had gone to watch one of his bands 18-Wheeler but turned up early because he went with his sister and caught the Oasis gig. The rest, as they say, is history. He knew the story and he knew how to get noticed by the creator of Creation, but there was a major problem with this strategy; that gig did not happen for nearly 3 years. The date 31st May 1993 was engraved into Tim's head. Had this been an option of dates to travel back to, he would probably have chosen it. He wished it had.

The new playlist, along with some of the originals, were going down well on the circuit as they regained the impetus they had before the accident. The demo tape was poor quality, recorded live in the shed in Marple on a tape cassette by pressing record and play on the Aiwa cassette player. They had to do it in stages when the pub was quiet with one of their mates standing outside telling people to shut up.

The tape was upgraded to a CD by a mate of Moody's at the Institute. Across the road from the main building was a new annex known as Eagle House which, among other subjects, covered media and communication studies. It was a mini recording studio with all the latest recording equipment, including video cameras. In 1990 it was the latest in cutting-edge technology producing a CD no better than Tim could have knocked up on his phone in 2015. But it was a vast improvement on the tape and the ability of Moody's mate to burn extra CDs, when no one was looking, universally impressed everyone. Compact discs were still new and the domain of the established bands and having one burned in a recording studio was ridiculously expensive. Even the Stone Roses were not recording on CDs.

Moody was micromanaging the band, pulling in contacts; strategically placing the expensive CDs in the hands of those worthy, until one evening he called a band meeting at the Student Union. The Bolton Institute Student Union was small but well laid out and always busy. Mad Ferret had played a few times and they were often recognised, especially since the latest 'Definitely Maybe' gig a couple of weeks ago. The new material was causing a stir in the handful of tiny venues they had played.

'Cheers for the pints lads but can you give us some space we have a band meeting?' Moody said to a couple of lads sat next to them and had bought a round for the band. Four pints was a generous act for students and he felt guilty asking them to leave before they had even knocked the froth off, but there was a big announcement to make.

'Right then lads, can you give me a drum roll Adam?'

Adam obliged by drumming his index fingers on the table as Moody sat with a ridiculous grin on his face.

'We've been offered a record deal!'

'Yes,' shouted Adam banging his fist on the table, 'brilliant, well-done Moods.'

'Yes,' Quinny confirmed looking skyward, 'well-done pal. I bet Bobby's up there punching the air.'

'But you've not heard the best part yet,' teased Moody.

'What you fucker, just tell us,' Adam demanded.

'It's Silvertone Records.'

'Who are Silvertone Records?' Quinny asked.

'Silvertone Records,' Moody explained, leaning back in his chair with his hands behind his head in a moment of self-congratulations, 'are the record company of the Stone Roses.'

'No way!' exclaimed Adam leaping up and punching his fist in the air, 'oy lads,' he shouted to the two students sat with them earlier, 'you've just bought a pint for the next Stone Roses!'

'How did you manage that?' asked a stunned Quinny, 'the fuckin Stone Roses record label.'

'You wouldn't believe it. I've been asking around for months and giving the CDs out and nothing. Then I go round to my mum and dad's for Sunday tea and my dad starts telling me about this bloke at work. My dad works in Sale selling mortgages and the guy next to him knows someone, who knows someone who is mates with one of the Roses. When the Roses signed their record deal with Silvertone they didn't have a manager and didn't want to get ripped off so asked this bloke at my dad's work if he could look at the contract.'

'Hang on,' said Quinny, 'why would a mortgage salesman from Sale be overseeing a record contract?'

'Because he works with contracts for a living. It's all contract law and I would imagine they're pretty much the same. So, when I'm explaining to my dad about trying to get a record deal he tells me this story, but can't remember the name of the band, so I don't pay much attention until a couple of days later when he rings me up and asks me if I've ever heard of the Stone Roses. I gave dad a CD, he gives it to his mate and a couple of days later this dude from Silvertone rings me up saying he proper loves the demo. He thinks we'll be bigger than the Roses!'

'Fuck me,' Adam gasped.

'And my dad's mate says he will come over with us on Saturday to look over the contract like he did for the Roses. And get this – we will be their only two signed bands because they used to be called Zulu or Zombie Records, or something but they've formed a new label for this kind of music. So it's us and the Roses – best buddies. We can get free tickets for any shows they play. Fuck that we'll be supporting them.'

'Fuck that for a game of soldiers,' laughed Quinny, 'they'll be supporting us.'

'This is all down to you Troy, my boy. A guy is coming up from London on Saturday from Silvertone and we are going to meet him at Piccadilly Station with my dad's mate at 11 am. I thought we could go around Manchester after and celebrate. What do you reckon?'

'Yes!' shouted Quinny

'Fuckin deffo.' Laughed Adam.

''What d'you reckon Troy?'

'No.'

'What do you mean?' gasped Moody. 'I thought it would be a good idea to go around fanny brown to celebrate.'

'No,' repeated Tim, 'I mean no, I'm not signing the record deal.'

'You're kidding, right?' said Moody, 'you don't want to sign a record deal with the Roses label when it's the only offer we have. You *are* pulling my plonker, right. Right?'

'No, I'm serious, I'm not signing with Silvertone.'

'Why? Why the fuck not!'

'I've heard bad things about them that's all.'

'From who? They're a new label.'

'On the grapevine that's all.'

'The grapevine? You know the same people as me, less even. What fuckin grapevine do you know about that I don't? The closest thing you get to a grapevine is that disgusting two-quid red wine you keep buying. I know we're students but that stuff's shit. You're telling me you won't sign the record deal?'

'No.'

'Well, it's tough shit anyway. It's a democracy so we'll have a vote. I'm in. You're out.'

'I'm in, obviously,' Adam added.

'Come on then Quinny, tell us you're in,' prompted Moody seconds later, clearly irritated at the minuscule pause Quinny allowed himself.

Quinny looked at the floor silently.

'Come on.'

'I'm thinking.'

'What's there to think about? It's a no-brainer. You said yourself how happy Bobby would be. He'd be in there like a rat up a drainpipe.'

'I know but Troy's got me thinking. Shouldn't we get proper advice from a proper solicitor or something, not some mortgage guy from Sale? You always hear about bands getting ripped off. I heard the Clash were only paid fifty quid a week when they first started cos they signed a shit deal. And it's not just that though, is it?'

'Well, what else is there?'

'It's him,' he mumbled nodding toward Tim.

'Troy. What about him, you can make your own mind up you know. If he told you to jump off a cliff would you?'

'No, but you would have up until now.'

'Fuck you.'

'It's true and I can see why. This album he knocked up in a few weeks is genius. That's the only word for it. Genius. None of us can get near that. We've tried before he came along and you know it. Why upset the only genius in the band. And before you start crying like a baby, we all appreciate what you do Moods. You put the graft in and get the contacts. We need you. My dad calls it sweat equity. Someone in business who works harder than other people around him to make up for having less ability. We all do it a bit. Put in that extra so we can cling to Troy's coat tails. But it's no substitute for raw genius. He just knows stuff. He has this aura around him and if he has doubts about the deal then so do I. I can't believe I'm saying this, but I'm voting no. And that's a tie and it has to be a majority.'

'So, you're telling me I have to ring my dad up and tell him to call his mate to tell him to tell the guy from Silvertone to not come up from London.'

'I'm sorry Moody, you'll have to trust me on this,' explained Tim.

It was the first disagreement in the band and the first sign the bond between Moody and Tim was not impenetrable. Moody was a clever man who knew Quinny was on the money, but that did not stop the seeds of resentment from taking root.

'Well, you're wankers the, lot of you,' shouted Moody as he stormed out of the Union.

'But,' muttered Adam as his friend disappeared. 'I said yes.'

Chapter 28

Rock 'n' Roll Stars

Bands have split up over smaller creative differences than looking a gift horse of a record deal in the mouth. But these bands didn't have Definitely Maybe locked and loaded. Madchester was in full swing and with the energetic gigs showcasing the Ferrets musical masterpiece it was no surprise a record company came knocking. It was equally as unsurprising it was Factory Records.

He had set his heart on forming his own label at the recording studio they used and calling it Institute Records, but he didn't know how to do it. Besides if he turned down another high-profile label Moody's head would have exploded.

Tim was not keen on signing to Factory due to what he read in the music press and the Shaun Ryder biographies he devoured before becoming a time traveller. Despite the impressive list of signed bands and infinite kudos seeping from the label they ultimately failed to get the basics of business right. It was fun to look at from the outside, but did he really want to join New Order in financing the failing Hacienda? But then at least Factory were based in Manchester and doing it for the right reason – music not money. One of the reasons Factory were never bailed out was because the bands owned the rights to their music. That was the deciding factor in Tim signing on the dotted line.

They didn't mess around getting the album recorded. They had top producers and engineers and were connected to everyone in the city. They knew about music, even if they couldn't organise a piss-up in a New York-themed nightclub. Had they employed somebody who could work a calculator they would have been unstoppable.

Thursday 18th October 1990 was announced as the album release date and the publicity machine ensured Mad Ferret were busy boys. The only thing to decide was which track to release as the debut single. Factory wanted to release two singles before the album and one to coincide with the release at two-monthly intervals and a fourth and final single as the album fizzled out. Factory left the choice to the band, who decided the fairest way to do this was to pick the four songs they wanted and scored them accordingly. Their top choice received four-points – the final single one.

Moody
Slideaway	-	4
Supersonic	-	3
Live Forever	-	2
Cigarettes and Alcohol	-	1

Adam
Rock 'n Roll Star	-	4
Supersonic	-	3
Live Forever	-	2
Cigarettes and Alcohol	-	1

Tim
Cigarettes and Alcohol	-	4
Whatever	-	3
Bring it on down	-	2
Married with Children	-	1

Quinny
Slide Away	-	4
Rock 'n Roll Star	-	3
Live Forever	-	2
Shakermaker	-	1

TOTAL

Slideaway	-	8 (2)
Rock 'n Roll Star	-	7 (2)
Live Forever	-	6 (3)
Cigarettes and Alcohol	-	6 (3)
Supersonic	-	6 (2)
Whatever	-	3 (3)
Bring it on down	-	2 (1)
Married with Children	-	1 (1)
Shakermaker	-	1 (1)

The results were close and with three songs tied; Supersonic, the choice of the Gallagher's for debut single, was relegated on goal difference as it was chosen by the least band members. It was decided this would be the way they would choose single releases in the future. It was Tim's idea and although only one of his songs made it onto the list, he had created a blanket democracy within the band which, after the Silvertone incident eased the tension between him and Moody.

With the singles decided they embarked on a huge UK tour starting in Ilford in July and finishing a few days before Christmas at the Hacienda, with a couple of festivals mixed in for good measure. There were a dozen gigs each month at a variety of small venues, mainly clubs, pubs and student unions; the first gig corresponding with the release of Slide Away.

The Island Club in Ilford was a large venue, similar in appearance on the outside to their favourite venue back in Manchester, the Apollo. But it wasn't the appearance of the building, which was reassuringly familiar, it was the reception from the crowd. All the gigs they had played so far were up north and they were not sure how a London crowd would react. The vibe was electric. It was like being home. The sense of music fuelled optimism wasn't just in Manchester. It was everywhere, and they had lit the blue touch paper.

The tour manager was a guy in his mid-twenties from Thirsk called Ollie with an infectious love of music, a bounce in his walk and a ready smile on his face. He knew everything there was to know about Bob Dylan, a topic he and Tim would discuss whenever possible and often late into the night, dissecting every Dylan song and nuance. Even by his standards, he was looking happy as the Ferrets marched triumphantly off stage.

'I can't remember a northern band getting a reception like that down here since the Roses. This is on guys, trust me. There's no us and them – no north and south, it's just the music and they love it. I was here in November for the Roses gig at Ally Pally. When Ian said, "it's not where you're from it's where you're at" the hairs on the back of my neck stood up and all the crowd started singing Madchester la la la. In London! They opened a door that day and you've just walked through it and nailed it to the fuckin wall lads. That fucker is staying open. And that's not all. The numbers have come in for Slide Away and its number 37. Well done lads you're in the Top 40. Keep playing these gigs and Rock 'n' Roll star could get high enough for us to push for Top of the Pops. Why not? The Roses and Mondays did it!'

This was the first time he noticed the unavoidable guilt. Oasis's fourth album was called 'Standing on the Shoulder of Giants', which was ironic as he was doing exactly that. There were so many ironies since he gate-crashed the era that he could only focus on one at a time. But with each gig, the guilt grew and then contracted. It would always be there, but he had it under control. Besides, what could he do? Did a cuckoo feel guilty after he pushed the other eggs out of the nest? Of course not, it flew around happily being a cuckoo. He had killed Oasis, so he owed it to the Gallaghers, no he owed it to himself, no he owed it to the country to be the best British Rock and Roll band of the decade.

Chapter 29

Reading Festival 1990

The Ferrets arrived at the Reading Festival 1990; unaware they were on the cusp of greatness. Rock 'n' Roll star had been released a week earlier and gone straight in at Number 17, resulting in their first appearance on Top of the Pops the day before the festival. On the back of their television appearance, they had been bumped up at the eleventh hour from the Mean Fiddler Stage to the Main Stage on Friday night, at the expense of a band called Mega City Four, who became the latest egg pushed from the nest by the time travelling cuckoo.

Despite the relative success of the two singles and the sold-out tour, the Ferrets were in awe of the situation and had never been to a festival together let alone play the main stage. The sold-out gigs had been small intimate venues and Slide-Away had grazed the charts largely unnoticed by anyone other than friends and relatives. Rock'n' Roll Star had only just been released. But what they had not realised was the impact of their appearance on Top of the Pops the day before on national television. Tim had no idea of the importance of the music programme and the reach it had in a country of 55 million people with only 4 TV channels to choose from. Within seconds of entering, they were surrounded by festival-goers asking for autographs and throwing them cans of beer. Moody somehow managed to end up with a bottle of Jack Daniels.

'Saw you guys on Top of the Pops. You were brilliant. Rock 'n' Roll motherfucker!' shouted a young lad with scruffy shoulder-length brown hair, light blue baggy jeans and a white T-Shirt with a stoned cow on the front. 'You and the Carpets man, you're gonna kill it! It'll be like when the Roses and Mondays took over Top of the Pops. The north is taking over man. We're gonna conquer the south in this fuckin field man. Madchester la la la!'

Fellow Manchester band the Inspiral Carpets were an indie tour de force and headlining Saturday night. Tim had been watching their commercial success with interest. He had heard of them through his dad, but never realised how big they were. They were more commercially successful in

1990 than the Stone Roses and their debut album had made its way to number 2 spawning a couple of hit singles. The first single 'This is How it Feels' made its way into the top 10, whilst the latest single 'She Comes in the Fall' was a music worm in Tim's brain. Their music was a fresh mix of indie dance cross-over and were the first of the Madchester bands to strike commercial gold.

Mad Ferret hit the stage at 2 pm with a smaller set than usual, with all songs from Definitely Maybe. Despite the early start the glorious sunshine and beer-fuelled atmosphere ensured the festival was packed and the Ferrets got the party started in style. They left the stage to a rousing chorus of 'Madchester' echoing around the field.

As usual, Ollie was the first to congratulate them.

'You get better boys. Tom and Clint from the Inspirals were back here watching. They loved you. They want you to watch them tomorrow and party after. We've got a week's break in the tour, so we can stop all weekend if you want?'

It wasn't the memorable performance by the Inspiral Carpets which stuck foremost in Tim's mind that Saturday; the set of a band at the top of their game spearheading the Madchester movement.

The reception the Ferrets were getting throughout the day as they walked around the festival was the first indication things had changed. The rock star treatment they received was new enough to be fun and exciting, with fans falling over themselves to take pictures and get autographs of the band. Their set was lauded as the best performance of the festival so far and they were destined for greatness. It was a defining moment in the career of Mad Ferret. But this was not what stuck in his mind either.

Neither was their first big after-show party following the Inspiral Carpets set. They had after-show parties of sorts after all their gigs. They were young, full of energy, and loving their new life; of course, they had after-show parties. But this was the next level. This was big-time baby.

What stuck in his mind was what happened in the early hours of the morning.

'Troy, Troy,' shouted Moody, walking towards him, with his arm around Noel Gallagher. He was much younger than the many times he had seen him in concert, but it was him. 'Troy, you need to say thank you to this guy.'

'What?'

Moody laughed, 'This is my mate Noel and you owe him a big thank you. Without him, none of this would have been possible.'

'How do you know?' a stunned Tim replied.

'What? Are you pissed?'

'What do you mean owe him?' Tim countered. Moody couldn't have figured it out. A rush of blood shot across his face as he took a breath of composure.

'You remember the first night we met in the Dry Bar and I bought you a drink because I thought you were a mate of mine? Well, this is him. He's a roadie for the Inspirals. I forgot that. Just bumped into him backstage with the sound guy talking bollocks about the Beatles, as usual. You've got to admit it, Troy. You're dead ringers.'

'I don't see it,' Tim Replied.

'Me neither,' Noel agreed.

'Oh, you do, especially from the side. And he's a musician. If you ever get ill or go missing, we can bring him in and nobody would notice,' Moody howled. 'Or if we get famous, he can start a tribute band and be you.'

'We could scour the country and not find anyone ugly enough to be you though,' Tim replied.

'True. Oy Sarah wait up,' Moody shouted running towards a girl. 'See you later boys.'

'I saw you lot yesterday. You were brilliant. Proper Indie Rock 'n' Roll. I was jealous,' Noel said.

'Jealous?'

'Yeah. I love the Beatles, but my dream is to be in a proper band, you know, like the Stones or the Clash. The Jam even. The eighties were a vacuum for proper guitar music, but it's on its way back and what I saw yesterday is what I'm talking about. You guys are gonna be big. Bigger than the Inspirals.'

'You think?'

'Easily. They are good and I like all the indie dance crossover stuff, it's brilliant. I even auditioned for them last year. Lead singer.'

'I take it you didn't get it then.'

'No. They said I wasn't good enough, but I know I am. It's their loss. I'm not sure if it would have worked anyway.'

'Why?'

'I'm more of a songwriter and guitarist than a frontman. They're already established and write their own stuff. I like to write but I'm not sure if it would have worked writing with other people. I prefer what you are doing.

And the lyrics. I love the lyrics. You have a real talent. I wish I could write like you.'
'Are you in a band now?'
'No, but I want to start one. Unless I can join yours?' he laughed. But seriously man if you need a roadie, give us a call. I'll drop my number off with Ollie. I spoke to him earlier. After your performance, I think you're going to be touring a lot. I could try a few of my songs out on you.'
'That'd be good,' Tim replied.
'Just don't laugh at them. They aren't as good as yours.'
'I'm sure they're fine. Look I've got to chip now. I'm knackered. See you around Noel.'
'Yeah, cheers for that pal. And don't forget, if you need a roadie, I'm your man.'
But Tim wasn't tired. He couldn't sleep that night. Meeting Noel reinforced what he had done to him and he couldn't get away fast enough. He'd stolen his intellectual property just to be famous. What kind of person did that make him? The kind of person who made up an excuse to get away from somebody who under normal circumstances he would have spent all night talking to. In 2015 he would have loved to have met Noel Gallagher and to have the chance to compare songs and jam together.

And Noel was right about the touring. By the time their third single, Live Forever, cruised straight in at Number One in unison with their debut album, they were the biggest guitar band in the UK. The stratospheric rise had taken a few months and Tim finally had everything he wanted. Life was an all you could eat buffet, but Tim wasn't hungry. His meeting with Noel played on his mind and alongside Bobby's death, the cumulative effect weighed heavy on his soul. He had an opportunity to ease the guilt when Ollie approached him about taking Noel on as a Roadie. He refused. He couldn't face a constant reminder of what he had done.

By the time December 1990 arrived, Definitely Maybe was the bestselling album of the year by a British band having gone 4x platinum and the final single, Cigarettes and Alcohol was tipped to be the Christmas number one. Mad Ferret had the world at their feet.

Chapter 30

1991 -The Second Coming

Saturday 1st December 1990

The guilt came in increasingly small patches, dwarfed comparatively by the time spent happily living out his rockstar status. Unlike other songwriters, he didn't need to worry about the 'difficult second album'. Not when he had the greatest album of the Nineties safely tucked away in the locker. Did Noel Gallagher feel this confident after the success of Definitely Maybe? Did he realise his second album would be as good as it was?

Oasis were mega confident with an arrogant Manchester swagger, but a lot of that came from Liam, who didn't write the album. Tim may have stolen Noel's thunder, but he was no Liam Gallagher; no one in the band was. There was only one Liam Gallagher and Tim wondered if Mad Ferret would suffer from not having him in the band. Maybe he should have asked him? Mad Ferret were a four-piece with Tim as the Lead singer and guitarist. He could have taken a step back to backing vocals and let Liam do his stuff. He was the best frontman of the Nineties by a country mile. But it was too late now, besides he wasn't sure how old Liam would be in 1990. He could still be at school for all he knew. He was a few years younger than his brother.

Moody wasn't cool enough to carry it off and despite being the best looking in the band, Adam was stuck behind the drum kit. The closest to Liam was Quinny, a man who never dipped his toe in the sea of self-doubt. He already had a reputation for being a wild man with an eye for the ladies, which the press loved. And as for Tim, he looked the part, had a cool name and already knew his next album was a blockbuster.

Tim was worried about the albums which followed What's the Story. The remainder of Oasis' albums were not as good as the first two and after all his bragging he couldn't afford to release a substandard album. But then again, the first two were so good it was difficult to maintain such a high standard. Should he release an album that was previously a compilation of

B sides, The Masterplan, as their third album? That was a better album than most, if not all the other studio albums. Or maybe he should cherry-pick the best songs from all the later Oasis albums. By purging them into a couple or three good ones, he would be able to stretch it out until the internet was invented. Then he could find out which songs he liked had not been recorded yet and steal them.

But for now, he had a masterpiece on his hands, allowing him to display the arrogance needed to do justice to his heinous crime. When asked how he would follow Definitely Maybe, he proclaimed the next album would be the best album of the decade and cement them as the greatest Rock 'n' Roll band in the world. Whether anyone believed him or not was irrelevant, all that mattered was the press loved it and so did the fans. Besides, as far as he was concerned, it was true. The only lie was who wrote it and he was managing his guilt by packing it away in the back of his mind for now, in a room with a 'do not disturb' sign hanging from its handle.

Unlike Definitely Maybe he didn't need to change any of the songs and would guide the other band members into which to pick as singles and in which order. He would celebrate the album by making 1991, the year of What's the Story; adding Champagne Supernova and She's Electric to the four singles originally released by Oasis.

He called a press conference on the first Saturday morning in December on the roof of the Main College Building at Bolton Institute. He knew how to play the media, calling a selected few journalists from Q magazine, NME, the Manchester Evening News and students from the Institutes media department as a thank you for recording the demo to Definitely Maybe earlier in the year. It was good PR, the rooftop was a vague reference to the Beatles final performance and he could see the flats he and Moody used to live in before upgrading to a 'Yuppie' flat in Manchester City Centre.

Moody and Adam thought the idea ridiculous and arrogant with only Quinny, with who he now seemed to have the most in common, happy to attend the press conference. Tim thought Moody and Adam took themselves too seriously, whereas Quinny was on the same page as him. All they wanted to do was be young and have a good time. So, as they sat behind the classroom desk, carried up the fire escape by the four media students, there were a total of ten people on the roof and only two Ferrets with manager Ollie.

Word had got around about the meeting and small crowds were gathering to the car park at the rear of the building and on a grassed area to the front. Sat in the middle of the table was a giant bottle of champagne, Tim insisted Ollie brought with him. He wanted the largest bottle available, and Ollie had turned up with one 8 times bigger than a standard bottle. With the number of people on the roof, the bottle seemed gigantic. It was almost a bottle each. But then two were Rock stars and four were students, so it might not be enough.

He stood to the right of the bottle with his left hand on top, Quinny mirroring him as the press took photographs. Only the students were allowed to film proceedings. Over the top of the Eagle Building, where the demo was produced, he could see his old student accommodation and his flatmates were stood out on the flat roof with the trip hazard parapet wall. As he waved, they waved back, shouting and screaming. He missed them. He missed the flat. He recalled the Only Fools and Horses Day when Moody had the demo tape in his back pocket. He remembered how guilty and misplaced he felt. Those feelings were not gone but had diminished fantastically. The longer he stopped in the nineties the more he belonged there. Soon he would be a resident, not a refugee from another decade he thought, casting a glance towards the Derby Arms across the road. It seemed a million miles from where he was now but, with a strong wind behind him, he could reach it with the champagne cork.

'Does anyone want a glass of champagne?' shouted Tim attempting to pick up the bottle. 'On second thoughts I'll open it on the table.'

Eventually, Tim and Quinny between them managed to pop open the cork, which flew high into the air, blowing backward towards the grassed area. The Derby Arms was safe.

'There's a souvenir for someone,' Ollie grinned nervously. He wasn't comfortable with the meeting, trying on several occasions to talk them out of it.

'Can you give us a hand pouring this lads?' Quinny asked the students who took delight in pouring the contents of the giant bottle into the half-pint glasses taken from the Student Union Bar. They didn't have any need for champagne flutes in the Union.

The champagne which was not spilled on the table was unceremoniously distributed to the selected few as Tim regretted his decision. Coffee would have been better as the wind began to bite on the exposed roof. But then he wasn't about to record a song called Coffee Supanova, was he? And thirty years from now nobody would know how cold it was on the rooftop, they would just look at the photographs.

'I have a plan,' Tim announced raising his glass. 'But first a toast. To 1991. The year Mad Ferret will become the greatest Rock and Roll band of the decade.'

'Oh yeah,' laughed the guy from the NME. 'What makes you so sure? You've released a great album; I'll give you that. Sold more in the month after the Reading Festival than any other British band sold the entire year. But that's the problem, Troy. How do you follow that? You can't assume you can just do it again. I've seen plenty of bands fall flat on their faces. Haven't you heard of the difficult second album?'

'Oh ye of little faith,' Tim responded, shaking his head theatrically. 'I have the second album written and it's not only better than the first but will outsell it. We start recording next week, releasing it in the middle of next year. We will release a single every 2 months throughout the year starting on the first day of January, to have a song in the charts every week of 1991, culminating in a second successive Christmas number one with the grand finale, a masterpiece of a sonnet called Wonderwall!'

'So, let me get this straight,' the NME guy chirped in laughing, 'you're going to release SIX songs from ONE album and have a single in the charts every week in 1991. And for the record, you haven't even had a Christmas number one yet, let alone successive ones. And what on earth kind of a name for a song is Wonderwall?'

'I love it,' said a girl in her early twenties, from Q magazine. 'It's what Rock n Roll is all about.'

'Would you like some more champagne?' asked Quinny rhetorically, walking towards her with the giant bottle he was carrying in one hand, demonstrating his superior strength to Tim. If he were a peacock his tail feathers would have popped open en route.

'Sure,' she giggled coyly.

'Jesus Christ,' muttered the guy from the NME, putting his head in his hands.

Chapter 31

Butterflies and Moths

SUNDAY 1ST DECEMBER 1991

They never imagined how quickly they would get rich, or just how rich they would get. Two years ago, they were skint. After Moody packed his job in to focus on the band, only Adam had a proper job. But suddenly they had more money than they knew what to do with. Quinny's parents told him he had more money than sense; a good analogy in his case but being the sole songwriter, Tim was the richest in the band. "Don't Look Back in Anger" made him a millionaire twice in one day. And "Wonderwall" was tipped to eclipse this and cruise to the Christmas number one spot.

The seemingly outrageous claims Tim made about Mad ferret in 1991, exactly a year ago, looked understated with all expectations - and boasts - having been eclipsed. Everyone associated with the band had benefitted financially from association with the Mad Ferret brand. Outside of the four band members the record label and Manager had done particularly well. Mad Ferret had a single in the UK top 40 throughout the entirety of 1991, with all previous 5 singles rereleased on the first day of December alongside the second album's final song Wonderwall; presales suggesting all 6 songs would go straight into the Top Ten. They were shattering records as fast as they were selling, leaving the legendary Beatles in their wake. Even Tim was surprised by the impact "What's the Story, Morning Glory" made. He knew it was a great album, but would the earlier release date adversely affect record sales? Were the public ready for it? The opposite happened. Maybe it was the presence of other bands in Manchester or even the influence of Factory Records, but whereas in 1995 the public wanted the album; in 1991 they needed it. Mad Ferret and the Stone Roses were feted as the resurrectors of British guitar music.

Each of the band members used their money, fame and influence differently.

Quinny was spending his money in the here and now, using his fame to sleep with as many women as he could. He was a decent-looking man, but his money, fame and notoriety allowed him access to women who under different circumstances, would not have noticed he was in the room. But he was very much in the room. He was King of the room. Aside from his penthouse flat in the centre of Manchester and a few watches, his money had gone on things that either depreciated or swallowed up money. He had an array of sports cars, clothes, and trainers. He started a clothing company called Pink Carnation in the Arndale Centre which, after 6 months, was closed, losing a significant sum of money. 'The rest I've spent on drink and drugs,' he used to say, 'otherwise I'd just waste it!' He lived life like the Mad Ferret gravy train would last forever.

Adam had a loft apartment in Manchester City Centre. He used his new platform of fame to come out as gay and was the happiest anyone had ever seen him. He and his partner had started a property development company called Urban Wave and had been buying old factories and warehouses and converting them into accommodation in the city centre; having taken the attitude this level of success was unsustainable.

Tim and Moody had moved to the suburbs. They could have gone to Cheshire and hob nobbed with the footballers, who were beginning to take residence in the area. Instead, they chose to buy large houses next door to each other in the Lostock area of Bolton, only a stone's throw away from Giovanna's house. Fortunately for Tim, Giovanna had moved to London and married a Yuppie who worked 'in the city' killing any chance of an embarrassing explanation of why he never called her back having slept with her. For months Moody would shout, 'I told you we'd live in Lostock if you pulled your finger out!' over the privet edge in the morning.

They were rarely in their matching mansions; more often frequenting the finest hotels as they toured the world. Despite this Moody had, in six months, managed to completely re-model his mansion, the centre piece of which was an art installation in the huge garden, forming part of a newly installed swimming pool, featuring a partially submerged Rolls Royce car. The art installation had become the talking point of the latest party in Moody's mansion, thrown to celebrate the year anniversary of the rooftop press conference. It seemed everyone except Tim had forgotten that Moody refused to attend the 'arrogant and unnecessary' meeting. Even Ollie was lording it up with the VIP guests despite trying to persuade Tim not to have the meeting in the first place, but at least he attended the rooftop shindig.

The party was full of record executives from the label, selected journalists, other acts from the label, local bands and random ace faces from places scooped up in the tidal wave which was Mad Ferret.

'So Moody, what inspired you to design such an extravagant and provocative piece of artwork?' asked a press guy from the NME.

It was the same guy, Carl, from the rooftop meeting; the one who scorned Tim's claim. He had become a familiar face over the past 12 months, unlike the girl from Q magazine who, after a brief fling with Quinny, no longer reported on the band.

'It's a parody of the excess of Rock 'n' Roll; set in a scene of serenity,' Moody waffled back pretentiously. 'The Rolls Royce has been driven into it by, I don't know – let's say Keith Moon – and left to rot because he can afford to go out and buy a new one, whilst millions of people in the world starve. Just look at the famine in Ethiopia and the juxtaposition of multi-millionaire Rock stars, who probably didn't really care about getting involved in Live Aid. I imagine most of them got involved for the publicity.'

At the top of the oval-shaped swimming pool was an elevated circular hot tub area with the excess hot water forming a waterfall into the main pool area, giving the impression of a giant exclamation mark. Partially submerged in this area was the chocolate brown convertible Rolls Royce which served as both an existentialist statement of decadence and a mini bar. Quinny and a girl were sitting at the bar in their underwear. Moody had not figured it to be a pool party due to the weather and did not ask anyone to bring swimwear; both minor details to Quinny.

'Mmmm, interesting. Which part of the installation signifies the famine?'

'None of it, but the giant exclamation mark is saying – like what the fuck!'

'Oh yeah, I didn't notice the two pools formed a giant exclamation mark. But then I'm not much of an art critic.'

'You're not much of a music critic either,' Moody riposted, 'you're only here because we wanted to rub your face in it after the comments you made at the rooftop conference, you twat!'

'Hey up,' said Quinny emerging from under the water and standing up before them in the shallow end. He had been working out in the gym in his penthouse and steam rose from his trim physique, much to the delight of his female partner wrapping her arms around his chest.

'Is the pool warm?' asked Carl.

'Warmer than your lukewarm review of What's the Story,' replied Moody.

'What? I've given the album and you guy's some great press recently.'

'Only since the album took off, you fucker. Your reviews were shit. 7 out of 10, for fucks sake! See for yourself how warm it is,' screamed Moody as he pushed Carl into the pool, to an eruption of cheers.

Carl stood up in shock, soaked from head to foot, only to be dunked back under the water by Quinny.

'And that's for the roof conference,' he laughed.

'Yeah, brilliant. Thanks a lot,' moaned Carl, casting a glance at the woman with Quinny, her underwear soaked to the skin. He had to admit Quinny had done well for himself again.

'You like what you see? She has a nice pair, doesn't she? I'll probably be having some fun with them later.'

'You'll definitely be having some fun with them,' she said.

'Jesus Christ,' Carl sighed putting his head in his hands.

'Is that your catchphrase?' laughed Quinny, 'you said it on the roof with the girl from Q magazine. I had some fun with her as well.'

'You should be ashamed of yourself,' announced Carl, looking at the girl.

'Oh, lighten up, all I wanna do is have a little fun before I die,' she said out of nowhere, splashing water in his face, 'Perhaps I've got a mate for you if you take that stick out of your arse.'

She seemed sweet, or as sweet as she could be with her nipples showing through the wet white bra.

'She's out of your league. She's only with you because you're in Mad Ferret, you know. What will you do when all this is over?'

'I'm in Mad Ferret now and that's all that matters,' he replied holding out his hand, 'shake for a truce? It's all water off a duck's back to me pal. I don't hold grudges. This is a wicked party. Go put some of Moody's clobber on, dry off and let's have a laugh.'

'Ok,' said Carl, holding out his hand.

It was classic Quinny; as arrogant as he was annoying, but for some reason, everyone loved him.

Since the bands' stratospheric rise an invisible gulf had appeared between Quinny/ Tim and Adam/ Moody. The Quinny and Tim dynamic partied hard at every opportunity with Adam and Moody still partying but knowing when the night was over. It rarely caused problems; they were a rock 'n' roll band after all, but the divide was there.

Quinny and Tim's party fuel was a mix of drink and drugs, depending on what was available: tonight, an ecstasy pill with a butterfly stamp on the front was the recreational pharmaceutical of choice. As the main party died down Tim, Quinny and an entourage of hard-core partygoers consisting mainly of people they didn't know made the short trip to Tim's house. Carl staggered along with his arm around Quinny, his new best friend.

Tim's house was even bigger than Moody's, but he had done nothing with it since he bought it. It was already better than anything he had lived in before and he saw it has a party house. He wanted to hold the party here but knew Moody wanted to show off his fancy interior designs and art installation. He knew if he had not let Moody have his way he would have sulked, so he gave in. Besides, the party was always going to end up at Tim's as Moody's house pride would make him twitchy when things got rowdy. Adam and his partner had spent most of the evening looking around the house and chatting to the interior designer and builder.

With no shortage of musicians and wannabe DJs to showcase their skills, the music soon took centre stage, with Tim's guitars and CD collection taking a hammering. For the truly ambitious the prospect of a record producer or a band member hearing their set, or an acoustic version of their latest song, was irresistible. For the less ambitious, there were plenty of beautiful young women with their inhibitions seeping out through their pores, to be wooed by a homemade sonnet.

'Wonderwall!' shouted Carl his right arm holding aloft a bottle of Bollinger, his left wrapped around a girl egging him on, 'come on Troy, sing Wonderwall.'

'Wonderwall, Wonderwall, Wonderwall,' they shouted, the chant reaching a crescendo as the entire kitchen joined in.

'OK, OK!' shouted Tim grabbing an acoustic guitar. He was used to it by now and happy to oblige. He liked being the centre of attention. After years of doing the pubs of Sheffield with nobody listening, he appreciated a captive audience. The kitchen was large and open plan with an island unit in the centre, which he climbed on for his stage. The island had a black granite surface half full of empty bottles and cans, a few of which he kicked on the floor to make space.

From his elevated vantage point, he could see there were about 50 people there, but the only two he knew were Quinny and Carl; and he barely knew Carl. Where had they all come from? His house was full of strangers.

'Ladies and Gentlemen, the new John Lennon, TROY GOLD!' announced Carl to an eruption of applause.

'John Lennon!' Tim thought. 'He was killed by a crazy fan. What if one of these is crazy?' There was only Quinny he trusted, and he was too loved up on E to be any use if anything happened. There had been security at Moody's house, but they must have gone. He noticed a kitchen knife set in a wooden block on the worktop, but one was missing. Had it always been missing; or had it been taken? He didn't have a clue, it had come with the house, but it would be easy for a crazed fan to stab him, just to make a name for himself as Mark Chapman had done when he shot Lennon. He panicked, throwing the guitar onto the floor.

'Get out!' he yelled, 'everyone get out of my fuckin house. I don't know who any of you are!'

An embarrassed silence shrouded the kitchen as Quinny jumped up on the island and put his arm around him.

'Are you OK, Buddy?'

'Yes. Can you all leave? Please?'

'You heard him, folks. The parties over. Now get out.'

As Quinny ushered out the final guest, Tim slumped in a settee in an offshoot part off the kitchen, facing out overlooking the garden. Over the laurel bush edging, separating his house from Moody's, the back of the brown Rolls Royce nosediving into Moody's pool could be seen. If he didn't know Moody, he could probably get the Council to remove it. Something as big as that probably needed planning permission.

'All gone buddy. Just me and you.' Quinny confirmed, handing him a beer.

'Thanks, Quinny. I couldn't face throwing them out after screaming at them like that.'

'What happened?'

'I freaked out. When I looked down, I realised I only knew you. I had visions of when John Lennon was shot. What's to stop one of them just grabbing a kitchen knife out of the block and using it on me. I'm no John Lennon but you never know. And one of the knives is missing. Where the fuck is the knife?'

'It's in the dishwasher pal. I chopped some resin up earlier.'

'OK, but d'you know what I mean?'

'Yeah, yeah,' Quinny replied, 'Its paranoia pal. Butterflies and moths.'

'Butterflies and moths?'

'Yeah, the E's you dropped turned dark on you. The butterflies turned to moths. These things aren't made by qualified chemists, you know. Did you hear about me last week when I was in that club and my butterflies turned to moths?'

'No.'

'I can't believe you haven't heard. I was in this dodgy club on the edge of town, and I'd dropped a couple of E's. A few people recognised me and came and started chatting and, being loved up, got all huggy, you know like

they do. So, I start thinking – just like you tonight – I don't know anyone here and a few moths arrived. Then there's this one guy who's all smiley but I take an instant dislike to him. I just don't trust him at all. Then I'm thinking about how rich I am and how I could get kidnapped. Then I start thinking what if he wants to smack me to tell his mates he smacked one of the Ferrets? Suddenly he walks toward me...' Quinny paused to take a sip of lager. 'Fuck me, man, you can see that stupid art installation from here.'
'And?'
'And what?'
'The guy in the club?'
'Oh, right. He gives me a big hug and starts rubbing my hair. Telling me how much he loves us, but then he says a weird thing.'
'What?'
'He says – but you don't belong in this club.'
'What?'
'I know right? So now I'm proper fuckin paranoid and I look over and he's back with his mates laughing. So do you know what I do?'
'What?'
'I run up to the toilet and start washing my hair in the sink.'
'What?' laughed Tim, 'Why?'
Quinny was also laughing, 'I read in some dance clubs they pick someone out who is new to the club and they call them the club chicken. And as an initiation ceremony, they rub Immac in their hair and they all stand around laughing as their hair falls out.'
'Is that a real thing?'
'I think so. I might have seen it on TV as well. Anyway, I'm convinced this has happened to me, so I'm washing my hair in this shit hole bathroom and all they have is this one tiny bar of soap – like this big. It's one of those you used to have at school, you know off white but all cracked and black around the edges. I bet the bog roll was the stuff you used to get at school as well, like greaseproof paper. I literally washed my hair in the sink of the worst bog in Manchester with a tiny bar of soap in front of loads of people and it never even made the papers.'
'Jesus, you must have been out of it.'
'But was I though? How do you know he hadn't put Immac in my hair? We were on Top of the Pops the following week. Imagine my hair falling out? He could have bragged about it to his mates.'
'Sounds unlikely.'

'But you don't know. When you're as famous as us, people will do surprising things out of jealousy, or to get noticed. It's only the same as what happened to you tonight.'

'Do you think?'

'Yes, pal. It's just butterflies and moths.'

'Fuck, man. So, what do we do? I can't live the rest of my life like this.'

'We need to give it a rest, dude. Have a break over Christmas and go away somewhere. Leave behind the drugs and get our heads straight. Just because you're paranoid doesn't mean people aren't out to get you. We need to be ready for them – and we won't be if we are off our heads.'

'True,' agreed Tim. 'Where shall we go?'

'Dunno, we'll get Ollie to sort us some flights out. The important thing is we stop the tablets. The drugs don't work, anymore. Remember when we were skint and used to have to chip in to get a teenth of resin? That's how skint we were. But we enjoyed it. I guess my parents are right; I've got more money than sense. I can buy what I want but I've overdone it. I don't enjoy it anymore.'

As Tim stared at the brown Rolls Royce, he knew Quinny was right. They couldn't go on like this, but they could sort it out together; his bond with the guy he was initially at odds with was strengthening.

'Sorry to hear about Pink Carnation, pal. What happened?'

'Fuck knows. Business stuff. Nothing to do with the threads though. I had some great designers. Student designers, all young with great ideas. It wasn't just revivalist stuff from the sixties either, trying to recreate the Mod generation. There was some of that because that's the heart and soul of the whole Madchester indie thing. But it fused all of that with what is going on around town and all the little stores in the markets and Affleck's Palace. It's a shame, but I wasn't interested in the business side and I think every fucker was ripping me off. I can't believe the store didn't turn a profit. The stuff wasn't cheap.'

'It was good stuff. I was upset it got shut down.'

'Don't worry Troy, my boy, I've got a better plan to invest my money now.'

'How?'

'Stocks and shares.'

'What do you know about stocks and shares?'

'Nothing, but I have a financial advisor now. Ollie put me onto him. He advises loads of rich people. You name it - footballers, musicians, bankers – the lot. He comes highly recommended. Turns pence into pounds this guy; he's a license to print money. I'll pass you his number if you want?'

'Maybe. What sort of thing does he invest in?'

'It's all blue-chip stuff, Troy. High tech companies in the States are his specialty. I've just stuck a wedge into this company from Florida called Blockbusters. They rent out videos, but on a massive scale and they get first dibs on the latest films, so they get them before any of the other shops do. They'll be opening stores in the UK soon; they'll be massive. I've got in on the ground floor. I'll make a killing.'

'Blockbuster,' Tim commented, 'sounds interesting. You have to be careful with these companies you know. Technology changes quickly and you have to know when to sell.'

'But that the thing. Ben – my Financial Advisor – told me about this new bit of technology called a DVD. It's like a CD but for films. You know when they fine you at the video store if you forget to rewind the tape. None of that bollocks. It doesn't need rewinding. It's genius.'

'Yeah but even that will be outdated one day. So you have to have an exit strategy, for every investment. I read that somewhere.'

'Outdated,' laughed Quinny, 'a CD for films which never needs rewinding. How could that ever be outdated? Maybe the discs could get smaller or something, but you'll never get better technology than that. It's like music. Vinyl to cassettes and then finally CDs. Films are the same except we missed out the vinyl. Nothing will ever get better than CDs. Have you seen the size of them? They are tiny compared to records and you can't scratch them, and they can't get tangled up like cassettes. It's perfect.'

'What if you didn't need a CD or DVD. What if you could have the film sent directly to your computer? You wouldn't need shops or anything.'

'What?' Quinny puzzled, 'I don't get it. You must have some kind of product. You can't sell fresh air.'

'You would get the film, or music you wanted but there would be no physical product as such.'

'What, down the cables and into the computer?'

'Or wireless, through the air. Bounce it off a satellite or two.'

Quinny laughed, 'You do talk bollocks at times. A film flying through the air! I doubt technology like that will ever exist and if it does, we'll both be long gone. Besides no one would buy it. One of the best parts of an album is the cover, especially on vinyl. I remember when I got the Beastie Boys Album – the first one with the jet crashing into the mountain. I loved that cover. Spent ages looking at it. I bet kids in the sixties did the same with Sgt Peppers.'

'What if I told you I'm from the future and I've seen it? In 20 years, that's how we will listen to all music. CDs will be collectors' items.'

'I'd say those pills were stronger than I thought. Or you'd taken that guy in the Castrol GTX jacket too seriously. Remember him from the Roses gig in Blackpool? Said you were a spaceman from the future.'

'Yeah.'

Tim often joked about being from the future. The Castrol GTX guy's comment had opened the door for him to make seemingly tongue-in-cheek comments about his vision of the future. He took a perverse pleasure in it.

'20 years,' Quinny mused, 'that will be roughly when the second Back to the Future film is. Mmmm...'

Quinny giggled as he spiked his hair up. He always did this for his Dr. Emmet Brown impersonation.

'So future boy, tell me who the President of the United States is?'

'Err,' replied Tim, 'Donald Trump.'

'Donald fuckin Trump!' spluttered Quinny, before reverting to character, 'I mean Donald Trump, the billionaire businessman?'

'Yes.'

'Wasn't he in Home Alone 2?'

'Yes.'

'Well, who's Vice President then Macauley Culkin?'

They burst out laughing.

'I could see him being President one day though,' said Quinny, he's popular enough.

'Donald Trump?'

'No, you idiot. Donald Trump won't ever be President. I mean Macauley Culkin. He's one of the most popular people in America. Give him a few years and he'd walk into the Whitehouse. Ronald Reagan was an actor and he was nowhere near as popular as Macauley Culkin. Donald Trump for fuck's sake. But you did well to come up with off the top of your head.'

'Yeah, it was inspired.'

'But if we did go to 2015, which of the new inventions in the film would be around, Troy? A hoverboard. Do you reckon they'll have hover boards and flying cars?'

'No, and no,' Tim responded.

'No! Five minutes ago, you had films flying through the air and now you don't think they will have flying cars. I reckon they will; all you have to do is strap some wings to a car, like in James Bond.'

'James Bond isn't real you know?'

'Obviously, but how difficult can it be. And hover boards. They are even easier. Haven't you seen a hovercraft? If they can get one of those across the Channel, I'm sure they can get a skateboard to hover. So, I disagree with you there Troy my boy. Further proof you are not from the future. What else is in the film?'

'What about those boots and jackets which fit themselves to your size?'

'Yeah, I forgot about those. Pink Carnation wouldn't have gone bust if I'd had some of them. I'm gonna say yes. They can't be difficult to make,' commented Quinny.

'I'm going to say no again.'

'No? Really? Well, what about the TV telephone he has and fax machine?'

'Fax machine?'

'When he gets a fax to tell him he's been fired.'

'Oh yeah, we'll have all that. But none of the other stuff.'

Quinny gazed into space and sighed. 'So, your future consists of invisible albums and fax machines and mine consists of flying cars and hover boards. I know whose future I prefer.'

'You're right,' laughed Tim, 'let's hope you're right, and I'm wrong. But thanks for tonight. I needed this when it all went Pete Tong.'

'No problem, pal,' said Quinny, raising his bottle to Tim's, clinking them together before toasting, 'to the butterflies, not the moths.'

'The butterflies, not the moths,' Tim replied.

Chapter 32

On Yer Bike

The Artist's Retreat, Stinson Beach, Nr Mount Tamalpais, San Francisco

JUNE 10^{TH,} 1995. 7 AM

Tim peered over the small but well-pruned hedgerow. It was an L-shaped timber-clad 2 bedroomed studio with large windows revealing a living room with fireplace and 4-seater red settee. In the next window was a double bed with a powder blue and white striped duvet. The contents of a third room were hidden behind a silver Venetian blind. There was a large decking area and blue cushioned outdoor furniture savouring views over Stinson Beach. It was a glorious location and a glorious morning.

This must be it; his bike is over there leaning against the wall. It's not even locked. That's sloppy John. I'll not be needing these bad boys, he thought, tapping the pocket of his cargo shorts containing the mini bolt cutters.

He stood up and carefully strode over the thigh-high privet bush and headed toward the bike. It was red with white writing and as he lifted it was lighter than it looked. He paused, oddly full of confidence, as his former nervousness disappeared. He looked around the grounds, over the perimeter fence and out to sea before glancing at the window obscured by the blind. A small, relaxed grin grew on his face until he saw one of the slats in the blind raise. He was stood at an angle to the window and could not have been seen, but perhaps he had been heard. Frozen to the spot, he considered his next move. To reach the gate he would have to walk past the window and risk being seen. Had he been heard or was he just checking the weather? It was too risky to push the bike, so he would carry it back over the privet hedge and up the steps to the gate.

He went for it, quickly skipping across the decking and expertly striding towards the steps. Turning around to check the window, he misjudged the bottom step, tripping up the first flight and falling on top of the bike.

'Is there anyone there?' a voice shouted from the studio. Turning around, he was relieved to see he was out of sight of the window. He grabbed the bike and ran up the steps and through the gate he had jarred open with a stone.

He jumped in the saddle as the bike began its slow and unsteady journey down the steep lane.

'Fuck, which is the back brake?' Tim was puzzled as the bike began to speed out of control, zig-zagging down the road with clouds of dust appearing as he used his feet as makeshift brakes.

He left the road and onto a footpath and with the trail becoming steeper and windier, he pushed his feet to the ground until it stopped. After testing the rear brake, he allowed himself to pick up speed deliberately using the brakes to skid around the switchbacks in the path. As he became familiar with the bike he cruised through the light undergrowth, onto the coastal road. It was a good bike.

He had a mountain bike in 2015 and went trail riding most weekends in the nearby woods. The gears were like his bike as he rode the short distance along the main coastal road towards a small slip road, which peeled off to Stinson Beach. It was still early and there were few cars on the road, but he kept his head down in fear of being spotted. He was one of the most famous men in the UK and was started to get recognised in the US.

At the beginning of the access road, he stopped on a bridge over a small river with hardly any flow but surrounded by lush green undergrowth. After checking the main road was empty and there was no movement from the few houses he could see on the beach road, he picked the bike up and threw it into the undergrowth. It sank deep into the greenery and once the plants had rearranged themselves the bike could not be seen. Glancing around one final time, he lowered his head and walked toward the beach.

The sandy, flat beach was empty except for the occasional jogger or dog walker passing behind as he stared into the sea. Looking left, he tried to spot the Golden Gate Bridge as the brisk wind blew his hair over his face. His presence in the past would naturally change the course of history but he never intended to deliberately change something which he knew happened. This was the first and only time, but as he continued to stare out to sea, he was happy he made an exception. He didn't regret being deliberately awkward and using his influence to change the tour schedule, so they ended up in San Francisco the same time as the Stone Roses.

Nobody gave it a second thought; they knew the Stone Roses well and assumed Tim wanted them to meet up for a night out in San Francisco. Over the past few years, the two bands had drummed up a healthy rivalry with each other in the press. The two Manchester-based indie rock bands were the biggest in the country, each pushing the other to new heights. Tim had been instrumental in encouraging the Stone Roses to expand on the indie/dance crossover aspect of their music, resulting in a collaboration with the Prodigy which elevated them to one of the most critically acclaimed bands in the country. Mad Ferret continued down the Oasis setlist producing a string of number-one singles and albums. The Stone Roses encouraged Mad Ferret to step out of their comfort zone which, along with a chance meeting in Brooklyn, resulted in Tim agreeing to a collaboration with the Beastie Boys later that year.

Although they shared a lot of the same fan base there were a hardcore of fans for either band who claimed theirs was the best. The record companies suggested they release a single on the same day to find out who was the most popular. Tim objected on the grounds it wouldn't be a fair indication of anything except who released the best single. One band could win the singles battle but get blown away by the others next album. Besides the bands were friends who helped each other, not competitors.

Despite the request to change the bands' schedule seeming innocuous, Tim's request caused a major headache for the management team, who refused to comply until Tim threatened to pull out of the tour. Eventually, as always, Ollie and his team gave in to the inevitable.

Finding out where his good friend John Squire was staying and his itinerary of mountain biking, whilst the other band members visited Alcatraz was easy, but having never stolen anything before he had been so nervous he hardly slept.

With his master plan complete he casually paddled into the shallows to retrieve an egg-shaped grey pebble, picking it up and throwing it as far as he could into the vast blue expanse.

'Happy birthday, Dad. Hope you have a perfect night. I miss you.'

Chapter 33

The Last Supper

THURSDAY 7TH JUNE 2012

'Do you think we should get a hot tub?'
'Aren't they expensive, dad?' asked Tim, surprised at the question.
'Not an actual hot tub, it's like an inflatable hot tub with bubbles. Think they're called lazy tubs or something. Mick at works got one. Say's they're great and only cost a couple of hundred quid at Argos. We could put it over there in the corner of the decking.'
'I suppose so.'
'I'll look into it when I get back,' mused Matt, his eyes doing a brief reconnaissance of the garden to see if it would fit. 'Or do you think we should move to a new house?'
They had lived together in the three-bedroomed mid-terraced house for as long as Tim could remember. They had lived in a bigger house about half a mile away before his mum died. It was a stone semi-detached house with a large bay window on the front and a huge back garden overlooking the River Don. He could barely remember living there himself, but as it was on the main road, he passed it most days. He often cast a glance as he passed in the car, pondering if they would still be there were his mum alive. His dad would also glance when they passed. He probably wondered the same as Tim, but they never discussed it. He knew his dad missed his mum and couldn't decide if living so close was a comfort or a hindrance to moving forward. Either way, they could have fitted lots of hot tubs in that garden.
Matt regretted selling the house but had to downsize after his wife died. He was a self-employed Architect who struggled to come to terms with working after her death to such an extent he had to sell the family home to pay off his debts. He wanted to repurchase when it went back on the market a few months ago, but the subsequent rise in house prices and only one moderate income meant it was unlikely he would ever be able to afford the property again.

'No dad,' replied Tim. 'I like it here. It's where I grew up. It's full of happy memories.'

Matt smiled as he opened another couple of bottles of lager.

'You'll be alright when I'm away? Do you have money for food and a few beer tokens?'

'Yes dad, thanks. You enjoy yourself. It sounds like a good laugh. Where are you going?'

'Corfu.'

'Whose stag do is it?'

'If I'm being honest, I've only met him once, but he seemed OK. He's a Wednesday fan so he's bound to be a good lad. But there's a whole bunch of us from the golf society at the Wadsley Jack, so it'll be a laugh. We've got a nice place near this private harbour. Someone's hired a speedboat, so I might have a razz on that bad boy,' Matt replied, passing Tim the bottle as the Stone Roses came on the Radio.

''Did I ever tell you about the time I nearly saw the Roses at the Leadmill, son?'

'No, but I know you saw them a few times.'

'Yeah, I did. Saw them loads of times. Blackpool, Spike Island, Paris, Bridlington twice on the Second Coming tour, Leeds Town and Country Club and the Arena.'

'Which was best?'

'Manchester Apollo. It was a few days before Christmas and the first time they had played Manchester in 6 years. It was brilliant. The Empress Ballroom and Spike Island were great but, I like a small venue. It's more intimate. The Apollo is a smaller venue. It's a great venue. I've watched a few there. Must have seen the Charlatans half a dozen times there. And Weller.'

'So how come you only nearly saw the Roses at the Leadmill?'

'They were due to do a secret gig as a warmup to Glastonbury, but my mate Bob worked there and he let me know. He got me loads of great tickets like that. I remember Weller once, played a secret gig in about 96, just after he released Stanley Road. He was supposed to play a few years earlier but had to cancel because he was ill but promised to play later to make up for it. The thing is when he was due to play the first time his solo career was stuttering a bit after the Style Council and some other stuff he did. But when he did the re-scheduled gig, he was at the height of his powers but kept his word and came back. He's a top bloke is Weller,' Matt concluded despite having never met him. 'Probably the best gig I saw him at, although there was an acoustic gig in Bradford. Saw some great gigs when Bob worked the Leadmill. There was this one James gig which was number 6 in the NME's gigs of the year. But the Roses. It was all set up and John Squire fell off his mountain bike and the whole thing got cancelled. I was gutted, as you can imagine.'

'They cancelled the gig because he fell off a bike?' Tim laughed.

'Yeah and Glastonbury. Pulp took over and blew everyone away. That gig made Pulp. Great for Jarvis Cocker, but not so great for me. Can you imagine that? Seeing the Roses at the Leadmill. My favourite band in my favourite venue. I'm not sure if my head would have coped. I think it would have exploded. I was music crazy back then.'

'Back then?' Tim laughed.

'OK, I still love music but back in the day I was current and cool. But now I'm just an indie music dinosaur; a nineties refugee.'

'But going back to John Squire, they missed playing Glastonbury because he fell off his mountain bike?'

'Yeah, typical Roses. They toured America in mid '95, and on a day off John Squire fell off his mountain bike in some mountains near San Francisco. They only ever did two albums and never headlined Glastonbury. It was criminal how much they underachieved.'

'Perhaps that's why they were always so popular. They didn't overdo it. Kept everyone interested with the air of mystery they had.'

'I know what you mean but no. It was the music, especially the first album. It changed the landscape completely. It's difficult to explain unless you were there, but that album changed the direction of everything. The nineties were the dawning of a new era, a brighter future. The eighties were bleak and difficult. But not the nineties. The nineties were beautiful. It was like a switch was flipped overnight on new year's day 1990 and everything became good. England got to the Semi-Final of the world cup and Wednesday were one of the best teams in the country and actually won something. I imagine this is how Beatles fans think about the sixties. Imagine being there at the time – and England won the World Cup. What a decade that must have been. I love the Beatles, that's why I'm collecting all their vinyl at record fayres, but I wasn't there. But I was with the Roses. The nineties were a bit like the sixties. Decades like that don't come around often son. I wish you could have been there with me; you would have loved it.'

'Yeah, that would have been something, bouncing on the Leadmill dancefloor to Resurrection when it was in the charts.'

'Not sure it was ever in the charts, not the full version anyway, but yeah, that would have been something else. My only regret was that fuckin Roses gig at the Leadmill which, by the way, would have been on my 25th birthday; it would have been perfect. I could talk all night about the nineties, but I've got an early start tomorrow.'

'OK Dad, have a great time.'

'Love you, son. See you Tuesday.'

But he didn't.

Chapter 34

Come Back to What You Know.

Sunday 3ʳᵈ September 1995

Tim stood before 125 000 people with his arms aloft. It was the second and final day of a record-breaking music festival, headlined by Mad Ferret. In front of him was the Grade 1 listed English Baroque-style Wentworth Woodhouse Country House which, when framed by the sea of adoring fans, was the most beautiful building he had ever seen.

'Don't be sorry that it's over,' he shouted, 'just be glad it happened.'

He had heard those words before, but he couldn't remember where. Was it in the past, present, or future? It was impossible to differentiate anymore. But the words he uttered in a moment of reflection as he savoured the nuances, would be scrutinised by fans and media for years to come. But the fact they were the last words he spoke in public as the frontman of Mad Ferret, was as big a surprise to him as anyone.

They were the biggest band in the world, who had just nailed the ultimate concert; but there was a sense they could not get any bigger or better. Had they reached a plateau? It felt like the beginning of the end. When you are at the top where do you go? Many of the reporters, fans and fellow band members attributed Tim's unexpected departure to this. It seemed the logical explanation, but no one knew because Tim never explained his actions. The truth was very different. Standing there, soaking in the plaudits, Tim was blissfully unaware that two events in the space of a week would persuade him he had no alternative other than quit the band.

The Wentworth Woodhouse Music Festival was Tim's idea, or at least it was his version of Knebworth if you could call that his idea. His dad had been to Knebworth, describing it as the pinnacle of the nineties. When he put the idea forward, Knebworth was one of the venues mentioned and was considered until he realised it was in Hertfordshire. He had assumed it was somewhere in Lancashire and could not understand why Oasis chose a venue so far down south. He was keen to have the festival at Chatsworth, which turned out to be impossible before Wentworth Woodhouse was proposed as location.

Wentworth was perfect for Tim; it was a stone's throw away from where he lived with his dad and the owners were keen to raise cash for repairs to the stately home set in the 87 acres of land. Within the grounds were 5 blocks of modernist former student accommodation not occupied since Sheffield Polytechnic ceased using the site a few years earlier and ideal for temporary accommodation for the band and crew. The suggestion that the band should stop in a luxury hotel nearby was pushed aside by the Ferrets, who preferred to mix with the crew. The 5-block accommodation was designed for students and perfect for the band and crew to socialise early into the morning.

Close to the accommodation was a Palladium-style stable block, so huge it could be confused for the main house itself, wrapped around a courtyard. This was used as a smaller venue to showcase up and coming local bands, with the area ironically being called 'Shed 8' in reference to the band Shed 7 and a comment by Quinny about how the elaborate entrance to the stable block looked like a posh shed. Shed 7 were a regular support act for Mad Ferret having met at a festival a few years previous. Most of the other support bands were from Manchester, so Tim enjoyed hearing the dulcet tones of fellow Yorkshiremen. He also felt oddly connected with the band as he remembered Lyla's comment about her mum fancying the lead singer Rick. It was one of the few reminders he had of his previous life. Shed 7 were one of the many support acts and crew still at the after-show party as Tim headed for his room.

His room was small and did not have a bathroom, causing Moody to complain about them not choosing the fancy hotel option. However, Tim liked it, but it had an odd, sickly sweet smell. It probably was marijuana. Maybe one of security had been smoking when he wasn't there? But he liked the simplicity of the room; he was bored of the exuberance of his existence, pining in a small way for the simplicity of his previous life. Lying in bed he wondered who had used the room in the past when it was used by Sheffield Polytechnic. What did they study? What did they do now? Had they enjoyed being in such a fantastic setting? It must have been odd being students in such a tiny village. What must the villagers have thought about it? Would he have enjoyed being a student? Would he have enjoyed it here? Yes. A shared bathroom or not Tim could see himself here. What would he study? Marine biology? No, that sounded better than it was. English literature? Yes, he could see himself wandering around the rolling countryside reading Thomas Hardy on a spring day. Would it be a better life than he has now, or is happiness relative?

He awoke sharply and out of breath as if disturbed in the early stages of slumber.

'Are you awake?'

'What?' he replied, unsure if he was dreaming.

'It's me,' replied the female voice, 'I've come to save you.'

She had a soft Irish accent which reminded him of Lyla. It must be another dream. He often dreamt about her.

'Lyla,' he said putting his hand on her cheek. He didn't want the dream to end. He never did.

'Tim,' she whispered. She was the only person to call him Tim. The name died when he failed to return to 2015, replaced by the ill-prepared and ridiculous pseudonym of Troy.

'I've missed you,' she whispered, leaning forward and kissing his forehead. As her soft lips gently grazed his forehead the sickly-sweet smell further assaulted his nostrils.

'What?' he gasped, jolting upright in bed. It wasn't a dream. 'What the fuck? Who are you?' he screamed jumping out of bed, turning on the light.

'It's me, Lyla.'

Stood before him was an 18-year-old girl in denim dungarees. Her blonde hair was tied in knots and a small silver stud glistened in her nose.

'You're not Lyla.'

'Yes, I am.'

'Who told you about her?'

'Come on Tim, it's me, Lyla. You must remember me.'

'Oh, I remember Lyla alright. Believe me, I remember Lyla. But who are you, and how do you know about her? I must have been talking in my sleep. How did you get in here, there are security guards everywhere? I think there's one asleep in the next room, the useless fucker. Tell me who you are, or I'll bang on his door.'

A small smile appeared as she coyly bit her bottom lip, 'You remember me, alright. Well, that's a start.' The smile increased.

'I remember Lyla, but I don't know who you are. Now tell me how you know about her and why are you calling me Tim?'

'Tim's your name,' she giggled.

'What's so funny?'

'Troy? Troy? Why on earth did you call yourself Troy? If you're gonna pretend to be someone else, then why not go the whole hog and use his name?'

'What?'

'Noel. Why not just call yourself Noel? Or Liam. Whichever one you're pretending to be.'

Tim was stunned. 'What are you talking about?' he spluttered, struggling to get the words out, his heart pulsating in his chest.

'You were in an Oasis tribute band in 2015. Now I come back to rescue you and you've stolen Oasis. You are Oasis. Well, Mad ferret. You really are terrible with names,' she laughed, jumping onto the bed. 'You must realise it's me now. Did you think Clint would only be able to send one person back? He's proper pissed at you for not coming back as you promised.'

'You're not Lyla. It's impossible.'

'Why? Clint sent you back and then I insisted he sent me back to get you.'

'But you're the same age as she was when I left. That was six years ago. You'd be older if you were her.'

'It was six years ago to you, but six months to me. I don't understand how it works but it was something to do with the traversable wormholes. He can't use the same destination or exit at the same time either. So, whereas you ended up in 1989 somewhere between Sheffield and Manchester I ended up in 1995 on the outskirts of Nairn.'

'Nairn?'

'Don't ask. It's a little town in the highlands of Scotland, near Inverness. So, I land in Inverness, this small town at the top of Scotland, and I'm an 18-year-old girl driving a DeLorean. I've got to drive down to either Manchester or Sheffield – because I don't know where you are yet – and I don't have a penny to my name.'

'Didn't he give you any money?'

'No. He didn't have any 1995 currency because he spaffed his last 10 grand on you. That's another thing he's pissed off about. It's not easy to come across old currency, apparently. His dad left him that money, which sounded dodgy, but I didn't push him on that. So, I'm in this DeLorean, sticking out like a sore thumb....'

'Why the DeLorean? Why not the Beemer?'

'And that's another thing he's pissed off about. When the Beemer came back it shot down the ramp and into a column. It didn't look too bad until he took it to this BMW specialist and the car is completely knackered. It would cost twice as much to repair it as it was worth, so he sold it for parts. He wasn't happy that day, I can tell you.'

'So, you've been hanging around with Clint then?'

'You jealous? When you didn't call me, I used the find my I phone app and traced you to the industrial unit next to the golf place. Then I forced my way in and made him tell me where you were,' her triumphant tone dipped in pride.

Tim sat next to her, staring blankly at the wall.

'You believe me now? As I was saying, I was driving around this tiny town in Scotland without a penny, but I needed money. Clint sent me over with 5 vintage Rolex watches, all with proof of authenticity which I was to sell when I got here one at a time until I found you. Because we didn't know where you were, he gave me ten weeks before the wormhole reopened and then another month after that for the final one. He reckons the watches are worth a minimum of a grand each. I tried to sell them at a jeweller in Inverness, but they didn't believe they were mine, so I decided to drive down to Edinburgh. But I'm not sure how far it is and if I've enough petrol and there's no internet. Can you believe there's no internet?'

Tim laughed, 'Yeah, that takes some getting used to.'

'Right? So, I travelled down this beautiful road to Edinburgh and I make it there, just in time. And I mean I'm running on vapours as I pull up. I get ripped off at the jewellers as I only get 300 quid, but I wasn't bothered as I have 4 more. I'm sitting in this hotel in Edinburgh, next to the Zoo, and I'm wondering how to find you without Google, and there you are on the front page of the Sun. Even without the internet, you aren't a difficult man to find. So, here I am.'

'Wow,' said Tim.

'I know. It was a nightmare.'

'No. I mean your hair. Wow. Who do you think you are Bjork?'

'There he is,' she laughed, the smile on her face broadening as she brushed away a tear rolling down her cheek with an equal measure of defiance and annoyance. 'I just wanted to fit into the nineties style. I've seen a few girls like this, so I went for it. Plus, I didn't want you to recognise me until I had a chance to explain myself. I know it's been a few years for you. You weren't necessarily gonna believe me. And you aren't easy to get to meet. You can't just walk up to someone as famous as you. There's always an entourage.'

'How did you get in here tonight? There's security everywhere.'

'I didn't get in here tonight. I've been here since midday when you lot went for breakfast. I'd been hanging around Shed 8, watching all the bands and I saw you all head up to the main building, flanked by security. You were busy getting mobbed by fans and security were dealing with them so I just snook in unnoticed. I knew exactly which room you were in as I've been watching since you got here. I was one of the first in yesterday morning, so I found your room and hid under the bed. There's nowhere else to hide here. I would have thought a megastar would have a better room than this.'

'I like it, but there's an odd smell in here. Sort of sickly sweet.'

'Is this it?' she asked, putting her wrist under his nose.

'Yes, that's it. What is it?'

'It's a marijuana scented perfume I bought from a stall outside. It's awful but I've been under the bed since I snook in waiting for you to finish the show.'

'Hang on,' he mused, 'I came back here before the show, got changed and had a nap. You were under the bed then? That explains the smell. I thought security had been smoking in here.'

'Yeah. You snore by the way.'

'No, I don't. Why didn't you say something?'

'The show, stupid. I didn't want to freak you out. Do you think you would be able to do the show if you'd have seen me?'

'Perhaps not. But why does that bother you? I thought you'd come to take me back? Why would you care about the show?'

'Well,' she said, sighing, 'that's the thing.'

'What do you mean?'

'You know I said I had been given ten weeks, followed by another 4?'

'Yeah.'

'I've been here since June. When I got here you were on a tour of America. I didn't have the money to fly over find you; I'm down to my last watch as it is. This is the first chance I've had to get past your security.'

'So how are you going back. How are we going back?'

'We can't. Did you want to, Tim?'

'Not really. I don't know. Wouldn't it be odd if I just disappeared in 1995 and turned up in twenty years? Look at that guy from the Manic Street Preachers. He vanished earlier this year and everyone is looking for him. You don't think he's a time traveller, do you?'

'He could be. We are.'

'But if he turns up in twenty years, people will ask questions.'

'No, they won't.'

'Why,' exclaimed Tim, 'he turns up in 20 years and nobody says anything.'

'Think about it. He's the same age as he was when he disappeared. Nobody will think he's a time traveller. Who believes in time travel? No, he will just be a dude who looks like the guy from the Manics, who never turned up. He was still missing in 2015. Maybe he is in 2015, but still the same age. He could get on with his life without any fuss. What do you reckon?'

'I hope so. Or he could have come from the future and then be rescued by his girlfriend and gone back to his proper time, a bit like me.'

'So, I'm your girlfriend, am I?'

Tim put his hand on hers, still staring at the wall, 'Why did you do it? All this for me and after just one night.'

'I wanted to make sure you were OK. For all we knew you may have regretted your decision and wanted to come back. It's been six years?'

'I know, but why did you miss the wormhole? You could see I was OK; more than OK. What if I didn't remember you? What if I had a girlfriend? What if I had come back with a girl earlier? I could have easily. You would have been lying under the bed, listening to the live show. Like Monica with her parents in Friends.'

'You watch Friends?'

'It's the nineties, everyone does. And Only Fools and Horses. I'm always dying to tell them what happens next. So why?'

'If you'd have come back with a girl, you wouldn't have got that far. I'd have jumped out and smashed both of your faces in. I know you don't have a girlfriend. It's not that hard to find out about you in the press. You went out with an actress about a year ago. Can't remember her name but you and her had a John Lennon style "Bed-In" on the Chris Evans Radio show. I went to the library and read about it on this Hi-Tech CD Rom they have,' she laughed, 'I know all about you. Who needs the internet?'

'You still haven't answered my question. Why didn't you go back in the wormhole?'

She put her fingers between his gently, before quickly squeezing them together.

'Ow!' he yelped, pulling away his hand and staring at her in puzzlement, 'what did you do that for?'

'Why the fuck do you think I stayed? Why do you think I risked my life coming back in the first place? You know, so why are you trying to make me say it?'

'Say what?'

'What do you think, you thick bastard?'

'Oh.'

'I'm not saying anything until you start talking. Are you glad I came? Have you thought about me, even for a second? I bet you haven't. I bet you've been filling your boots with all the groupies. Typical man. You all think with your dicks. I don't know why I bothered. I feel such an idiot.'

'Calm down. You've made a few leaps there without giving me a chance to answer. Typical woman.'

Tim leaned forward, opened the drawer of the white MFC bedside cabinet and took out a blue leather Fred Perry wallet; inside was a flap with a press stud to a secure compartment.

'What's in there? If it's a condom, I'll ram it up that big nose of yours.'

From inside a crumpled TSB plastic money bag, he carefully retrieved a thin silver necklace between his fingers.

'Is that the necklace I gave you?' she gasped, attempting to grab it.

He pulled it away. 'Careful. It has one of your hairs trapped in the links. That's why I keep it in a bag. I don't want to lose the hair. Part of you has been here with me all the time. When I feel homesick, I look at this.'

'Can I look?'

'Yeah, but be careful.'

'Why? You can have as many hairs as you want now.'

'I want to keep that one for old times' sake.'

She held the necklace in he hand, slowly caressing the hair, 'You've had this all the time?'

'Yeah. Bet you feel guilty now? Especially after the nose comment. I don't even have a big nose. Besides, I don't know how you have the cheek to take this piss with those on,' he said tugging on her dungarees.

'You don't like these? Then they're gone,' she replied standing in front of him, lifting the two metal clasps over their buttons, sending the dungarees cascading to the floor. She peeled her white ribbed skin-tight T-Shirt over her head and threw it to the floor. She was naked except for a pair of sky-blue pants.

As Tim's gaze moved around her body she felt as powerful as she did weak. She had a hold over him; the bulge in his boxer shorts told her that much. But was that it - just the typical male reaction to a naked body? But she was in deep. She hadn't stopped thinking about him since they met. One night together and he was all she thought about. She hated herself for it. But there was nothing she could do. For a woman normally in control, the whole situation drove her crazy. But, secretly, a part of her rejoiced. She was happy; the happiest she had been. If only she could lose the need for control. She was his, there was no denying it. She had thought about this moment constantly, especially alone at night. She needed to know if she was wasting her time. Was she stuck in the past for no reason? Had it all been for nothing? She was terrified to find out, but the necklace gave her hope.

'It's all yours,' she conceded.

'What is?' replied Tim, looking up at her.

'Everything.'

She took his right hand and slid it up and down her thigh slowly, advancing to the curve of her hip. She moved it across her midriff, sliding it up to her left breast.

'Especially this.'

Tim could feel her heart pounding the blood around her body, as he softly held her breast. Was his heart pounding as fast? He hadn't felt like this since the last time he was with her. He thought about her a lot; she was the only thing from the future he missed. How could he love her - he had only known her one day? Was it love; or could it be he hadn't had time to get bored of her?

Fame and fortune afforded him the luxury of meeting many beautiful women who wouldn't have looked at him twice otherwise. But none had come close to the night they had in 2015: they were white noise in comparison.

He was still holding her breast as he stood up.

'My whole life's been an adventure,' he replied, looking into her eyes, 'not just Mad Ferret or the time-traveling - but my old life. Being in an Oasis tribute band and hanging around with Clint. And my parents. My dad dying in such a stupid way. Everything. So many things have happened. But if I wrote a book about my life, it wouldn't be complicated. Yeah, I've been through stuff most people haven't. I've just played in front of 125,000 people for fucks sake. Did you know we had 6 consecutive number ones in 1991? But none of it matters. Not in the end. If I wrote that book, it would only have two chapters; before I met you and after I met you. That's how I see things. Everything changed when I met you. Just two chapters. That's all.'

She wrapped her arms around him.

'That's exactly what I wanted to hear,' she whispered, 'and you've just hit the jackpot tonight, mister.'

Chapter 35

Low Flying Birds

THURSDAY 7TH SEPTEMBER 1995

'So, what do you think of the room?' asked Lyla, 'only £10 per person per night.'
'That much? It's a shit hole,' laughed Tim, 'but perfect. Nobody will expect to see me here. Why did you pick this one?'
'It was in this big yellow book, called the Yellow Pages. How they manage without the internet is beyond me.'
'You get used to it.'
'I hope so. I picked this one because the receptionist said they have live music on Thursday. We could check out the bar downstairs before we head out. I think the Yellow Pages suit this hotel.'
'Why?'
'Because I wouldn't have booked it if I'd seen it first.'

When you are as famous as Troy Gold it's difficult to go out without being noticed, impossible in Manchester. He'd been reunited with Lyla for 5 days spending every minute hauled up in his mansion.
The day after the Wentworth gig, she drove the DeLorean into his garage in the dead of night. Tim was all too familiar with the intrusive nature of the press and wanted to shield her from its gaze for as long as he could. A young lady driving through his gates in a 'Back to the Future' car would-be be front-page news. Mad Ferret made the front pages for less.
It was the end of festival season and the Ferrets had a month's downtime to recuperate after another successful year. Tim had just one thing to do before he could relax – pop into the studio and put the finishing touches to the next single.
With Tim in the studio, Lyla took the opportunity to explore 1995. The novelty of being in the nineties was still in its infancy for her, having so far

spent her time tracking down Tim; but now she could acclimatise to the decade without distraction. With Tim up early to drive to the studio, she headed for Meadowhall in Sheffield, to feel the difference in timelines in familiar surroundings.

She walked a mile or so from his house before calling a taxi from a phone box to Bolton Train Station and, after changing trains at Manchester Piccadilly, headed for Meadowhall, armed with a pocketful of cash. On the train, she hatched a scheme to buy a disguise for the most famous man in Manchester, so they could wander around the city incognito. When Tim returned from the studio just before midnight, the bedroom was full of clothes and a reservation to the budget Drop Inn Hotel, on the edge of town, had been made.

'So, what have you got for me to wear tonight? It can't be any worse than this bloody jumper. The Sweater Shop? Where on earth is the Sweater Shop and why does it say the Sweater Shop in big letters all over it? I'm a walking advertisement for the place. I feel a right idiot.'

'I wanted to get you looking like Mr. Average and this shop was the busiest in Meadowhall. It was packed. Everything in the shop said Sweater Shop on it. Besides, it worked didn't it? Who would think the great Troy Gold would walk around looking like that? If anyone recognises you your record sales will plummet.'

'I doubt it. More like sales in the bloody Sweater Shop would go through the roof. I can't do anything wrong,' moaned Tim.

'Aww diddums. I feel sorry for you. Poor little rich kid!' she teased, 'but you will like this T-Shirt I have for you tonight. It's brilliant.'

'It's just a purple T-Shirt with some writing on the front. Global Hypercolor.'

'It changes colour to suit your body temperature, so when you put this on the colours will change and the T-shirt will be lots of different colours. It will go with your disguise.'

'What disguise?'

'I'm going for a hippy surfer look. I've got some baggy Thai dye joggers. You put these on, and I'll put the finishing touches on before we go out.'

'Finishing touches?'

'You'll see.'

'I look a right knob,' moaned Tim as they entered the ground floor bar area.

The bar area was big but sparsely occupied with a small stage in the corner next to the shopfront.

'You look fine,' replied Lyla, trying not to laugh.

'The clothes are bad enough, but this hat is stupid.'

'It's not a hat, it's a cap. A newsboy cap, they call it. I like it and let's face it, you've got one of the most recognisable haircuts in the country. Without the cap, the disguise doesn't work. If I'd have had time, I would have dyed your hair.'

'No, you wouldn't.'

'Yes, I would. Just look at yourself in that mirror behind the bar. I did that. I own you now, boy,' she laughed slapping his bum, 'now get me a drink, you sexy mother!'

Tim shuffled reluctantly to the bar as a happy Lyla headed off to claim a table near the stage.

'I didn't realise people still wore them,' the barman commented as Tim approached.

'The hat, I mean cap?'

'No, I like that. I mean the T-Shirt. They were massive a few years back but dropped off the face of the planet. A mate had one, but he hated how it kept changing colour around his armpits.'

'Great,' Tim thought. 'Yeah, they're making a comeback. Everyone wears them where I'm from,' he lied.

'And where's that?'

'Err, Newquay. Is there a band on tonight?'

'Yeah.'

'Are they any good?'

'Dunno?'

'What are they called?'

'Not sure. The Highflyers. Or Flying Birds. Or Flying Turds. Something like that.'

'The High Flying Birds?' asked Tim.

'Yeah, that's it. Have you heard of them?'

'No, but it sounded right. A pint of lager and a bottle of orange Hooch, please.'

'You'll never guess what this band is called?' Tim asked, placing the lager on the table Lyla had picked, which was next to the stage.

'It's not Oasis, is it?'

'What? Why would it be Oasis? It's the High-Flying Birds. Noel Gallagher's band were called that after Oasis split up.'

'That's what I'm trying to tell you. I've just seen the band. Noel Gallagher is in the band. I've just seen him. No Liam or Bonehead or the others. Just him and three others, I've never seen before. He looked so young. But then I suppose he is.'

'Why is he playing a shit hole like this? There's no one here and they're on soon.'

'Why is he playing a shit hole like this? You nicked his songs that's why?'

'Sssssh, quiet.'

'Nobody can hear me, there's nobody here. Besides who would believe it anyway? You killed them before they were conceived; you're basically an Oasis condom,' she laughed.

'Come on, let's go,' Tim snapped.

'No chance. I want to see this. Front row seats to watch Noel Gallagher, whoever he plays with, is brilliant. I can't wait. The Tim I knew would have been beside himself with excitement. Why do you want to leave?'

'Why do you think?'

'I don't know. That's why I'm asking.'

'Are you gonna make me say it?'

'Say what?'

'Guilt. Are you happy now? It's the guilt. Sometimes I wake up at night and it's all I think about. I can't get back to sleep. I'm alright sometimes, but others I can't live with what I've done.'

'I didn't realise. I thought you would have gotten over it after 6 years. And Manchester isn't that big. Especially the music scene. This can't be the first time you've bumped into him?'

'No. I bumped into him in 1990 at Reading when he was the roadie for the Inspirals. He asked me for a job and I said I'd get back to him, but didn't.'

'Why didn't you help him out? I would have thought you would want him around the band, bouncing ideas off him?'

'I couldn't bear the idea of him being there every day to remind me of what I'd done.'

'Oh, I see,' said Lyla. 'I'm not going to sugarcoat it, but I'm disappointed in you. I don't agree with what you've done, but I get it. I get how you got carried away with the success and fame, but why didn't you help him out? The others you stole from, Suede and Pulp, are still bands. But Oasis you blew out of the water. And they are supposed to be your favourite band.'

'You say you understand but then make me feel like shit.'

'You should feel like shit after what you've done. You should have helped him out. Not just him but Liam and the others. What are they doing now?'

'I think they're in a band called the Rain. They aren't particularly good from what I've heard.'

Lyla sighed and crossed her arms.

'I don't need you to tell me what I've done, but it's too late now. I get hot sweats every time I think about it.'

'I can see that,' she said, nodding at the dark purple patches forming around his armpits.

'Brilliant. Like I don't look stupid enough.'

'I reckon they're just gonna keep getting bigger tonight,' she said nodding towards the stage as the band started setting up. 'It's definitely him. It's Noel Gallagher.'

Tim leaned forward in his chair, his arms resting on his knees as he wrung his hands together. He wasn't used to being talked to like this. Everyone loved him. Everyone told him what he wanted to hear. But not Lyla. She was the only one who knew the truth. It wasn't the first time they had discussed what he had done but, although she wasn't happy, she understood why he had done it. Part of her found it funny and liked the idea of living the lifestyle with him. She certainly enjoyed his huge mansion. But another part of her, the part which knew right from wrong, wasn't happy about it. Nevertheless, he had done it and she understood the reasons why. But she wasn't happy about him not using his money or influence in the industry to help the others out. She was right, he could have done it many times over, he had helped the Stone Roses and Shed 7 out. Their careers were better now than in the original reality. But he was too much of a coward to face up to the people whose lives, and music, he had stolen.

'Eleven. Eleven,' wafted over the microphone, in the undisguisable tone of Noel Gallagher, 'no, I'm not saying we're going to crank it up to eleven. That's how many people are in her watching us! Eleven.'

The silence in the audience was broken by Lyla's high pitch giggle.

'Did you like that one love?' Noel replied, over the microphone despite being close enough to speak to her directly.

'Yes!' she screeched clapping her hands.

Tim cast an angry glance at her. She was doing this on purpose to draw attention to them both; to make him feel even more uncomfortable.

'What's your name?'

'Lyla.'

'Lyla. I like that. I could write a song about you with a name like that. But your boyfriend doesn't look happy. Is he your boyfriend?'

'For now,' she laughed staring him up and down. Tim knew how ridiculous he looked. Lyla had made him look this stupid and was now drawing attention to him in front of everyone, especially Noel Gallagher.

'Mmm, I wouldn't have put you two together,' he smiled mischievously, giving her a wink,' I'm only joking pal. I wouldn't want your armpits to get any more purple.'

It wasn't just Lyla laughing now.

'I'm getting another, do you want one?' growled Tim, snatching his empty pint pot and heading for the bar.

'Just joking, pal. Just having a laugh. Don't go!'

Tim's mood wasn't improved as the barman did not attempt to hide his laughter as he served him.

'I lost my job a couple of weeks ago,' continued Noel.

'Awww,' sympathised Lyla.

'It was sadder than that!'

'Awwwwww,' she giggled.

'I hated it, but the girlfriend is giving me grief and so is my landlord. I could have had another job by now, but I've been too busy writing a song about not having a job to look for one. But don't tell the girlfriend. You lot are the first to hear it. The lucky eleven. It's called the Importance of Being Idle.'

I sold my soul for the second time
'Cause the man don't pay me
I begged my landlord for some more time
He said, "Son, the bill's waiting"
My best friend called me the other night
He said, "Man, are you crazy?"
My girlfriend told me to get a life
She said, "Boy, you lazy!"
But I don't mind
As long as there's a bed beneath the stars that shine
I'll be fine..

'Two quid pal,' said the barman. 'Hello pal, two quid.'

A statuesque Tim looked up and threw a fiver on the bar, 'Sorry pal, keep the change.'

'Nice one pal. Ignore the singer he's a twat.'

'Didn't you get me one?' Lyla asked.
'I asked but you were too busy laughing at me.'
'Don't be jealous it doesn't suit you. What's wrong, you look like you've seen a ghost?'
'It's worse than that,' replied Tim.
'What is?'
'You know that song we laid down a couple of days ago while you went to Meadowhall?'
'Yes?'
'This is it. The Importance of Being Idle.'
'Woops,' she laughed.
'It's not fuckin funny.'
'It is a bit. Although maybe not for you.'
'I can't go back on it now. All the production is done. And what if someone hears him sing it? They'll know I've stolen it.'
'I doubt it, there's only 9 other people in here. This is the first time he's played it. Unless anyone in here was in the recording studio, you're OK, for now. Do you know anyone in here?'
'No,' replied Tim looking around. 'But when it gets played on the radio a couple of weeks after I've seen him play it live, he will know.'
'He doesn't know it's you.'
'No, but he knows you and eventually he will see us together in the press. Imagine the front page of the Sun. Troy Gold dresses up as the world's worst-dressed surfer and steals another band's song. I'll never prove I wrote it.'
'You didn't though, did you? This was bound to happen sooner or later, and it will happen again.'
'Fuck, fuck, what am I gonna do?'
Lyla sighed, 'I don't know how you managed to get as far as you have without me. Oh yeah, you stole all his songs. But still, you are looking at this from the wrong angle. Life is all about angles.'
'What do you mean?'
'This is an opportunity.'
'An opportunity?'
'Yes,' she replied, picking up his pint and taking a large swig, followed by two more, to build up the suspense.
'What opportunity?'
'To right a wrong.'
'To right a wrong?'
'Yes, if you want to pull this off, listen carefully and do exactly what I say.'

Chapter 36

Deal or No Deal?

'Good set tonight, pal,' Tim uttered as he joined Noel at the long stainless-steel urinal.

'Cheers,' he replied, spinning his head sideways. 'Oh, it's you. I was only messing around earlier. Having a laugh.'

'I'm not bothered, I saw the funny side.'

'Good, the last thing I want is you pissing angry and splashing all over the place.'

Tim laughed.

'Do I know you?' asked Noel as he spun his head around for a second time.

'I've got a business proposition,' Tim replied.

'No,' asserted Noel firmly.

'No, what?'

'I don't want any drugs.'

'What? I'm not selling drugs.'

'Well, there's only one other thing you could mean and that's a big fuckin no.'

'To what?'

'You fuckin know what. I thought you stood a bit close to me at the pisser,' snapped Noel, reeling away to the wash hand basin.

'What? God no. Fuck no. I've got a girlfriend. You should know, you've spent half the night chatting her up. No wonder your girlfriends pissed off at you.'

'She's not really pissed off. It just makes the song sound better. She likes my music and wants me to make it, but I doubt I will ever will.'

'Really? I think you're good. Some of the songs were brilliant; especially the first one. Did you write it?'

'Thanks. Yeah, I write all the songs. I had high hopes a few years ago. Dreams and schemes, you could say. But I'm 27 now. If it were gonna happen it would have by now. That job I was on about earlier, was with the council. I had an accident at work a few years ago and hurt my foot so they put me in this supply cupboard where workers would come and pick stuff up. But most of the time I was on my own. I wrote loads of songs that I thought were gonna make it happen. But nothing ever did. I used to call it the hit hut. Guess it turned out to be the shit hut.'

'No man, you've written some top tunes there and the band is tight. You *are* a good band.'

'Sometimes that's not enough though. I know we're good. My younger brother is in a band. They *are* shit. I know the difference.'

'Why don't you start a band with your brother. Maybe that's what you need; the dynamics of youth.'

Noel laughed. 'You've obviously not met my brother.'

'What do you mean?'

'There's no way we could be in a band together. We'd kill each other.'

'You never know until you've tried it.'

'Oh, I *know*, pal. There's no way on this universe, or any fuckin universe we could be in a band together.'

'Not even a parallel universe?'

'Especially a parallel universe,' replied Noel, squinting at Tim. 'Are you sure I don't know you?'

'This business proposal. I think you'll like it,' Tim deflected.

'Go on then.'

'I want your first song. The Importance of Being Idle.'

'Want it?'

'To record.'

'To record? Who the fuck are you to record my song?'

Tim took off his hat and unruffled his hair, 'Imagine me in a Fred Perry on Top of the Pops singing Wonderwall.'

Noel stared, his jaw-dropping. 'Troy Gold. *Troy fuckin Gold*!'

'Sssssh, I'm in disguise.'

'I can't believe I'm talking to Troy Gold. I can't believe Troy Gold wants one of my songs. We've met before. You won't remember but....'

'I remember, it was Reading 90. You asked me for a job, but I couldn't get you one. But I remember you.'

'I can't believe Troy Gold remembers me. I can't believe you want my song.'

'It's a great song. I could record it for the next single. We're in the studio tomorrow, so I'll need to know tonight.'

'Tomorrow! I'll come along and teach you the chords.'

'That's OK, I think I got them.'

'Of course, you're Troy Gold. You're a pro. Hear a song once and you know how to play it.'

'I'll do my own arrangement. Just write me the lyrics down, with your telephone number and I'll be in touch.'

'So how much do I get?'

'It depends on sales. As a joint songwriter, you get half of the songwriting royalties.'

'Joint songwriter?'

'Yeah, sorry about that, but the band wouldn't go for it if it were written by an unknown. They'll only trust it to be a hit if I've been involved. Look upon it as a collaboration.'

'OK. I get it, but any idea how much I will get?'

'No idea, but let me tell you this,' Tim said holding up three fingers.

'Three? What do you mean?'

'That's how many times Wonderwall made me a millionaire in the same day!'

'Three million quid. Fuck me! But this isn't as good as Wonderwall though.'

'I dunno. It's a great song.'

Noel laughed, 'No way is my song as good as Wonderwall. I'm not blowing smoke up your arse but Noel Gallagher versus the great Troy Gold. There's no comparison.'

'I wouldn't say that, it's different but has a similar feel. They could have been written by the same person.'

'Fuck off. You're saying the Importance of Being Idle is good enough to have been written by Troy Gold.'

'Or maybe Wonderwall is good enough to have been written by Noel Gallagher? Who knows if you'd had the accident earlier, you might have beat me to it?'

'I wish,' laughed Noel, 'they say you should never meet your hero, but here I am with mine and you're a top bloke. Me, write Wonderwall? It's a brilliant song and it does speak to me. Lots of your songs speak to me. It's like you've scooped thoughts out of my head and turned them into songs I could only dream of writing.'

The crippling pangs of guilt once again began to build inside Tim. Noel wasn't the only one who stood in front of his hero, but he was the only one who had earned the status of hero honestly.

'So, is it a deal or no deal?' Tim held out his hand, anxious to leave the crime scene.

'Aren't you forgetting something?'

'What?'

'To wash your hands. You may be Troy Gold but I'm not shaking until you've washed them. Then we have a deal. I'll write the lyrics and my number down and casually drop them on your table as I walk past. Then what?'

'Then you sit next to the phone and wait for your life to change.'

'How did it go?' Lyla asked as he returned from the toilet.

'Just as you said it would. He's gonna pop over with his details in a bit. And the lyrics. I know the lyrics, obviously, but I couldn't pretend I remembered them all after one listen. Then can we piss off somewhere else?'

Lyla smiled. 'You're welcome.'

'Ok, I'll give you that. Well played. I don't suppose you could get me out of this mess I'm in. Every time I write a new song I wonder if I'll get found out. I'm like an escaped prisoner looking over his shoulder all the time. I can't go on like this.'

'I know how to get you out of this. You've already righted one wrong tonight – in part anyway – you could do it again. You could put the whole thing right again.'

'How?'

'Do you want to put things right?'

'Yes.'

'How serious are you about putting things right, because it won't be easy, and it will take years.'

'100%'

'OK. First, when you go to add Noel to the songwriting credits tomorrow you have to tell them you are quitting Mad Ferret.'

'What? Tomorrow? As soon as that?'

'Yes,' she affirmed, 'or you might change your mind. Can you do that?'

He took a deep sigh as Noel Gallagher approached the table with a handful of beermats.

'Here's the autograph you wanted,' he said loudly, before whispering, 'the barman didn't have any paper, so I've written everything on these beer mats. You don't know what this means. You're a good man. I've got to chip, or I'll miss my bus. Thanks, pal.'

'Well?' prompted Lyla.

The thought of Noel Gallagher rushing to catch the last bus was the clincher.

'OK, he conceded, 'I'll do it.'

Tim returned to the studio the following day to clarify the writing credits for "the Importance of Being Idle," before quitting the band. The fallout was immediate as the rest of the band was contacted.

Moody took the news badly, at first angrily accusing Tim of the ultimate betrayal and arrogance. This anger turned to remorse as he later apologised before begging him to change his mind. Realising his pleas were falling on deaf ears, he reverted to defiance, proclaiming Mad Ferret would continue and become bigger and better without him. It's no wonder his name was Moody.

Adam was philosophical. He thanked Tim for being part of an amazing journey, which he would never forget and had set him up for life. He also thanked him for his friendship and support over the years, referring to the conversation outside the apartments in Blackpool after the Stone Roses gig. The conversation had been more important to Adam than Tim had realised.

Quinny just cried. Maybe he was upset at the ending of the chapter, or maybe it was the realisation he would see his friend less often. Or maybe he could foresee what was coming next.

Mad Ferret took a break for the rest of 1995, with The Importance of Being Idle topping the charts as the news of Tim's departure filtered through. It would be their last Number One single.

They returned to touring in early 1996, with a new frontman and, accused of being a glorified 'greatest hits' band, also took to the studio to record their first post-Troy Gold album. The album was never finished.

By the summer, with the confidence provided by Tim's talent gone and Moody's desperate insecurities growing, large cracks in the band were exposed.

Mad Ferret imploded on an infamous Saturday night in August 1996 during a disastrous gig as they headlined the main stage at the Reading Festival. The significance of their failure was exacerbated the following night as their friends and former equals The Stone Roses played a triumphant set, highlighting the gulf which now existed between them. Mad Ferret were no longer relevant.

The speculation in the music press was led by Carl from the NME who, despite becoming friends with Quinny and accepting the benefits of his association with the band whilst at their heights, was quick to jump off the rapidly decelerating gravy train.

Maybe he was still upset at being pushed into the swimming pool or was envious of the attention Quinny got from women, or maybe it was the money or other trappings associated with fame. Maybe he wanted to use his inside knowledge to further his career. Or perhaps he just wasn't a very nice person; he was a journalist after all.

Carl made a name for himself doing a hatchet job on the band with headlines such as 'Mad Ferret reputation dragged into the pissiest Portaloo at Reading.' And 'Roses v Ferrets was like watching an elephant squash a ferret under its mighty foot'. If further clarity was required the article was accompanied by a cartoon elephant squashing a ferret under its foot, a caricature of Moody's face on the ferret.

Carl's attempt to desecrate the memory of the band was complete when the image became a popular T-Shirt sold outside Stone Roses gigs.

Two months after Reading 96, Mad Ferret was as dead as the one on the T-Shirt.

Chapter 37

The Reunion - Part 1

WEDNESDAY, OCTOBER 7TH, 2015

They knew the metal personnel door would swing open, even though the large car park was empty. They had been following him for a year, gradually increasing surveillance over the past couple of months, culminating in Tim 'bumping' into Clint in the bar at the driving range the previous evening. It was two weeks before 'Back to the Future day' - the day Tim was sent back to 1989. Tim was born in 1993, Lyla in 1997 and were now middle-aged people in a time they were previously young adults. Not much had changed in the world, but as they no longer existed as young people in this era, the micro world they previously occupied was different. From the surveillance and previous evening's conversation, Clint's existence was reassuringly similar to the one Tim had exited. They needed to know if they could follow their plan and, as usual, Clint was the key.

'Hi, Clint. Bet you're surprised to see me, aren't you? I enjoyed last night. I need to talk to you about something. Oh sorry, how rude; this is Lyla.'

'Hi, Clint. Lovely to meet you,' Lyla responded holding out her hand.

'Is Lyla your real name?' asked Clint.

'What?'

'His name isn't Tim. It's Troy. So, are you lying as well, or just him?'

'My real name is Tim. Troy is a nickname. It's a long story. How do you know that?'

'Because most of the people who drink at the driving range bar are middle-aged men who loved Mad Ferret and all that '90's indie music stuff. You were recognised, but nobody said anything until after you left. I'm amazed none of them introduced themselves. They never shut up about you after you left.'

'No, Lyla's not my real name, it's also a nickname which I've had for so long nobody uses my real name, which is Orla. But please, call me Lyla.'

'OK, But what are you doing here?' he snapped, glancing at Tim, ' I didn't mention this place and there's no car outside; but you've turned up the day after our chance meeting with, I guess, your wife? Is she your wife? Are you following me? Was last night a chance meeting or did you plan it?'

'Yes, she's my wife and if you let us in, I will answer all of your questions. We need to speak. But you must let us in to speak in private.'

'Please let us in,' Lyla added, 'we are your friends, what we need to tell you is important. And don't worry it's not bad. In fact, it's quite the opposite.'

The surveillance had produced mixed results. The occasional trips over the Pennines and internet searches had procured vital, but limited information. Clint still lived in the same house, had the same job and hung around in the relocated industrial unit in the old car park next to the driving range. But as it was difficult to guess when he would be at the unit, little else was known. There was no sign of the red BMW, instead he drove another classic, a white Triumph Herald convertible.

It was great he still occupied the building, but what they really needed to know was on the inside. Was the big white MRI scanner there and did he know how to use it? Had he already used it? Tim's conversation at the bar yielded fewer nuggets of information than there was chicken in the average chicken nugget.

It was impossible to steer the conversation in the direction of time travel except asking if he liked Back to the Future, which he did; but rather than discuss time travel itself they ended up discussing the film. The evening chat consisted of music, films and football. Tim was reassured to find Clint liked all the same stuff he did the first time around. He would have been mortified if he had developed shit taste in music or, worse still, was now a Sheffield United fan. He was the same old Clint he left behind but with a girlfriend he was smitten about and happier and more confident. Tim was delighted his friend was happy. He felt guilty for years about the way they parted and often thought about his act of betrayal by not returning in either of the wormholes. His guilt could dissipate now Clint was happy. But as fantastic as it was to catch up with his oldest friend, he had not gleaned enough information. They needed to get inside the unit.

'Ok, I suppose,' Clint muttered hesitantly, 'I'm a part-time artist and I've got a few art installations I'm getting ready for an exhibition.'

Lyla squeezed Tim's hand as they stepped over the threshold.

There were settees, a dartboard, a fridge and, parked next to the Triumph Herald, was the DeLorean. Tim had been in the unit enough times before to have a photographic recollection of the layout. It was similar but different in many ways, but most importantly to the right was a huge white plastic cylinder accessed by a timber ramp.

Lyla squeezed his hand even tighter as they stared at the structure.

'Oh yeah that,' Clint explained. 'It's an art installation I'm working on. The white cylinder is meant to be a giant MRI scanner, into which I am going to somehow insert the DeLorean to signify how we care more for our cars than we do other human beings. It's a metaphor. The money spent on research and development of the motor vehicle could be rerouted into healthcare for the poor in third world countries.'

Lyla cast Tim a glance as he sniggered. He couldn't help himself.

'Oh, you find that funny, do you? Well, that's a typical bourgeois attitude you would associate with a multi-millionaire. '

Tim burst into laughter, forgetting both his etiquette and the softly, softly approach he and Lyla had agreed to.

'I'm sorry pal, you were always full of shit, but even by your standards that was poor.'

'What?' exclaimed Clint.

'It's not an art installation. It's a fuckin time machine!'

'What? What do you mean? It's an art installation. I'm a part-time artist.'

'Troy! We agreed on a strategy. What are you doing you knob head?' Lyla screamed.

Clint bent over with his hands on his head, 'either tell me what you are on about or get out.'

'A part-time artist,' Tim laughed, 'you haven't got an artistic bone in your body.'

'How the fuck would you know? You don't know me. One evening plying me with drinks doesn't make you my mate, so start talking.'

'Look I'm sorry about him,' placated Lyla, 'we were supposed to be treading carefully around this until that idiot started shooting his mouth off, but then in the long run it makes no difference; rip the Elastoplast off in one go. Get it over quicker.'

'Get what over quicker?'

'That big white cylinder over there is a time machine, right?' Tim butted in, 'just admit it.'

'What makes you think it's a time machine? Do you realise how ridiculous you sound?'

Tim continued, 'It is a time machine and I know because you sent me back to 1989, two weeks from now on Back to the Future Day.'

'Do you expect me to believe that?'

'In the film Back to the Future, which you love, Marty proves he has been sent from the future by showing him the sketch of the flux capacitor.'

'I told you I loved that film last night. We spent most of the evening talking bollocks about it.'

'Yes, but if you let me finish, I can prove that you sent me to the past by explaining how that thing works. Well as much as I understand anyway.'

'What?'

'If I explain to you how that makes time travel possible will you stop fucking around and accept that you sent me to the past?'

'Go on then, explain to me how the "time machine" works,' Clint laughed, air quoting the words time machine.

'The only kind of artist you are is a piss artist. We used to practically live in the Leadmill. Your talent lays in science, not the arts. You are easily the smartest person I have ever met. Easily. So clever, you find even the best Universities too easy, instead opting to take menial jobs at Sheffield University so you can use their equipment for your experiments, which is how you came up with using the principles of an MRI scanner for your version of the flux capacitor.'

'OK, but I could have told you some of that last night, and I've already told you it's an MRI scanner.'

'But you didn't tell me you use electromagnetics to create traversable wormholes, did you? To be fair that's as much as I remember before you lost me with your explanation, but apparently, the tricky part is finding a suitable exit at the other side of the wormhole. It must be somewhere which won't have changed over the time period travelled and isolated enough for someone not to stumble across accidentally; because if they do and wonder in their body will explode, or implode, I think. This is possible as the wormhole stays open for 5 minutes. Any Tom, Dick or Harry can wander in. The only reason the car doesn't crush like a tin can is some exotic matter you spray on before, whatever the hell that is. The wormhole then reopens in exactly a week and stays open again for 5 minutes. It can be re-opened again in another week's time but it's less stable and if you don't get in that one you are stuck in the past. Am I right?'

Clint looked stunned, before scratching his head and replying, 'So if this thing works, how come I don't remember you?'

'What do you mean if this thing works?' Lyla asked, 'you must know it works?'

'All the numbers add up, but I've not tested it yet. I'm just in the process of doing that. You say I sent you back in two weeks, but I'm nowhere near there yet. I can't locate a safe exit location. As you said, that is tricky. The Clint you remember must have been in front of me?'

'The Clint I knew didn't have a girlfriend. Love steals your time,' said Tim.

'True, but why don't I remember you?'

'Because when you go back in time you exist in people's memories until the point when the past passes your conception. After then you no longer exist. The last time I was in 2015, I was your 22-year-old best mate.'

'Of course, you passed your conception date. A different sperm will have fertilised the egg. I knew that. Fuck me. I really did send you back in time! I sent the lead singer of Mad Ferret back in time. Awesome!' he laughed, dancing around the unit, 'I know how Emmet Brown felt when he first met Marty. This is mega. Thank you, thank you.' he cried, briefly losing composure as he hugged Tim.

'But hang on. What went wrong? Why did you end up stuck in the past, old friend of mine who I don't remember?'

'Grab a few bottles of ice-cold Asahi out of the fridge and I'll tell you all about it. I've dreamt of this moment for years.'

'How do you know I have Asahi in the fridge?'

'It's the only bottled lager you'll drink.'

'Correct, you must be my best mate,' Clint laughed.

Tim told him everything. Clint was spellbound, hanging onto every word and asking questions throughout. By the time Tim finished, the beer fridge was empty.

'I can't believe I sent you back to 1989 in that machine. I mean I know it works theoretically, but I haven't tested it. And you say that Mad Ferret were called Oasis in the first reality, and you stole their records. That's crazy, mate. I wish I could remember you. I bet we were good friends?'

'Like brothers.'

'I have a question,' Clint spewed out unable to contain his excitement. 'When you landed in 1989, what were the 3 things most different to now. What surprised you about 1989?'

'Good question,' Tim mused. He loved chatting with his best friend again. It didn't matter Clint couldn't remember him; he remembered Clint like it was yesterday. 'Number one had to be the technology; or lack of it. Obviously, 1989 is in the past but it isn't that far in the past when you think about it in terms of the history of the world, its only 26 years ago, so I wasn't expecting them to be so far behind us.'

'Example?'

'Mobile phones didn't exist. I mean they did but they were huge, and I never met anyone who had one until the mid-1990s. I saw them on the TV and that was about it. But crazier still was there was no internet. So, get this, if you wanted to find something out you had to go to the library and either look in encyclopedias or – if you were lucky – get the latest information from a CD. I did that a couple of times and you had to sign the CD out like it was made of gold. Number two had to be AIDS.'

'The disease AIDS?'

'Yeah.'

'Really?' asked Clint, 'why?'

'It was huge at the time. It hadn't been about long and not much was known about it, which wasn't helped by having no internet. Everyone was terrified. There was even an advertising campaign by the government with giant tombstones falling to the ground.'

'That's mental.'

'Number three is how busy the pubs and clubs were, especially the pubs. If you went into a pub on a Friday or Saturday night, it was rammed and they would all shut at the same time, so when last orders came it took forever to get served. And they used to drink so much and if you were a man it had to be a pint. You couldn't have a short unless it was a chaser. It took me ages to get used to drinking so much volume but, after a while, I got used to it. There was a real pub drinking culture and the pubs were brilliant. Much better than they are now.'

'So, which is better 1989 or 2015.?'

'1989. Without a doubt,' Tim smiled.

'Really?' asked Clint.

'Yes,' interrupted Lyla. 'Which is why we want you to send us back there.'

Clint laughed, 'You're joking right?'

'No,' she replied, 'we need to go back.'

'Back to when exactly?'

'To a couple of weeks before you sent me back to last time,' answered Tim, 'anytime in July 1989, should do it.'

'Why?' asked a perplexed Clint, 'If you go back, you will stay the same age. You know that. You've had the 90's experience whilst you were young and it sounds like you have a great time. So why go back? You'll be old by the time you get back here. And if you go back further than before you will undo everything that happened before. Mad Ferret will never exist. You can't take your money with you, so you'll be skint.'

'Don't worry about the money. There's more to life than money. I need to go back to right a few wrongs I created,' explained Tim.

'Like what?'

'It's not important,' Lyla replied, squeezing Tim's hand again.

'Well, it doesn't matter anyway, I can't send you back. I've not tested this thing yet.'

'But we know it works. We're living proof. We've been there and got the T-Shirt, literally. And we both went separately. You sent Tim 6 months before me, so it must be safe.'

'I can look into it, but it won't be soon, it could be years until I've tested it properly.'

'That's not good enough,' snapped Lyla, bullying the new Clint the same as she did the original. We need to go back before Back to the Future Day.'

'Why?'

'Because unless we do that we will go back after the young Tim, and we won't be able to change the future.'

Clint rubbed his chin. 'That's not right. Tim doesn't exist anywhere now, ever since he went past his conception date. All traces of him have disappeared.'

'Are you sure?'

'Yes, of course.'

'OK,' she said, 'that buys us some time, but we still need to go back as soon as possible. Tim can't live with himself because he changed the future negatively for some people. You must do it as soon as possible.'

'You don't understand how difficult this is. It's not just flicking a switch. It could still take years.'

'That's not good enough we need to go back sooner than that.'

'Look,' said Tim, 'If he says it will take years then we will have to bide our time here, I will be settled as long as I know I can go back and put things right at some point.'

'Well, I won't,' Lyla commented.

'Why?'

'Because I want our baby born in 1989 not now 2015.'

'What!' exclaimed Clint.

'She's pregnant. I'm going to be a dad!'

'Congratulations. But are you sure you want to go back to 1989? You've said yourself how we're more advanced now. Wouldn't it be better for your child to be brought up in 2015?'

'No, we've made our minds up, pal,' Tim responded, 'I can't live with some of the things I did in the past. I changed too many things and people suffered. Sometimes it was by accident and sometimes on purpose but, either way, the effects were devastating.'

'Besides,' continued Lyla, 'just because you have the technology, it doesn't mean these are better times. How is this technology being used? Bullying each other on social media and looking at porn. People sat opposite each other in pubs and restaurants staring at their devices rather than looking at each other. The nineties are simpler but better times. People are nicer and look out for each other. And more fun. And the music is better. I don't know about Troy, but I can't wait to get back.'

'100% agree. But the question is can you do it before April, Clint?'

'I suppose, but the tricky part is finding where to exit the wormhole, but I don't see why we can't use the position of the one I used before. Do you know the coordinates?'

'Co-ordinates? No.'

'I mean, could you take me to the exact location of where you exited before? Can you remember where it was?'

'Yes.'

'It has to be the exact spot. Are you sure you remember?'

'Yes. I'll never forget. I went back twice to make sure nothing wandered in and disintegrated after I decided to stay in 1989.'

'Is it far?'

'No, it's just off the Woodhead between Sheffield and Manchester. Probably about 30 minutes from here.'

'OK. If we drive over there, we can get the coordinates and I can start the calculation. Can you go first thing in the morning? Meet here at 8?'

'OK.'

'Anyone fancy a nightcap?' asked Clint, 'I have a nice whisky.'

'OK'

'So where are you staying?'

''We've booked into the Peacock Room at the Whitley Hall in Grenoside for the week,' Lyla replied, 'It's lovely and only 10 minutes from here. Troy wanted to visit a few of his old haunts to see if anything is different.'

'That sounds fun,' Clint replied, passing the glasses of whisky, 'are you going to visit anyone else you know? If you were born in Hillsborough, won't your family live there?'

'No, I'm an only child and both my parents are dead. My mum died of cancer when I was young and my dad a couple of years before now in an accident. Nice whisky by the way.'

'Sorry to hear that. My Dad died when I was young. It's tough.'

'Yeah, I remember. He was friends with my dad. They used to go to school together. And the Leadmill when they got older.'
'Your Dad knew mine. What was he called?'
'Matt Bauer.'
'Matt Bauer!'
'You remember my dad?'
'The whisky you're drinking. The first time I had it was when Matt bought it for my 18th and I've drunk it ever since.'
'Blair Atholl. The stuff they make Bells with?'
'That's the one.'
'Wow. I feel emotional thinking about him and my mother. The fact that you knew him makes me feel even closer to him and you. It means a lot,' Tim explained as his eyes welled up. 'I'd like to propose a toast to the best dad in the world. Matt Bauer. Hope you are still watching Wednesday from up there.'
As Tim and Lyla raised their glasses, Clint was agitated.
'What's up Clint? Why won't you raise your glass?'
'I don't need to. Matt Bauer isn't dead!'
'He's alive,' Tim gasped looking into the glass before downing the remainder of its contents, 'are you sure?'
'Me and Lucy see him all the time. We go up Grenoside on a Saturday and sometimes bump into him. And I still see him at the match. He goes with his mates, the ones him and dad went to school with. He always buys me a pint. He lives up Grenoside.'
'Are you sure he hasn't had the accident? When did you last see him?'
'It was only last Sunday when we went for a walk in Greno Woods. His house is next to the footpath, he shouted me as we walked past.'
'You know where he lives?'
'Yeah, I don't know the name of the road or number, but I can tell you exactly where it is. It's easy to find.'

Chapter 38

The Reunion - Part 2

'This is the house,' announced Lyla, 'are you excited? Are you sure you want to go ahead with this?'
'Do I want to see my dad, who I thought was dead? Of course, I want to go ahead with this. I can't believe you don't want to go to Ireland to check out your family.'
'I'm not like you, Troy. I love my family, but I'd rather remember them as they were. It would be weird seeing my parents again after all these years and them being the same age as me. Aren't you worried about being the same age as your dad?'
'No. I can't wait. We'll be best mates. Besides, it's not the first time I've done it. I saw him back in the Leadmill in 1989. I told you about the night out we had with Jarvis Cocker and Richard Hawley?'
'Yeah, you've told me a hundred times. If you tell me again, I'm going to start calling you Bungalow Bill.'
'Why?'
'Because you've only got one story.'
'Oh, very funny. Are you sure this is the one?'
'Yeah. Left at Pete's Chippy, up to the top of the road and the last house before the woods, next to a gunnal, or something.'
'Gennel. Next to a gennel. This is more of a footpath than a gennel, don't you reckon?'
'Are you serious? I've no idea what a gennel is; it's just a path to me. But I can hear someone in the back garden. Let's walk down the damn gennel and see if you can see anything.'
They stepped over a timber style onto a grass footpath leading towards the woods. To the left was a timber fence surrounding an expanse of grass occupied by horses in the distance; to the right a shoulder height bramble edge separating the public right of way from the private garden. At the bottom of the garden was a middle-aged man with medium-length brown greying hair, kicking a football with two young blonde-haired girls in matching pink dungarees. He looked how he imagined his dad would look.'

'Excuse me pal, is there a chippy around here?' he shouted.

'Really?' laughed Lyla, 'It's only half ten?'

'Err, yeah,' replied the man turning around, 'but it doesn't open until 12...' His voice trailed off as he caught a glimpse of Tim.

'Don't I know you?' he asked, raising his hand above his eyes to shield the sun as he walked towards him. He was wearing dark blue jeans and a black T-Shirt with the Def Jam logo. 'Aren't you Troy Gold, from Mad Ferret?' he gasped.

'Yeah, I am. I recognise you. Didn't we have a night in the Leadmill back in the eighties with Richard and Jarvis?'

'Yes, yes we did! I can't believe you remember me. Someone as famous as you remembering me. I've told loads of people about that night, and no one believes me. Would you mind posing for a photograph so I can show the missus and prove it happened? She just laughs at me when I tell her. I once bumped into the Arctic Monkeys in High Green when they were only about 16 and they asked me to get them some beer. She doesn't believe that either.'

'Did you get them the beer?'

'Of course not, they were too young. It was them though. Alex lived just around the corner. You were asking about the chippy. If you're hungry I can make you something to eat?'

'How about a coffee?'

'I can make you a coffee. I'd love to make you a coffee. Ever since that night I've followed your career. I've seen you loads of times. It would be an honour to have a coffee and a chat.'

'The honour will be mine,' said Tim, 'By the way this is Lyla.'

'Pleased to meet you, Lyla.'

'Likewise.'

It was a 1970's stone-clad one-and-a-half-story detached house with large dormer windows to both roof slopes. It was bigger inside than it looked, courtesy of a single-story extension to the rear forming a large kitchen and dining area.

'How do you take your coffee?' Matt asked cleaning out a large silver mocha pot.

'White with half a sugar for both of us,' Tim replied looking around, 'you don't have to go to all that trouble, we'll be fine with instant.'

'It's OK. It's not every day Troy Gold comes around for coffee. I'm hardly gonna give him Nescafe, am I?'

His two daughters were sat at a large island bar, the focal point of the kitchen.

'So, who are you two?' Lyla asked.

'I'm Rosie,' replied the oldest, who looked around 11 years old.

'Lily,' replied the smallest, around 3 years younger.

'They are beautiful girls, you must be proud?' she asked, 'do you have any other children?'

Tim knew why she asked that question. Since seeing the girls outside and Matt mentioning his wife, his head was full of questions he needed to shoehorn into the conversation. Lyla was less patient and had decided to go straight for the jugular.

'No, just these two. Do you have any?'

'Not yet but there's still time,' she replied. She didn't want to mention she was pregnant to avoid the inevitable questions. 'I'm a fair bit younger than Troy.'

She mentioned the age difference at any opportunity, but for once Tim wasn't irritated by the obvious attempt to wind him up. He spotted a photograph in a large Art Deco style frame on a side cupboard of his mum and dad dressed up in sixties gear. He had seen it before; it was his favourite photo of his mum. It was the night they met at a Mod theme night at Sheffield City Hall called Brighton Beach. They used to go there every month, but this was the night they met. His dad used to look at the photo a lot. Seeing the look on Tim's face, Lyla nodded at the photo mouthing the word 'mum'. Tim nodded back.

'Is this your first wife? She looks pretty?' Lyla scrutinised, as Tim shot her an angry glance.

'Yeah. That's right; but why did you say first wife?' Matt replied, spinning around.

'I hope you don't mind me being nosy, but Troy talks about that night you had in the Leadmill with Richard and Jarvis and how well you got on. You're a mate of Richards, right?'

'Yeah; but why did you say first wife?' Matt reiterated uncomfortably.

Tim was frozen to the spot, mortified, preying the ground would open and swallow him. This was a part of Lyla's personality he did not like; it was bossy and borderline bullying. She did it a lot. He had seen his dad upset at his mum's death enough times to recognise the pained look. He could have got this information out of him in a subtle, less devastating, manner; it would have taken a little longer, that's all. He was furious but couldn't say anything.

'It's just that we keep in touch with Richard and he told us your wife had cancer a long time ago. You see Troy still mentions the night out you had just before he got famous. He says it was one of the best nights of his life because it was before all the fame, money and complications which come with it. When playing music was still pure,' she spluttered out in desperation, not her usual composed self. It was a complete lie. She had overstepped the mark and was clumsily digging upward to get out of the hole. Fortunately, starstruck Matt's judgment was distorted by the story.

'It was a great night. I remember it like it was yesterday, but I assumed it would just be white noise to you. A blur in the life of a true Rock and Roll legend. I can't wait to tell Stacey when she gets home, which should be soon. She's been working nights; she's a doctor.'

'Stacey?' muttered Tim. That was his mum's name.

'Yes, that's my wife. My first and only wife,' he laughed, 'Yeah, she had cancer years ago, but fortunately we caught it early and the doctors were able to treat it. It's one of the reasons she became a doctor.'

'You caught it early,' Tim stuttered.

'Yeah. Before we had the girls Stacey fell pregnant years earlier. It wasn't planned but we decided to make it work. We were young but with a few sacrifices to our careers, we could make it work. It was a boy. But something went wrong early on and we had to rush to the hospital one night. It was then they spotted the cancer.'

'And she's OK now?'

'Yes, she's fine. It's funny how things work out. I guess it just wasn't meant to be. Some of those little swimmers aren't strong enough to survive, even though they win the race. But every cloud and all that. We were told the cancer was spreading so fast if it hadn't been spotted then it would have become terminal. It saved her life. So, we decided to be careful and waited a few years until our careers were established until we had a family. I doubt Stacey would be a doctor or I would have a successful Architectural practice in the centre of town had we started a family so young.'

'Look, I'm sorry about Lyla, she shouldn't be asking such intrusive questions.'

'That's OK. I don't mind. It's good to talk about it from time to time if only to remind me how lucky I am.'

'But the point is, everything worked out and his wife is still with us.' Lyla established, widening her eyes as she stared at Tim.

'Yes,' he replied in shock.

Tim's head spun as the news sank in. His mum, whom he had not seen since he was too young to formulate lasting memories, was alive. He was nervous enough about seeing his dad, despite his previous denials to Lyla, but he wasn't expecting this. It was a lot to take in; too much perhaps. Did he want to meet her? Would he be able to string together a coherent sentence? She wouldn't know him. And who was he anyway? He no longer existed. He had no parents anymore and just like Clint they were happier without him. He could handle Clint being happier, but what was he supposed to make of this? His own parents living the dream because he didn't exist. They were happier because they didn't want him in the first place; he ruined their lives. They were better off without him.

He looked at the girls, colouring in on the island bar. What were they to him? Were they parallel universe stepsisters? He suddenly realised why Lyla had decided not to travel to Ireland. She was right; he had made a mistake.

'Look, I don't want to put you out?' Tim muttered, 'I think we'd better get off. Your wife will be tired if she has been at work all night. The last thing she wants is us here spoiling things. She'll most likely want to spend some time with your daughters.'

Matt looked shocked and offended, not just with the words, but the way they had been delivered. His friend's demeanour had changed in an instance.

'Oh, but I've nearly finished, she'll love to meet you both. And she will be back any minute now. I'm surprised she's not here already.'

'Nonsense, darling,' Lyla said, walking over and grabbing Tim's hand. Seeing his panic-stricken expression, she gently caressed it with her thumb, 'I'd love to meet Stacey and your friend seems happy to see you. Of course, we'll stop Matt, it's just Troy is over-polite at times. He worries he will overstay his welcome. You wouldn't think a big Rock n Roll star would be so polite and lacking in confidence, but there you go. It's one of the things I love about him.'

'Seriously pal, I'd love you to meet the missus,' Matt confirmed, the smile returning to his face. 'Besides, you may as well stay now as I've just heard the car pull up on the drive.'

'What was that text you sent me about the guy from Mad Ferret drinking a coffee?' Stacey shouted as the front door slammed shut, 'I don't think I got the whole text; the punchline was missing. Anyway, whatever happened to him? They were really famous and then disappeared from the face of the earth. Is he still alive?' her voice trailed off as the kitchen door swung open to reveal the answer to her question stood there, her stunned expression surpassed only by Tim's.

Despite the shock of seeing his mother for the first time in forty years Tim managed a reply, 'I'm standing in your kitchen, that's what happened to me. And yes,' he added, theatrically checking his racing pulse, 'I'm still alive. Just.'

Chapter 39

The Reunion - Part 3

She looked just how he imagined; shoulder-length black hair brushed back at the front and held with a clip, just like the Brighton beach photograph. Her complexion was clear and her skin youthful. In his head, he tried to work out how old she was. Was she much younger than Matt; she looked it? He couldn't work it out and was conscious he was staring at her, although this went unnoticed as she hurriedly put a bottle of milk into the fridge.

'The milk you wanted is there,' she said to Matt before turning to Tim, 'I'm sorry, I didn't mean to be rude, I was just shocked to see you in my house.'

'I warned you in the text,' Matt whispered with futility, aware they could hear.

'But why would Troy Gold be in our kitchen?' she whispered back with equal futility.

'I told you I knew him?'

'But I didn't believe you.'

'I know, but why would I lie? And I did get asked to buy beer for the Arctic Monkeys that time as well,' he snapped.

'Where are they; in the bloody front room?' she replied.

Lyla burst into laughter, 'Hi Stacey. As neither of these so-called gentlemen are going to introduce me, I'll do it myself. I'm Lyla. And don't worry about what you said, it's the funniest thing I've heard in ages. You're not the first to ask if he's still alive. And the Arctic Monkeys are washing their socks in your utility room.'

'They'd have a job; we don't have one.'

Lyla laughed even louder, 'I can see we're gonna get on,' she said hugging Stacey, 'It's lovely to meet you.'

The warmth of Lyla's response melted away the awkwardness, with Matt delighted the two were getting on so well he could spend time with one of his heroes.

'Ooh, you must still be pretty famous though if Matt has dusted the mocha pot off and made a coffee in it. I'm surprised he found it?'

'I use it a lot, just not when you're here,' he grunted.

As Lyla cast a smug glance in his direction, Tim could not believe she had got away with it, or that he was stood casually having a coffee with his mum and dad in their kitchen. Seeing his dad was remarkable but he had not seen his mother since he was 3 years old. At that moment it did not matter to him whether or not he existed, or that he was the same age as her; just that she was standing in front of him and he felt like a little boy again. It was like his whole life, or at least his time travelling adventure, had led him to this moment. He couldn't run up and give her a big hug as he wanted, but he was happy just to see her and get a feel for what she was like. His dad had described her to him many times. He was right about her being funny and kind.

Tim was determined to make the most of the opportunity. The previous day he, Lyla and Clint had driven to the wormhole exit under the Woodhead pass, igniting Clint's enthusiasm and optimism. He was confident he would be able to send them back to the past in a matter of weeks, so moments like these were to savour. Now he had met his mum, he began to wonder if they were doing the right thing going back. He knew Lyla wanted to go back more than him so they could bring up their child in simpler times and he needed to clear his conscience of the things he had changed in the past. He still felt responsible for Bobby's death. Even if they stayed, what kind of relationship could he have with either of his parents? They were happy and had an even better life than before, just like in the first Back to Future film when he returned in the end and his family were more successful and happier; it was life imitating art. It was better to live in the moment and soak up the unique and unexpected treat fate had dished up. With their 2015 departure imminent, there would be little point or opportunity to call again.

'So, what happened with Mad Ferret?' Stacey asked, 'I mean one minute you were everywhere, battling with the Stone Roses for the best band of the nineties then you were gone in a puff of smoke like Keyser Soze. Do you like my nineties film reference? I'm proud of that one.'

'The Usual Suspects. Nice,' Tim replied. He already liked his mum. He could see why she married his dad; they had a lot in common.

'I don't know what to say, I just didn't want it anymore. It wasn't what I thought it would be. I mean, I enjoyed parts of it and achieved what I wanted, but once I made my mind up it was simple, so I just quit. If you stop doing interviews and keep your head down, it's surprising how quickly people forget about you. I still get contacted by the NME and the TV for all those stupid 90's revival programmes like top 100 songs of the nineties, or whatever. I just hang up. Besides, the Stone Roses hit their groove and they were always the best band anyway. We did our bit and weren't needed anymore, so nobody missed us.'

'I don't know about that. You were missed. I loved you lot; I was gutted when you split up,' Matt responded.

'But who do you think was best; us or the Roses. Be honest.'

'It's close but probably the Roses shaded it.'

'What's the best gig you ever went to?' Tim asked.

''I could name loads. You lot, Weller, the Charlatans, Shed 7; but there was this one gig at the Leadmill in 1995. My mate Bob worked there, and he got me tickets to watch the Roses do a secret Glastonbury warm-up. The Roses at the Leadmill. Can you believe it? And on top of all that it was my 25th birthday. It was the best gig ever. And just before they went stratospheric. Only played big venues after that. That gig was followed by the triumphant Glasto gig which made them massive over here; especially after they did that collaboration with The Prodigy. Is it true you had something to do with that?'

'Yeah, I set it up. I spoke to John and Ian one day and said, after Fool's Gold, they should do more Indie/Dance crossover stuff. I said a similar thing to Keith and Bob's your uncle. I was right.'

'Wow,' cooed Matt.

'Did you know it should have been us that did the Beastie Boys collaboration?'

'What? Dump the Rump? You should have done Dump the Rump?'

'Yeah.'

'But that's what made them the biggest band in the world. It could have been you with the Beasties, opening the first-ever TFI Friday? That song shot them into outer space. I've just bought their latest album on vinyl, King Monkey – It's their fifteenth album. I doubt they'll ever split up. They're like machines churning out one great album after another. You're telling me that could have been you?'

'Could have. Should have. It was me who set it up on our USA tour in 95. Me and MCA lined it up, but we split up, so I got him to call John instead. Moody went ballistic. But don't tell anyone. Nobody knows this.'

'You had a song lined up with the Beasties and you split up. Why?'

'Matt,' snapped Stacey, 'don't push him on it. I'm sure he doesn't want to talk about it otherwise he would have done interviews at the time.'

'Well, you started it.'

'Yes, and I apologise for that. I don't know what it is but normally when I come back from a nightshift I'm exhausted and want to go straight to bed but today I don't feel tired at all. There's a good dynamic going on here; it's like I've known you two my entire life, there's a lovely familiar feeling. I feel like cracking open a bottle of wine and having and having a natter. I bet the pair of you have some stories to tell about the nineties. But first I want to know how you met because I have a theory,' she said looking at Lyla.

'And what's that?' Lyla obliged.

'I bet you're the reason Mad Ferret split up. I reckon you're a bit of a Yoko Ono,' she laughed.

The couple of hours spent with his parents, before the wine and lack of sleep caught up with his mother, were the most surreal of his time travelling experience; and there had been many. She was everything his dad had said she was and everything he hoped she would be. She was kind, had a wicked sense of humour and a fun personality. They made each other happy. But as much as he loved their happiness, he felt sickened he had missed out on this growing up. He envied their daughters. He was happy they were happy, but those couple of hours were emotionally draining. They took a toll he couldn't pay again. Lyla was right, they belonged in the past; they didn't belong in 2015 anymore.

'Come on,' slurred an inebriated Stacey throwing her arms in the air, 'let's have a group hug.'

For a moment, all four stood on the front doorstep entwined before Lyla unentangled herself with deliberation, leaving the three unlikely musketeers in a lingering embrace. Tim's hands squeezed the shoulder of his parents as tears rolled down his cheeks. He knew this was it.

'Are we likely to see you again? I've really enjoyed today?' asked Matt, peeling away from the huddle.

'That would be nice,' Lyla jumped in as Tim turned his back to his parents, quickly wiping the tears from his face, 'we'll keep in touch. I've got Stacey's number.'

'Oh OK. I'd better get her to bed,' Matt said before repeating, 'I've had a great time.'

'Me too,' reiterated a newly composed Tim as he watched his parents disappear behind the black front door.

Two weeks later Tim and Lyla were back in 1989. He never saw them again.

Chapter 40

King Tut's Wah Wah Hut, Glasgow

MONDAY, MAY 31ST, 1993

'But you're not on the bill tonight. There's three bands on, Boyfriend, 18 Wheeler and Sister Lovers, but no Oasis.'
'What do you mean? We've come all the way from Manchester. We're mates with Sister Lovers. They said we could play with them.'
'I'm sorry but you can't play tonight.'
'Look it's cost us 200 quid to hire a van and get up here. There's 10 of us in the van and only two security, so if you don't let us play, we're gonna smash the fuckin place up. If I were you, I'd get on the blower and talk to your boss and tell him we are playing, or else no fucker will be playing because there will be no fuckin club to play in?'
After a brief telephone conversation, the shaken promoter confirmed they could play, but would be paid in cans of beer. They played four songs to muted applause before cracking open their wages. They had driven all that way to play 4 songs and made just one fan. But sometimes one is enough.
'All right boys. My name is Alan. Alan McGee, Creation Records. When you played the first song, I thought to myself. Fuckin hell, I still believe in Rock 'n Roll. I wanna do this. Do you have a record deal? I can have 20 record companies banging on your door by the end of next month.'
Noel walked over and shook his hand. 'Alright, mate. What's your name again?'
'Alan.'
'You think we were that good, Alan?'
'Fuckin Rock 'n' roll star good, pal.'
'Fuck me, Alan. I like you and your passion, but I don't reckon much to your timing? We're already signed.'
'No, you're not, I was talking to Sister Lovers when you were on stage and they said you weren't signed.'

'We weren't but we got signed tonight.'

'Tonight? But I've walked straight over to talk to you after you came off stage. You've not knocked the froth off you're Tenants yet. He's not even opened his,' he pointed out, nodding at Guigsy. 'This is meant to be. I wasn't supposed to be here tonight, its's fate.'

'We got signed before we went on stage. Some big shot from Sheffield heard about us and followed us up here.'

'Who?'

'That guy over there,' said Noel pointing at a middle-aged man at the bar sat next to a younger, blonde-haired lady.

'Him over there? I saw him earlier. I thought he was your dad.'

Liam spat his beer across the table, 'I told you, our kid. He's the spitting image of you. He even has your haircut.'

'He looks fuck all like me,' he snapped.

'Bollocks, he's the spitting image of you. I reckon our mam was lying. I reckon he's really your dad,' Liam taunted to the howls of the band and their entourage.

'Well, it would explain why you're such a dickhead if we're not related.' Noel countered. 'Besides, he looks nothing like me.'

'He does pal,' confirmed Bonehead, 'It's you in 25 years is that. At least he's still got his fuckin hair.'

'Fuck off.'

'Oy,' shouted Alan to the man, 'who are you, coming up here and signing my band?'

'They're not your band, they're mine,' he said casually walking the short distance with a smile and a swagger before holding out his hand.

'My name is Gold, Troy Gold from Mad Ferret Records. Who the fuck are you?'

EPILOGUE

Part 1 – The Church

Marple, Lancashire

3 FEBRUARY 1990

Have you ever had a feeling of déjà vu? Tim had been getting it a lot recently, which was hardly surprising as he had lived every day before. Not in the same way Bill Murray relived one day multiple times in groundhog day. For Tim, a 'new' day would follow the previous. He had today, tomorrow and yesterday like everyone else but, unlike everyone else, he had lived that day once before over 26 years ago. There were no do-overs if he got it wrong, the day wouldn't repeat itself. Some of these days would pass without any déjà vu, but for others, he was stuck in time. For him to experience a day for the first time, he would have to wait 26 years. He would be 73 years old before he saw the dawn of a day utterly new to him.

26 years was a long time to remember things and he never had a great memory anyway. The drugs won't have helped either. But there were things he did remember, mostly sporting and current events. After a while he decided to have fun with the phenomenon by testing his memory, betting on every Grand National race and FA Cup Final so successfully he had to spread his bets amongst different bookmakers.

He was a different person, with a different life to the one who first lived the day many years ago. The hedonistic lifestyle he pursued and craved as a young man had been replaced with a steady family life with Lyla. He was still 3 years away from managing the greatest Rock and Roll band of the decade but was finally happy. With Lyla, his daughter and a miniature chocolate coloured dachshund, he shared a modest 1950's semi-detached house in the Hillsborough area of Sheffield. He could even see his beloved Sheffield Wednesday's football ground from his bedroom; if he opened the window and leaned out a bit. It was ironically like the house he grew up in with his dad. He had gone full circle. It was a different type of Rock and Roll.

The guilt which lay heavy on him during his previous visit made it impossible to enjoy his dream, but his return had exorcised many of those demons. Having travelled far enough back in time for Mad Ferret to have never existed, Oasis would reclaim the crown which was always theirs. No longer would he be haunted by killing the very thing which inspired him to strive for greatness in the first place.

Seeing Clint was another burden removed. Tim's feelings of abandonment dissipated upon the realisation Clint didn't know who he was. It was a different 2015 to the one he left behind in the Red BMW; one in which he had never existed. He couldn't have abandoned him if he never existed. Besides Clint was happier in the new reality without him. But he knew Clint well enough to realise that knowing his invention worked was the greatest gift this passing stranger could have given him.

But there was still one thing that haunted him. One stone unturned. One final barrier to contentment.

It was the same Church and the same day, but a different time parallel. Bobby's funeral was the worst day of his life. His time travelling was indirectly to blame for his death, influencing events that would ultimately lead to that fateful night out in the Hacienda. The service began at 11 am and he could remember turning up with Moody and Adam nursing the mother of all hangovers. But today he arrived at 10 am, as fresh as the snowdrops scattered in the grass around the war memorial to the front of the church. He hadn't noticed the tiny flowers before. Were they there the last time? Of course they were, it was the exact same day.

He hadn't taken much notice of the church either. Why would a grieving young man with no interest in architecture pay attention to a church? He had become interested in architecture after he picked up a book on Gothic Architecture at a second-hand bookshop for a quid. Maybe it was in the blood. Most churches have gothic features, and this was no exception, but he could see from the windows to the main projecting gable they were revivalist, not built in the gothic period. The tell-tale sign were the three lancet windows, which should have adorned decorative traceries. A tall bell tower to the left was also decorated in the gothic style but were again not elaborate enough. It was unlikely the church was older than the mid-nineteenth century.

'I'm not interested,' Lyla commented, cheekily squeezing his hand as they strolled along the tarmac path to the large lancet double entrance door, one leaf of which was open. It reminded him of the door to Giovanna's house.

'What do you mean?' he asked.

'I'm not interested how old the church is, or whether it's proper gothic or not.'

'I wasn't even thinking about that,' he claimed.

'Yes, you were. Ever since you picked up that damn book you think you're some expert in architecture. I keep expecting to see you on Mastermind – specialised subject Gothic architecture. But you'd get them all wrong anyway. It's a thin book.'

'No, I wasn't,' he protested a little too hard, 'I was thinking about something else.'

A small smile appeared on his face as he remembered what awaited him behind Giovanna's double lancet door that night. He gave Lyla's hand a guilty squeeze as they entered the church.

From the small entrance lobby, they entered under the Nave, next to the font. Having examined the roof structure from the outside he expected the Nave and the layout of the church to be as he saw before him. He was pleased with his architectural detective work but had nobody to blow his trumpet for.

'Good morning,' said a friendly voice as the vicar appeared from behind the font.

'Good morning,' they replied.

'It's a lovely church you have here Vicar. When was it built? Mid Nineteenth century?'

Lyla squeezed his hand tightly and sighed.

'Actually, it was built in 1850, so you are spot on.'

Tim Squeezed Lyla's hand back.

'Except for the All-Souls Chapel to the Northside of the church which was installed in 1937,' continued the Vicar. 'Are you here for the wedding today?'

'Wedding!' Tim exclaimed jubilantly, 'I mean, what a fantastic day for a wedding at such a wonderful church. No, no we're not here for the wedding. Just visiting from Sheffield. We like to go walking and exploring little villages and churches,' he overexplained.

'We'd better be getting off if there's a wedding,' concluded Lyla, 'we wouldn't want to be in the way.'

'Nonsense, you have time to look around the church. We are proud of it. I recommend you visit the All-Souls Chapel; it is a beautiful setting for quiet prayer and contemplation. The glass used for the windows is ancient French and Flemish glass made during the 15th and 16th centuries.'

'Thank you, vicar,' said Lyla respectfully, pulling Tim down the aisle.

'Will you give over with all that architecture stuff, it's embarrassing,' she whispered.

'How's taking an interest in his church embarrassing, he was happy I took the time to chat about it.'

'Well let's have a quick look around and get out of here.'

''It's a lot nicer inside than it looks outside, I'm taking my time. If you're in a rush, I'll meet you outside.'

Nothing Lyla could say would dampen his elation. There was no funeral, it was a wedding, confirmed by a small notice next to the pulpit announcing the joining of Mr. Lee Brown to Miss Anna Harris in holy matrimony.

Tim sat on a chair in the All-Souls Chapel. The Vicar was right, it was perfect for prayers and reflection. He reflected upon how lucky he was to have been given a chance to make amends. He had been given a second chance to get things right. He said a little prayer to thank God for his benevolence and promised he would live his best life, before relaxing in his chair to soak up a little high-quality reflection.

The glass in the window was clear but had an opaque quality to it, maybe because of its age he mused; less sophisticated firing techniques. It was ironic the bride's surname was the same as Bobby's. A nice little touch there pal he smiled looking skywards. Anna Harris. Wasn't Bobby's sister called Anna? Yes, she was. "Of course, how could I have forgotten?" he chastised himself. His sister was due to get married, but it was cancelled when Bobby died. Replacing your daughter's wedding with your son's funeral was the most painful twist of the knife fate could have dealt a parent. He knew the wedding had been cancelled but didn't realise it was the same day as the funeral. Bobby had talked about it, he was good friends with the Groom, Lee, whom Tim had met once.

If it was Anna's wedding, not only was Bobby alive, but he would be here soon. And Quinny. The whole gang. He sprang from his seat, looking frantically for Lyla, who had already left.

'Goodbye, Vicar and thank you!'

'Thank you for what?' he smiled.

'For pointing me in the direction of the All-Souls Chapel. You were right, it is the perfect spot for prayers and reflection. I've had an epiphany. What time is the wedding?' he asked.

'It's not for another hour yet,' he replied, 'but I have already seen the Groom and his entourage make their way into the Angel pub, across the way. I'm not judging. It seems a popular spot to ease the nerves before the big occasion.'

Tim's heart raced as he knew Bobby and the boys would be there.

'Thanks again Vicar,' he spluttered as he hurried out of the church to share the news with Lyla.

Part 2 – The Angel

Marple, Lancashire

3 February 1990

'Without stating the obvious, I take it you guys are attending a wedding across the road?'
'That's right, how did you figure it out?'
Tim laughed. 'Are you the best man?'
'No, I'm an usher, It's my sister's wedding. The best man is Steve, he's the one sat over there next to the Groom.'
Tim had been observing the gang from his table partially obscured around the corner, unnoticed. He recognised Lee, the groom but not the best man. The others he knew well. There was Bobby, Adam, Quinny and Ged who was not inter-railing around Europe in this reality. Or maybe he had been, but it was just a happier and easier event to return for. But, whatever the reason, he was there, all six and a half feet of him.
'Do you get on with the groom? Are you happy he's marrying your sister?'
'Yeah, he's a good lad,'
'What can I get you?' the barman asked Tim.
'A pint of lager and half a lager and lime please and whatever this young man and his friends want.'
'Oh,' said Bobby surprised. 'Thanks, but that's too generous.'
'Don't worry about it pal, I love a good wedding and I'm feeling generous. I've just won a few bob on spot the ball. Besides, you guys remind me of me and my mates when I was your age.'
'But we're about to go in so I was getting a round of double brandies to settle the nerves. It won't be a cheap round.'
'That's fine like I say I won on spot the ball. Won a few grand. I'd like to share my good fortune with you and your friends. Me and my wife were saying what a fun bunch you looked when we walked in,' he explained nodding toward Lyla to show he wasn't some middle-aged pervert coming onto him. 'Double brandies all around please, and I'll have one myself. My name is Troy by the way.'
'Thanks, Troy, that's kind of you. My name's Bobby.'
'Cheers Bobby.'

As Bobby walked back with a trayful of brandies and told his future brother of the stranger's generosity the Groom shouted across to Tim.

'Thank you very much, Troy.'

'And Mrs. Troy,' Bobby added. 'Hold up guys, where's Quinny, we can't have a toast without that pisshead. Oops, sorry about my language Mrs. Troy.'

'He's gone to the bog,' said Ged as the door swung open with Quinny, as usual, arriving the same time as the booze.

'Hey Quinny, are you ready for the toast? The guy at the bar, Troy has bought them for us. He had a big win on spot the ball, lucky bastard. Sorry, Mrs. Troy.'

Quinny looked over at Troy, his expression turning to a frozen stare as their eyes met.

'Quinny. Are you OK? Quinny, stop pissing around,' snapped Bobby as Quinny's gaze broke from Troy's eyes to the space above his head.

Tim's heart skipped a beat as Bobby grabbed Quinny by the shoulder.

'Have you taken something in the bog, you knobhead? I told you none of that shit on Anna's wedding day.'

As Quinny's gaze returned to Tim's panic-stricken eyes, a smile spread across his face.

'Quinny,' shouted Bobby shaking him by the shoulder, 'Is everything OK?'

'Yes... yes. Everything is perfect. Just how it should be,' he drawled cryptically, 'I just thought I knew him that's all. He looks like someone I've not seen in years. Sorry about that pal and cheers for the drinks.'

'Well, that wasn't weird,' joked the best man, Steve. 'Now, raise your glass to our mate Lee who today loses his freedom. He had a good run, but now it's over. It's a good job he's marrying a top lass from a top family. To Lee and Anna.'

'To Lee and Anna!'

Tim wondered if he would ever see them again as they bounced out of the pub, the stranger who bought them a drink already forgotten with only Quinny glancing back as they left.

'What was all that about with Quinny?' asked Lyla.

'No idea.'

'Are you OK now sweetheart?' she asked leaning over and kissing him on the forehead. She knew how much this meant to him. Bobby's death had torn him apart. 'Is that it - the final piece of the jigsaw?'

Tim exhaled, 'Yes, it is,' his voice cracking as he sobbed gently, wiping his eyes with his sleeve. 'Ignore me. I'm being a soft arse.'

'It's hardly surprising you're crying, it's a weird time you've been through.'

'I suppose so,' he laughed. 'But the relief of seeing him alive was unbelievable. Probably a better feeling than seeing my mum and dad alive. That was just a wonderful bonus. But Bobby. I killed him – before you say I didn't, I did really; we both know it. But now he's alive again and I can move on. We can move on.'

'You know what I think is the weirdest part of all this?' Lyla mused taking a sip of her lager and lime.

'What?'

'You're relationship with your father.'

'What do you mean?'

'Well, when you set off the first time, he was your dad. He was dead, but he was your dad, right?'

'Obviously, I don't get what you mean.'

'When you went back the second time you were the same age, and you were friends. If we survive the next few years and if you go back to see him, you will be his dad. You'll be your grandad!'

Tim laughed, 'God, yes. I never thought of that. I don't think I'll bother going back if we make it to 2015. That last goodbye was perfect. All I wanted to do was say goodbye to him. He's an amazing man. A brilliant dad, but I bet he'd be a pain in the arse as a son, some of the stories he told me.'

'I doubt he could beat yours.'

'You're probably right. But it's been hard for you as well. It was brave to follow me. You hardly knew me and to trust Clint like that was amazing.'

'I was young. I wouldn't do it now. But I was infatuated with you. Can't think why looking at you now, old man.'

'I'm glad you did. You still want to stick to the plan?'

'Yeah,' said Lyla, 'I still want to manage Oasis. But like we said, you make the first contact in the club and get them to sign up before we tell them I'm really the manager. This is the nineties; I don't think they'll take me serious as a woman. You haven't changed your mind, have you? You don't want to do it?'

'No, I'm still up for the plan. I couldn't manage them; I don't have the energy for it. I'd rather stay at home with the family. Besides you're way smarter than me.'

'True,' she replied, 'I think a woman's touch is what's needed to crack America. The problem with you men is you're too busy getting pissed and massaging each other's egos to get any real work done. And when Noel and Liam start showing off at each other I'll bang their fuckin heads together.

Remember I come from a big Irish family. My mother took shit from no one.'

Tim laughed, 'I feel sorry for them. You do realise at least one of them will try to shag you? You're still well fit. Way out of my league.'

'I'd be disappointed, and a little insulted if they didn't. But why would I need one of them when I've got my own Oasis reject waiting at home?'

'And as you said, I'm slightly better looking than Noel. Definitely,' Tim laughed.

'Definitely, maybe,' she replied.

Printed in Great Britain
by Amazon